# THE

# MISERABLE
# SINNER

*by* Dolf Wyllarde

*Author of*
THE NUPTIAL NIGHT
THE WEEK-END WIFE
*Etc.*

*New York*
THE MACAULAY COMPANY

# THE MISERABLE SINNER

# CHAPTER I

MONTE CARLO, even in the season, is not what it used to be, Horace Crayshaw reflected. He was just old enough to have acquired the habit of looking back, of which he was just young enough to be rather proud. When he used to come over for the pigeon shooting (he was in his early twenties then), it had been about right, and now it was about wrong.

He had gone up by bus to the golf course at Mont Agel in the morning, and played a round with Curton, getting an excellent lunch at the Club-house there; but Curton had not wanted to play after lunch, and so they had returned to the hotel, where he was writing letters. The difference between the two men was signified in the fact that when Curton had letters to write he sat down and wrote them; but Crayshaw, who had also letters to write, put them off till to-morrow. He wrote a very good letter—far better than his friend—but he particularly disliked the hotel pens, and his own stylo was out of order, and the trifling disadvantage put him off. Curton's habit of routine was not possible to Crayshaw, or he thought so, while he was sufficiently intelligent to see that it was a good trait, and that Curton owed half his success in life to it.

"But then," said Horace lazily, lighting a cigar as he strolled down the gardens towards the Casino, "he doesn't get half as much out of life as I do."

His eyes twinkled at his own expense, liquid eyes as clear as glass and perhaps as shallow, until emotions rose

7

in them like fish. The simile is not a bad one, for it was possible to drop bait into those eyes, as women had found, and perhaps to land something. It was good sport, anyhow. Horace was a good sport, also. He was a singularly handsome man of forty, black-haired and gray-eyed, with the recognized fringe of lashes that made them "put in with a smutty finger." He spoke without the least trace of accent to soften the asperities of the English language, but nobody could be in his company for long without suspicioning that he had Irish blood.

Hugh Curton was so much his opposite as to suggest that the contrast had made them friends; but it was as much community of taste as any liking for each other. Of the two, Crayshaw liked Curton a good deal more than Curton liked him. But they were both good at games, and both experienced travelers enough to make them independent of each other as companions. They were staying at Monte Carlo for the same reason that people from the British Isles always stayed there. Because it had been a fashion for some generations. Because the winter had been vile and they wanted to get away to the sunshine. Because it was more amusing than Nice and not so expensive as Cannes. Because the golf was passable, and the Casino a resource when—as sometimes happened—Mont Agel was capped with snow and the bus could not get to the golf course. Because they were well enough off to take the trip and stay a month and had no ties to prevent them.

Crayshaw was married and Curton had a business to look after, but in their separate ways both men had been able to shelve their responsibilities. Curton no doubt had made the more ordered arrangements for meeting his obligations while he was away, but Noel Crayshaw had said to her husband, "You had better run over to Monte with this Mr. Curton. I can do anything you want here, and I will send on your business letters." Crayshaw dabbled in business, but he had not one of his own. He dabbled on the Stock Exchange, and on the Boards of Companies, and he dabbled a little in Commission Agencies; and on the whole he did much better than any of his friends would have expected. He had many friends, being a charming man, and he declared himself very fortunate in his wife to whom he was deeply attached, and to their crippled son—the heaviest cloud upon his life. He loved Valentine so tenderly that the child's misfortune was sometimes almost intolerable to him. He could not bear to be with the boy. It was fortunate that Noel was not temperamental also. Her love for Valentine never seemed to distress her as his father's did, and she preferred to be with him, nursing, teaching, bringing up, building a soul for a man out of the wreck of a boy's body. Valentine and Noel were so comfortable together that it left Horace free to take a few weeks abroad here and there, and to get the change that he needed. He knew that he needed change, with his temperament, and Noel silently agreed. He was Celtic. Whenever anything threatened Crayshaw's preferences, his opposition took the form of being a Celt. He could not, of course, help being a Celt. It was better than Charity as a covering.

There was the usual network of traffic coming from all points of the compass to the Casino this afternoon. Crayshaw crossed the Cheese, and stood on the steps outside the building for a few minutes, watching the people passing in and out. But they hardly claimed his attention. He stared at the palm trees and the beds of flowers in front of him, at the Hôtel de Paris on the left and the Café on the right, and in a momentary dissatisfaction he felt that even the Casino was shabby and wanted doing up. It was more amusing inside than out, and he was just turning to go in when the indifference suddenly vanished from his handsome eyes and they became stirred to the depths by the rising of emotions which have been already likened to fish.

An unusually large and sumptuous motor-car had glided silently up to the steps, with two men-servants, one of whom ran round to open the door for a lady to alight. She came up the steps rather slowly, followed by a small dark-skinned woman who was evidently an attendant, for she took the sable cloak from the lady's shoulders inside the doors and waited with it there. Crayshaw had turned instantly and followed them, for he had seen the lady's face.

She was the most beautiful woman he had ever seen— well, one of the most beautiful. For he had thought the same thing many times since his eyes grew masculine enough to set up a standard for the feminine. In this case, however, it is probable that he was very nearly right, because the lady riveted attention even from those who had come to gamble and cared little for beauty. She had a coloring that might be called both dark and fair, since her eyes were so dusky as to be black in some lights, and her skin was pale with the pallor of a brunette; but her hair was the true chestnut that is not auburn or dark red, and it had the freshness and richness of a child's. It was not dyed, nor were her brows and lashes either. Her features were as nearly perfect as is consistent with beauty, the recognized standard for beauty being as arbitrary in Europe as in Chinese Asia, and equally repellent. The contrast between this lady's bright hair, the glint of her brows and lashes, and her pallor and deep eyes, was so remarkable as to take the breath. It took Crayshaw's as he looked at her, and his gaze could hardly tear itself from her face to notice the lines and grace of her figure as she walked through the entrance hall. There seemed no blemish upon that body, whatever her mind might be.

The lady paused of necessity to give her cloak to her attendant, and to add some instructions as to the car, which was Crayshaw's opportunity to slip into the cloakroom and give his hat and stick over the counter. He was lucky in that he had not to wait thus early in the afternoon, but he almost ran back into the hall just in time to see his new beauty going towards the rooms and to follow her.

He had never seen her in the Casino before, though he had been there often enough during the past month. He could not have forgotten her or passed her in the crowd. He wondered, instantly jealous, if Curton had seen her and said nothing about it (for Curton was close-lipped), even while he followed her as irresistibly as the needle follows the magnet—through the loose crowd in the entrance hall, through the Kitchen, and into the Salle Privée, where she passed the baccarat tables and the *trente-et-quarante*, and sat down at the roulette table in a seat just vacated by an old man who bowed to her as if in distant recognition. She took a handful of hundred-franc chips from her wristbag, and began to stake on the even chances with an indiscrimination that was almost indifferent. The luck appeared to be against her, but she was no newcomer or débutante at the game. Crayshaw knew that from the way she played, from her obvious knowledge of the table, and from the people round her, who looked at her indeed—how could they help it—but looked as at a familiar beauty, as they might look at the lovely nudes in what is sarcastically called "The Bath Room," or at a specially brilliant bed of flowers in the gardens—admiring but expectant of it all, almost proprietary.

Crayshaw walked round the table and stood behind the chair of the player on the lady's left, an elderly man who was losing on the even numbers. On her right sat an old woman, an inveterate gambler Crayshaw had often noticed before, and who would not move for an hour. The man was the more likely to curse his luck in silence and leave his seat. But Crayshaw had stood there some twenty minutes before he got his chance and sat down beside his new divinity, and by that time he knew more of her and was no less intoxicated. Standing to the left of her shoulder he could see the length of her curling lashes over the somber eyes, the close thick ripple of her chestnut hair, and the line of her cheek, despite her hat, and he could smell the faint scent that seemed her very essence, it was so faint and yet so distinct from the coarse perfumes profusely used by the other women in the Privée. His blood took fire from her propinquity, and the longer he stood there the more intensely he desired to speak to her and begin the acquaintance that his ardor urged him to pursue. It was just one of those instant passions that he would have ascribed to his Celtic origin, and quite possibly with reason. The Celt has for ages held the serviceable position of being his own excuse.

As Crayshaw sat down on the chair at last left to him by the elderly man, the lady stretched out her hand and laid a hundred-franc chip on "Trente." Instantly Crayshaw laid his own stake on the same number, her sleeve actually brushing his as she withdrew her arm. She did not turn her head or glance in his direction, and they both waited until the croupier announced the winning number— "Trente!"—his assistants pushing the winnings over to the successful players. Then, still without turning her head, she spoke to Crayshaw, in English.

"You have brought me luck, Monsieur."

"You chose my lucky number, Madame. When I saw you stake I felt that it was a—coincidence." His voice trembled a little with his excitement—not of his winnings, but because she had herself broken the barrier of silence between them. It was surely a good omen! They were no longer strangers who had never exchanged a word or a glance, though her splendid eyes were still looking carelessly at the table.

After a minute she stretched out her hand again as if to stake, and he noticed the delicacy of her wrist and the soft, round arm; then, with an equally sudden caprice, she drew her hand back, tossed her winnings into her bag, and rose from the table. Crayshaw had already put his stake on the number over which her hand had hovered, but as the lady rose he rose also, and without waiting for the wheel to stop he followed her down the room as if she drew him beyond resistance. The croupiers raked in the eccentric defaulter's winnings without the least alteration of their immovable faces, and a good many people standing behind the players—and even some of the players themselves— looked up after the lady and the gentleman following her, with curious expressions. On some of the faces—and these were mostly old women's—was a cynicism that was as horrible as a leer ; and on others—and these mostly men's— male jealousy that was bestial. It was evident that the lady at least was well known in La Privée and that her notoriety had a flavor.

She went back slowly through the rooms, pausing to watch the *trente-et-quarante* for some minutes but without sitting down, and taking no notice of Crayshaw. Yet as he hovered near he felt that she knew he was there, and the blood quickened in his veins for a new adventure.

He had felt these symptoms many times for many women
—surely never for one lovelier !—but they did not fail to
make life once more worth living. The holiday that had
been somewhat dull became full of possibilities; the Casino
that had seemed shabby was gay and attractive; even the
sordid faces at the tables were interesting. In fact *the game
was worth the candle* because of the old enchantment of
a man by a woman. There she stood, a few feet distant, her
dark eyes oblivious of him, and her beautiful face turned
to the gamblers, and just because she was beauty and nov-
elty and temptation she had changed the face of the world
to the Celt in him. His hands almost trembled as he tried
to light a cigarette with elaborate unconcern, and something
—perhaps the sharp ignition of the match—made her move
back from the table, nearer to him.

"You did not follow up your luck!" he said softly.

She turned her head slowly as if she said, "Oh, are you
there?" and looked at him with a slightly insolent surprise.

"I did not feel that it would last," she said, moving away
from the crowd and slowly through the room towards the
doors. He followed her, walking almost at her side as if
he had the permission. "It is a mood. When I feel like that
I leave the tables. But you——?"

"I felt that there was nothing to stay for." His rich
musical voice had a laugh in it, and there was laughter also
in his treacherous eyes. She glanced up at him as if half
impelled and half resistant, and her own more somber eyes
smiled in answer.

"It was certainly sick with odors in the Privée," she said
as they passed through the doors into the lounge, where
people were sitting or standing about. "The crowd is worse
than last season, I think."

"Oh, were you here last winter? And I did not come

to Monte," he said with the impulsive disappointment of a boy. One of Crayshaw's greatest attractions was his air of youth even though his youth had gone.

"I am here every winter. I have a villa out at Roquebrune," she said carelessly. "I come in to Monte Carlo nearly every day."

"How can I have missed seeing you?"

"Possibly because I have been away, at Bordighera," she mocked him. "I only returned yesterday. And you, I suppose, have spent all your time in the Casino."

"Sometimes I have stayed outside it," he laughed. "I am never tired of looking at the flower-beds and speculating as to what they will put in next week—childish, isn't it? They seem to do it by night. It is like a transformation scene."

"They alter the whole scheme about every fortnight. It would grow wearisome if they did not."

"You like a change?"

"I hate monotony. I think if one won always, even at the tables, one would sicken of it!"

"And yet I can imagine cases in which one could not change or grow weary." His handsome eyes almost caressed her, and were so eloquent of what he meant that his audacity seemed to amuse her.

"You are faithful?" she said ironically. "You do not look it!"

"I can be faithful to an ideal!"

"I hope you may find it."

"I have at least seen it!" he murmured.

"Your ideals are then material? Something you can see, can hear?"

"Oh, I agree to that! Something I can see—can touch!" (Was it by chance that his sleeve brushed the soft lace of her gown?) "I couldn't adore something that was purely theoretical. Even one's Saint has an image in the shrine."

"And you adore the image rather than the Saint."

"Faith, I doubt if I could adore the Saint except in the shrine, in any case!" He laughed again, knowing what an asset it was, that light laughter with its suggestion of youth. "Give me something human to love. Is not that your ideal also?"

"I have no ideals." Her face lowered until its beauty was almost sullen. She had paused half-way down the lounge to talk to him in this desultory fashion, not always even looking at him as she did so. Now, with a movement as capricious as when she left the tables, she turned and with a slight bow to him walked deliberately towards the doors where the dark waiting-woman was still patiently standing with the sable cloak on her arm. Crayshaw hesitated a moment in his chagrin and surprise—he had never dreamed that she would leave him like that, with so little ceremony —and while he hesitated he was lost. For when he ventured to stroll after her, still drawn like the needle to the magnet, he was just in time to see her pass out of the Casino and down the steps, her attendant following, and signal to the big car in which she settled herself and was whirled away through the town in the direction of Cap Martin. He stood still on the steps of the Casino, hatless, with a curious air of homage.

"Who wouldn't be alive," he said to himself, "when there are women like that in the world!"

# CHAPTER II

CURTON was in the lounge of the hotel as Crayshaw came into it. He was still busy with his correspondence, and his sleek head and flat back were so unresponsive that they irritated Crayshaw who was reacting from the excitement of the lady in the Casino. There was something self-dominant and determined about Curton that expressed itself through his physical appearance long before people knew his character. His head was somewhat square, and the dark hair on it was always flattened as if a wet brush had just passed over it. His face was square also, with a heavy jaw and eyes which would have been more pleasant without a certain suspicion or secretiveness in them. He was clean-shaven, tall, and well built, and would have struck anyone as a handsome man until they saw him beside Crayshaw. Then the latter's beauty made him merely ordinary.

He was writing his letters with the habit of a business man, the addressed envelopes already lying beside him testifying to his diligence in the past hour and his orderly method. They seemed to accuse Crayshaw, who sprawled all over a writing-table when he attacked his own correspondence and frequently mislaid the written sheets when he came to the envelopes, which he invariably left till the last.

"Still at it?" he remarked idly, picking up an English newspaper from the center table.

"I have finished," said Curton quietly as he stamped the last letter. "Been out again?"

"Only to the tables."

"Luck?"

"I didn't play long—won on the even numbers and collared my winnings."

The memory of his reason for leaving made him faintly restless again, and he dropped the paper and turned round in his chair to face Curton. He had an insatiable desire to speak of the woman who had taken possession of his senses, that would not be gainsaid, even though he half wished to keep the experience to himself.

"There was a lady playing who was evidently a personality," he said, choosing his words under the cynicism of Curton's eyes. "She was a wonder! Other people stared at her, though they evidently knew her. One couldn't help it."

"There is always some oddity at the tables, if you are not engrossed in the game. How was she remarkable?"

"The most beautiful face and figure I think I ever saw!"

Curton laughed outright. "Again?" he said with a kind of contemptuous good humor. "Your capacity for admiration never seems to reach its limit. Last week it was that dancer at the Palais."

"Oh, she!—it was her dancing that took me, and you admitted that she made the Russians look silly. But this was a different thing altogether to the dancing girl—a lady, you couldn't mistake the stamp."

"Have you never seen her before?"

"No, never. Have you?" said Crayshaw quickly, for something in the other man's tone suggested recognition.

"I expect it was Mrs. or rather Madame Da Costa."

"Who is she?" Crayshaw's voice trembled with the eagerness of a boy, and again Curton looked at him with that half-amused cynicism.

"The wife of a very wealthy American who died in a rather suspicious manner in Santiago. There was some inquiry about another lover and Madame, who was said to be lucky to escape justice. She was rather under a cloud even in Monte Carlo. I saw her at the tables last year——"

"Did you get an introduction?"

"Sorry I can't oblige you, old boy—I didn't follow it up. I looked at her as you did because she was worth looking at —yes, she is a beautiful woman. Probably dangerous as well. I have not seen her this season."

Crayshaw took it for granted that Curton had never spoken to Madame Da Costa or he would surely have boasted of it—he would have done so himself if he had not intended to pursue the acquaintance, and he generally judged other men by himself. He was sufficiently infatuated already to be jealous of Curton having seen the loveliness that had captured him, and to be ahead of him in knowing her name; if Curton had admitted becoming acquainted with her, Crayshaw would have regarded him with a suspicion that might have smoldered for days and burst into the flame of a quarrel. But he did not think that Curton was lying, or even prevaricating, though he would have done so himself with the hounds of his imagination already hot upon the trail. Curton was too supine to accomplish an adventure, and had only discovered the lady's name, to Crayshaw's own ultimate advantage. Madame Da Costa—wife of an American. She was English herself, however married. His thoughts, wandering after her, were recalled by Curton's next speech.

"I am sorry to say I shall have to cut short this trip and go back on Thursday," was his unconscious remark, his own affairs wiping out the incident that was flooding the other man's immediate surroundings. He had, apparently, forgotten Madame Da Costa in his hold on his business. "I'm sorry, Crayshaw, and I hope it won't upset your plans. You'll stay, I suppose?"

"If I can find another man to take me on at golf. What a damned nuisance, Curton! Must you really go?"

He was secretly and instantly delighted that his friend should be so suitably recalled, but he really did not betray himself. With Curton out of the way, and not even an onlooker, he was free to pursue the headlong chase of his last divinity, and to involve himself as much as his luck would allow him. But his long liquid eyes were almost as sentimental as they would have been to a woman, as he looked at his friend.

"Sorry, old Thing, but there's no doubt about it. My partner is very ailing, and the managing clerk advises my return. I must get off on Thursday."

The day after to-morrow. Crayshaw's brain began to scheme to keep Curton employed during the next thirty-six hours so that he should get no chance to see or begin an acquaintance with Madame Da Costa. It was extremely unlikely that Curton would have taken the trouble, or indeed thought of the woman again, however beautiful she might be, unless she came actually under his notice without effort on his part. But Crayshaw's excited fancy could not believe it though his reason told him it was true. Every other man was a rival the minute he began the old process of falling in love. Curton had always been somewhat of a dark horse to him, and he could never forecast what he might do. Even now, under that nonchalant exterior, he might be planning to use his last day at Monte Carlo in a more secret pursuit of Madame than his friend. The idea was as tormenting as a goad.

"At all events we shall get another game to-morrow——"

Crayshaw spoke as if his whole soul were in golf. "You'll come up to Mont Agel?"

"I've got my packing to see to, and a lot of arrangements. But I might manage the morning."

"Leave your packing and the rest of it for the afternoon. Cook's will do the arrangements for you, or the tourist agencies. I suppose you'll come down to the Casino to-night, as you've been sweating indoors all the afternoon?"

He did not want Curton to go to the Casino at all, but he suggested it to find out his plans. If they played golf to-morrow morning, and Curton were busy with his packing in the afternoon, there were only the evenings to threaten danger. He would of course go to the tables in the afternoon himself in the hope of seeing Madame, and if she encouraged the acquaintance he could find out whether she played in the evenings. He did not know, (though both he and Curton had been down to the Casino most evenings), because she had been away. As she lived outside the town, at Roquebrune, he hoped not.

"I thought I'd go in and see a show to-night. That old boy at the table next to us tells me there is something good at the theater."

"All right. It makes a change. Do we dine any earlier?"

"I expect we shall have to. What is it now? Past six, by Jove! I'll go up and change." Curton took up his orderly pile of letters to give them to the concierge, and a thought seemed to strike him in connection with them. "I say, Crayshaw, I should be glad if you'd look after my letters after I'm gone, and see if there are any for me, will you?" he said. "I am leaving before I expected, and the posts here are uncertain. Something might be forwarded before I can get back or stop my clerks sending it on. If there were important letters I don't want them delayed or lost. Could you undertake to send them back to me?"

"Of course I will, old Thing. Anything I can do—always delighted." Crayshaw's careless good-nature always accepted a favor asked or bestowed.

"Then I'll tell the concierge that he can hand them to you. Awfully obliged to you." Curton gave his letters in at the bureau and went up to his room to change. Crayshaw followed him to the lift as if in charge of him. He did not mean to let Curton out of his sight for long until he bid him good-bye, if it could be avoided. The play at the Palais was a bit of a bore—he hoped it might be lively, but he would have endured highbrow stuff rather than suspect that Curton had met Madame Da Costa by some freak of fate while he was elsewhere.

The two men dined together as usual, apparently on the best of terms, though Crayshaw's secret restlessness had the effect of making him exert himself to be amusing so that other diners glanced a little enviously at the table where the two Englishmen seemed to be so well entertained. They told each other stories and incidents, generally on the subject of women, sometimes of men also in ridicule of sex instincts, and their laughter became hilarious. Later on they went down to the Palais and saw a French play that left nothing to the imagination, and Crayshaw to his relief was not bored. Afterwards they strolled into the Casino and looked at the tables before going back to the hotel, but did not play; and Madame Da Costa was not present.

"I didn't see the beauty to-night," Curton remarked as they left the Salle de Privée.

"I suppose she isn't an inveterate gambler, and the afternoon play sufficed her," Crayshaw answered carelessly. "Was it in the evenings that you saw her last year?" The question came in very well and did not betray his eagerness to know.

"I saw her both in the morning and the afternoon, as far as I remember. She was handsome even by daylight, and did not look jaded as most women do who play high. I heard there was a row about her at the Sporting Club—she is a woman who brings trouble wherever she goes—and for that reason she never went there. But she planked it a bit at the Privée."

Handsome was not the word for that bewildering beauty, but Crayshaw let it pass. He always thought Curton rather stupid about women. "What a night!" he said, looking up at the blue-black sky that was rich with stars. The gardens of the Casino were still bright with electricity and the flowers showed brilliant colors almost as by day. It was so artificial that it seemed impossible they could be growing. The two Englishmen passed the gardens and walked up the hill to their hotel, smoking, and enjoying the freshness of the night after the heat of the rooms. "I'm awfully sorry you must go home, Curton. England will be beastly until March or April."

"I shall be home on the 14th, Valentine's Day. I think of all festivals St. Valentine's is the silliest. Who would feel sentimental in the middle of February? No wonder the custom of sending cards and presents to your last flame is dying out."

"February 14th!"—Crayshaw stood still suddenly in the road, regardless of the rush of motor-cars. "Good Heavens, and I'd nearly forgotten. It's my boy's birthday. I must send him something." The shadow that always darkened his face as he spoke of his crippled son, was on it now, though he was so out of touch with that tie in England that Curton rarely heard him speak of it. He had not

known, indeed, until this year, that Crayshaw was married
or had a child, though they had met at Hyères and St. Jean
de Luz in former years and played golf together. When
Crayshaw eventually told him, briefly, of his wife and child,
Curton had been broad-minded enough to attribute his reti-
cence to the fact of the boy's misfortune. It penetrated the
comfortable armor of his own egotism now, and made him
offer to help his neighbor in spite of himself.

"Can I take something back with me, and post it on
landing? It would be nearly as quick in getting to London,
and you would avoid the Customs if it's dutiable."

Crayshaw jumped at the suggestion, partly because it
saved him trouble, and partly because he liked other people
to do something for him. It fed his vanity, which was almost naïve. "Old Curton is a funny customer; he wouldn't
raise a finger for most people, but he'll do anything for
me," he thought. He turned his charming face almost
eagerly to Curton, and smiled as if he had been praised.

"It's awfully good of you. I should be really grateful. It
will only be a small parcel. Something from Rumpelmay-
er's, I expect. He's inordinately fond of *marrons glacés,* and
*marrons* often melt in the Douane!"

"All right—give it to me to-morrow, will you, and I'll
get it through for you. How old is your boy?"

"Just twelve. It's no use sending him things like most
active boys, but he's wonderfully clever at puzzles or any
game that wants head rather than limbs. He had quite a
rage for jigsaw when he was younger. Now it's crossword."

Curton looked really interested. He went in for crossword competitions himself, and had even invented them.
"A good crossword is a general education," he said some-

what sententiously. "It's surprising to find how small your knowledge is when you begin."

"I wish you could see some of Val's solutions. He's really clever, though I don't know where he gets it. Neither his mother nor I are very brainy——" Crayshaw laughed, but the shadow was still on his face like a twinge of pain.

"I think you told me it was hip disease? He can't go to school, I suppose!"

"No—impossible. But we have managed to get him tutored. His health makes him fretful at times, but he is wonderfully bright on the whole. When I'm back again I should like you to come and see us, and tell me what you think of him. His future is rather a problem."

"I will, with pleasure. I like boys."

He did not add that they liked him, or indeed stop to think whether they did or not. There was no diffidence in Hugh Curton as to his effect upon humanity, nor much sensitiveness as to its opinion of him. Of the two, Crayshaw was the more uncertain of himself, for all his good looks and his successful personality. He would have been amused and amazed if he could have realized that Curton regarded himself as quite as attractive, even to women, but would not have feared him as a rival once he had made up his mind that they both wanted the same thing. Curton always expected to win at golf, and generally did so because he was the more reliable player. Crayshaw was erratic. He said that his game depended on his mood, and it was true that sometimes he was brilliant, and at others as bad as a beginner. When he was really playing well Curton put it down to flukes. He did not admit the potency of temperament. "But then you're not a Celt, old Thing," Crayshaw said good-humoredly. "You see, I am."

Crayshaw was certainly not at his best on the following

morning when the two men took their clubs up to Mont
Agel, and played over the course. The peculiarity of the
golf course is that half the course is out of sight of the other,
owing to its being on a mountain, and the players need to
have the agility of mountain goats to play certain of the
holes. It was cold too, at that altitude so early in the day,
and Crayshaw was more sensitive to atmosphere than his
opponent. Curton drew steadily ahead, until he was four
up, and Crayshaw looked a certain loser half-way round.
There were few other players on the course, but as he stood
watching Curton make a long and successful putt, he
chanced to look to the far side and saw three people walking over the course in a contrary direction, a man and two
women. Something in the outline of one of the women
sent his heart suddenly throbbing with a suspicion that it
might be Madame Da Costa. She was too far off for him
to be certain, but the sun caught the sheen of a sable coat
that he thought he recognized and a black and white hat.
He glanced at Curton, intent on his stroke. The three pedestrians were evidently not playing, but were making
their way over the course to that point of it from which
there is a glorious view of the country and the coast. They
vanished from Crayshaw's range of vision in a few minutes, but the mere sense of this woman's proximity went
like wine to his brain.

Curton was so satisfied with his position that he regarded the game as practically his. "We may as well play
it out as walk back to the Club-house," he said. "My honor
——" He took his stance, and swung the driver over his
shoulder, hitting the ball with a clean smack some hundred yards.

Then Crayshaw suddenly became brilliant. He drove the
longest ball of the morning, placing it exactly where he

wanted it. His approach might have been that of a professional, and he putted as coolly as if he had never suffered from nerves. Even Curton was a little surprised.

"If you had played like that all through, I should not have had a chance," he said. "I've never seen you do that hole in three before."

"I don't suppose I ever shall again," laughed Crayshaw. "It was like an inspiration." He continued to play as if inspired, with the result that the game that had seemed lost was finally drawn, and Curton could only congratulate him on having retrieved his luck, perhaps a little dryly.

"Come on into the Club and have a drink," he added. "I'm sorry we can't play another round after lunch, but I must get busy this afternoon."

"And I'll go into the town and get that tuck for the boy."

The figure which had resembled Madame's was moving into the blue distance, carrying danger with it and leaving safety behind. Crayshaw's spirits rose with the immunity, and the "inspiration" that had retrieved his game shone in his eyes and on his lips as he pledged Curton in a "sidecar" to their next meeting. It had really been a happy chance that had brought Madame within range—if it were she—and then taken her in another direction without Curton seeing her or her seeing Curton; for if she played golf, or came up to the course with friends who played, how easy to arrange meetings when Curton was safely away! Crayshaw was as ingenuous as a little boy who has fallen sentimentally in love with a little girl, and tries to keep the other fellows off her while he slinks out on her trail.

Curton's time was really taken up with calling on the Agents, arranging for his departure on the morrow, and packing his belongings. Crayshaw was free to buy *marrons glacés* of the *pâtissier,* and to stroll down to the Casino in case—but she was not there. It fretted him to think that she might have been playing after he lost sight of her up at Mont Agel, but it was necessary to keep Curton employed and not to rouse his rivalry, and the golf was a sacrifice to the gods of chance for future opportunities. He hoped that Curton's packing might not be finished by dinner-time, but like all things that Curton did it was dispatched with method and according to routine, and he announced himself free to go down to the Casino for a last gamble after dinner. Crayshaw dared not let him go alone, and so they strolled down the hill and across the flaring gardens as usual, where a few people were even now sitting on the bright red seats overlooking the Cheese. On some of the faces was the dull look that comes of a passion indulged until it becomes habit—drugs or gambling, it matters not, there is no more excitement in it, but the loss would rouse a craving. Curton looked at these as he did at the flower-beds—part of the *mise en scène*—Crayshaw with more attention if hardly more thought.

"It is a curious fact that often as I have been here I have never yet seen a suicide," he remarked. "I suppose the tales of their being so frequent are mostly exaggeration."

"I don't know about that. I fancy the authorities are expert in keeping them out of sight. Even a man who has made up his mind to it if the luck does not turn, will try to find a quiet place by instinct, as an animal hides itself to die. They would preferably go into those gardens on the left, without the flower-beds and the electric lights."

They had crossed the Cheese, and entered the Casino as they talked, and left their hats and coats in the cloakroom. "Not so much of a crowd to-night, is there?" Crayshaw began as they passed into the Salle de Privée. His voice suddenly died away, and he shot a quick glance at Curton to see what he had seen.

Amongst the people standing on the other side of the roulette table was the same beautiful woman he had noticed and spoken to yesterday. She was wearing a long black velvet cloak over her evening dress, and the rich fur that trimmed it threw the lines of her head and face into more prominence. How wonderfully beautiful she was! Crayshaw caught his breath with something as emotional as a sob. He had never seen such a perfect mold of features with such coloring. Women with good masks were apt to be vapid in expression and lifeless in hue—things like Greek sculpture, at their best, a hairdresser's wax model, at their worst. But this woman—this!—had the warmth of life in her rich hair and skin, and passion in her eyes and mouth. It is easy to say "as beautiful as a dream," suggesting that no waking sense can conceive it, but this was as beautiful as reality. Intensely real too, and intensely human. It stirred every sense in him.

The lady was watching the players beneath full, lowered lids, the shadow of her curled lashes faintly visible on her smooth cheeks. A minute later she raised her eyes to the two men who, as it chanced, were standing exactly opposite to her. As she looked at Crayshaw she smiled and bowed slightly. It was impossible to judge if she had looked at Curton.

Crayshaw's face had been irradiated by her notice, but the next instant he gave another of those sharp glances at his friend, and almost scowled. Curton was certainly looking at Madame, whether she had noticed him or not, quite cognizant of her and deliberately appraising without rudeness. His broad gaze only lasted for a few seconds, but it was essentially masculine. Then he looked again at the table, remarking to Crayshaw, "Is not that the lady you admire, opposite?"

"Yes—it was she that you saw last year, I suppose?"

"I did. I have told you all I heard about her."

"She seems to be alone——"

"I think the woman behind her is some sort of an attendant, a maid."

Curton's quick eyes had seen more than Crayshaw's, possibly because they were not focused on Madame Da Costa. The same dark woman who had attended Madame the preceding day was standing behind her, seeming more interested in her surroundings than her mistress was, for her quick dark eyes roved over the players and the spectators with equal zest. A minute later Madame had sat down in a vacant seat and began to play.

"There is no room here," said Crayshaw impatiently. "Shall we try the other tables?"

"As you like. But I generally have more luck at roulette."

"We shan't have any luck if we have to stand and look on—and we can't go on playing over somebody's shoulder!" said Crayshaw cynically, leading the way to the *trente-et-quarante* table where there was less crowding. He looked back, however, to be sure that Curton was following, and thought he cast another of those significant, straight looks at Madame before he left. Curton's eyes were only expressive because of their lack of expression. They dwelt heavily on their object, whether animate or inanimate, as if nothing could turn them unless their owner willed it. It gave a sense of power and of boldness without offense, the redeeming virtue being that he always did will to look away before he became too personal.

The mere fact that he had looked at Madame, obviously seeing and approving of her, maddened Crayshaw. He staked recklessly, and when he lost it seemed to him like an ill-omen. He could not watch his friend's play as well as his own, but he was aggravatedly aware that Curton was as calmly absorbed in the game as he had been in golf this morning. Nothing had happened to upset the even beating of his pulse, he was amusing himself with this last "flutter" at the tables exactly as he had meant to do, and the presence of Madame Da Costa in the room meant no more to him than that of any other attractive woman who might—possibly—appeal to his senses if he had the time to pursue that game also. Crayshaw was aware that it all meant so much more to him than to Curton, undeveloped though the situation was, that he had the helpless feeling of a child overridden by the indifference of someone much older who looks upon the tragedies of his play as passing shadows. He fell back upon the old sufficing explanation of his own violence in emotion.

"It's his breed—Curton's a typical Anglo-Saxon. He can't conceive of what we feel or suffer. If he had a strain of Celtic blood in him he would be amazed at his own impassivity." Which self-assurance was perhaps more truly Celtic in its ambiguity than all the rest of him.

The luck had changed for Crayshaw, though he went on playing with the same recklessness, hardly looking at the numbers on which he staked. But the accumulating pile of chips beside him began to catch the attention of other players, who watched him stake and followed his lead. It seemed that he could not go wrong, though he played without much attention to any system of averages. Curton, a little farther down the table, seemed to be losing, but with characteristic egotism he would not change his mind and follow his friend's reckless stakes. Crayshaw doubled on "Trente," then trebled, and when at last Curton rose as if satisfied with his losses Crayshaw had won over sixty thousand francs, or about five hundred pounds.

The success exhilarated him: but partly because he again regarded it as an omen, this time of good luck in his pursuit of Madame. And his sense of her presence, his anxiety to see if she were still at the roulette table was stronger than his satisfaction over his gains, so that as he gathered his winnings together his eyes hardly followed the motion of his hands but flashed a searching glance round the Salle de Privée. She was no longer at the table, and he was half regretful and half relieved. To-morrow Curton would be gone, and he himself freer to follow his infatuation. To-morrow!——

As they left the Casino Curton said, "You had extraordinary luck, didn't you? People were beginning to notice it."

"Yes, I won a pot—for me. Not so much compared to a real break. There was a man here earlier in the season who won six thousand pounds in a night, so they tell me."

"Yes, I heard of him. But I would not have grumbled at your winnings, anyhow."

"I'm sorry, old man. Wish you had followed me. Did you drop much?"

"My limit. I always give up when I've reached what I mean to risk. It's no use going on with the luck against you."

Curton was, naturally, a little annoyed with the fortune that had so deserted him and favored Crayshaw, and inclined to attribute it to the latter's obstinacy in not playing roulette. But he was a good loser, and—as he said—he never went beyond his limit and tried to regain his losses. He enjoyed gambling as he enjoyed golf and dining and a good play. But he was no gambler. He would never play for the sheer love of it. It was a recreation rather than a passion. Crayshaw had much more of the gambler in him, though to-night he had really played absent-mindedly, almost mechanically, and his luck was not due to any concentration on the game. It was blind chance, for his eyes were partly with Madame Da Costa's subtle presence near him.

The five hundred pounds would, however, enable him to remain longer in Monte Carlo, and to continue a headlong pursuit of his inamorata. He had no desire to play again, beyond an idle hour or so in the Casino—which he would have spent there, anyway—or time wasted there in the hope of meeting her. He handed his money over to the hotel safe on his return that night, as thriftily as if he meant to live on his winnings, and the few lines in his face seemed to have vanished in a renewed boyhood. Crayshaw's face always sharpened when he was in pursuit of anything—a woman or some other object. It could not keep its own counsel. But the momentary satisfaction of seeing his way clear before him made him radiant.

Curton only saw literal things, and ascribed the man's obvious pleasure to the fact of last night's gains. When Crayshaw came to the station to see him off next day he was faintly amused because it seemed that the fellow's success had made him in love with all the world.

"He is overflowing with good-humor, and he can afford to pay a little extra attention to me," he thought with some cynicism. "I hope he won't gamble the money away again before he gets home, but will remember his wife and that boy."

To bring it to Crayshaw's mind he said, "I'll post that parcel as soon as I reach Folkestone. Drop me a line when you come home yourself, and we'll fix up something. I should like to see your boy."

It never occurred to him that Crayshaw was relieved at his departure for the sake of such a remote thing as a beautiful face seen last night at the roulette table. But in his exuberance Crayshaw could almost have made him free of his whole family—in England.

"Of course I will. I want you to meet the wife and Val. I shall write to her and tell her you are coming. She'd be awfully glad—at any time—to hear of me——"

The train was moving. Curton stood at the window of the high compartment and nodded with his finely impassable face bent to Crayshaw's ingenuous one. The impression of the latter lingered with him for a moment after the station was gone from his sight and the train was beginning to run down to Monaco.

"Handsome beggar, Crayshaw," he thought. "But no ballast. Acts like a boy—and looks like one. I'm sorry for his wife. Women want a man for a husband—not a boy. Well——"

He settled down to the English papers, which he had not had time to read the evening before.

## CHAPTER III

THE evening was fair, and life was altogether delightful as Crayshaw strolled back to the hotel after seeing Curton off. He greeted two or three acquaintances so cheerily that they said what a delightful fellow he was, and what a world it would be if there were more like him in it. At dinner he ordered a bottle of very good white wine that he had hitherto denied himself, and ate with the enjoyment of a schoolboy. "It really does one good to see anybody enjoying themselves as that man does!" said one woman to another, and she caught Crayshaw's roving eyes across the room and laughed and nodded to him.

"I heard of your luck last night!" she called "I am so glad!" and she really meant it. Anyone so handsome and so jolly deserved to be fortunate.

"Thanks!" said Horace, raising his glass to his smiling lips. "*A vous, Madame!*"

Everything really did seem to be very satisfactory at the moment. He had got rid of Curton just when his companionship might have become a check and an embarrassment. He was five hundred pounds to the good unexpectedly, and could prolong his stay until the Spring did he choose, for his precarious business did not tie him like his friend's more definite profession. He felt young—as young as he had at five-and-twenty—and happy and healthy, and his ardent fancy for Madame Da Costa seemed in good chance of fulfillment. He did not take it seriously, even in his growing excitement over her. He had been through too

35

many affairs like this to do so. But he meant it to last long
enough to be the motive power of his stay in Monte Carlo,
and he meant to pursue it without scruple if the lady
proved willing. It was easy to represent the tables as the
lure that had held him, if Noel grew suspicious of his prolonged stay, and if the five hundred were nearly all spent
on his return what more easy than to curse his ill-luck and
say that fortune turned against him? He did not want a
row with Noel. She had not been quite so easy-going lately,
or so politely blind to his indiscretions. She had indeed
been downright rude over little Kitty Shillinger, and had
bluntly told him that he must keep his mistress and his
wife apart—she would not accept Kitty in the house. It had
been a nasty jar, because he had grown so used to her overlooking his absences, his telephone calls, his correspondence
with women. But perhaps it *had* been a mistake taking
Kitty home and introducing her to Noel and the boy. Anyhow, he could keep Madame Da Costa out of his wife's
knowledge and sight, as they were at such a comfortable
distance from each other. And as there was no need to mention Madame to Noel, perhaps there was none to mention
Noel to Madame when they became better acquainted. He
could pose as a bachelor—he need not even use his own
name to her, should she ask it. He could call himself
Browne with an E. or Smyth with a Y! English names
were cheap. The only difficulty was his being known at
the hotel.

And then a brilliant thought occurred to him.

He could borrow Curton's name.

Curton's unexpected departure had not only cleared the
way of a possible rival, but had made it impossible that he
could ever pick up the dropped threads of the incident and
know how far it developed. He was unmarried, which to

Crayshaw's circuitous mind made him a legitimate cats-
paw, since (even should it involve him in some remote
rumor) it could not cause him domestic trouble. Crayshaw's
brain, traveling lightly and quickly over the possibilities,
found that his friend's position and personal belongings
had a thousand advantages for him to adopt. He could de-
scribe himself as a junior partner in Curton's firm, but of
less importance than the real Curton (the cards needed a
little shuffling here) and his prolonged absence as a long-
earned holiday while his nephew attended to the clients and
reported to him. Curton really had a nephew, recently articled, whose communications had been the means of sending him back to England. Crayshaw had learned so much
through casual conversation, though he knew little of the
scope of Curton's business or of the standing of the firm of
Staine & Curton, Solicitors. He knew that Curton was also
a barrister of the Middle Temple, which would improve
his social position. He, Crayshaw, could assimilate that also.
As a young man Horace had himself been intended for the
law, but had found it irksome and had preferred the excitement of the Stock Exchange until he had drifted into
Commission Agencies with the remainder of his dimin-
ished capital. The law experience would at any rate give
him sufficient smattering of the profession to avoid pitfalls
in conversation. But he did not talk Law to ladies of Madame Da Costa's type.

His initials were the same as Curton's. They had joked
over it when their laundry got mixed, or when a note-case
belonging to Crayshaw was lost and returned to Curton.
It was a small coincidence, but might prove useful some
day—somehow. Crayshaw was so practiced in intrigue that
he had learned the value of coincidence. Then again, the
forwarding of Curton's letters made it easy to correspond

in his name from the hotel did the lady wish to write to him—as of course she would, in time. He had only to watch the letter rack and detain his own letters while sending on the real Curton's.

The thing was becoming something like a game. His eyes sparkled and his lips laughed silently as he finished his wine and left the coffee-room, followed by admiring glances and salutations from other people finishing dinner. One or two men called to him as he passed to ask what he was doing that evening—they were going to play bridge, would he join them?—but he shook his head gaily—"I'm off to the tables!"—and they said amongst themselves what a pity he couldn't keep what he had won, but would assuredly lose it before the night was out!

Crayshaw, however, had no intention of risking his winnings that evening. He strolled down to the Casino, gave a swift glance at the people sitting in the lounge, and went into the Privée but did not sit down to play. One or two people recognized him as the Englishman who had wonderful luck last night, and exaggerated his winnings; but Madame was not at the roulette table, and after a tour of the rooms he realized that she either had not arrived or was not playing to-night. It was the first check to his good spirits, and though he lingered for some time, he had a foreboding that she would not come, and he went home at last to smoke and read in his room in preference to trying other distractions. She made him wait, this woman, and it enhanced her value. Something of the restlessness her actual presence had brought was upon him all night, so that he slept lightly and was glad when the clear gold morning came up and filtered into his bedroom. There was a house a little farther up the hill—a smaller hotel or pension—with a frieze below the flat roof, painted in delicate gold

THE MISERABLE SINNER          39

and violet and gray. He had never noticed it before, but in
the early morning it shone as delicately as a shaded ribbon
in a woman's hair. He stood at the window and looked
over Monte Carlo, and somehow it had never seemed so
innocent before—a red-tiled town with palms growing out
of it, and colored balconies, blue and green, clinging to the
houses.

It became colder as the sun strengthened, with a nip in
the wind; but at least it was fine. Crayshaw went down to
the Casino again about eleven o'clock; but again "drew
blank." The beautiful gambler was not there, and he passed
listlessly through the rooms and out on to the upper terrace.

There he suddenly saw her, when he had begun to give
up hope. She was seated just outside the Casino, under the
shelter of the balcony, talking with an elderly man, obviously not English, exquisitely dressed, and with one of the
"virgin" beards that foreigners rather affect. It looked as
soft and silky as vegetable down. He was chatting with
Madame animatedly, offering her the veiled devotion that
is all the more obvious for its restraint; but the animation
was certainly all on his part for the lady was listening with
a kind of insolent toleration, her down-bent brows almost
threatening a frown above her drooped eyelids.

The sun seemed to have gone under a cloud. The dancing
sea was as dull as where it broke round the icy shores of
England. The Casino was tawdry after all. Crayshaw
crossed the upper terrace, and walked aimlessly into the
recess near the empty bandstand. He leaned on the stone,
looking out to sea, as if the crowd below him, and the
pigeon shooting below the crowd, were not there. He saw
nothing, heard nothing, but the woman behind him and
her inaudible conversation with the Frenchman. His imagination pictured and heard all that distinctly, plainer than

the shots that dropped the unhappy pigeons to drown in the sea below. He said "Poor beggars!" without any sympathy for the pigeons but a general discontent at the world and a pity for his own discomfort.

He had fallen straight from the heights of illusion into the abyss of disenchantment and suspicion, according to his nature. Then he mechanically lit a cigar and wasted it because he noticed neither its flavor nor its soothing influence, while he leaned on the terrace, wondering savagely if he should go back to the tables and gamble recklessly till he lost everything he had won last night, or go back to the hotel and try to find a decent-looking woman to console him. Madame Da Costa was not the only woman in Monte Carlo, though she was, unfortunately, quite the most beautiful he had ever seen there.

He smoked the cigar so low that he hated it and flung the end over the balustrade regardless of the people below. There was a rustle behind him, and a voice said, "Are you thinking of swimming a new Hellespont to Corsica, Leander?"

"Why should Leander cross any sea when Hero is beside him?" said Horace gaily, turning, as if the bad moment was clean forgotten. His voice almost trembled with excitement, and the day was radiant again. For the gray-haired foreigner had vanished, and Madame was alone.

"I don't know," she said listlessly, moving to the balustrade that he had just left. "Leander had to return, hadn't he?"

"Not to Corsica, at any rate!"

"Have you been there?"

"No—have you?"

"Oh yes, I spent a winter there, at Ajaccio. If you took

the steamer instead of swimming, you might get to worse places, Leander!"

"While Hero is in Monte Carlo? Why do you want to doom me to exile?"

The two pairs of beautiful eyes met with a wordless avowal, for eyes become intimate long before the rest of the body. The long look was that of lovers, but their words had the guarded lightness of chance acquaintances. While their eyes met they neither of them spoke, but after that long minute Madame Da Costa turned her face away as if to release herself and spoke to him over her shoulder.

"I heard of your luck the night before last at *trente-et-quarante*. Or was it your friend's?"

"No, it was mine. He left the tables a loser, I'm sorry to say. If he would have followed my stakes he would have won, but he preferred his own game."

"Yes, he would prefer his own game," said Madame quietly. "Is he playing to-day?"

"He has left me and gone back to England, unfortunately. You take an interest in him?" The jealousy flamed out even in his voice, and she smiled as if a little bored.

"Not more than I do in any other Englishman."

"Did you think him good-looking?"

"I might have done so if I had not seen you with him."

Her tone was so impersonal that the compliment was more like a rebuff.

"But you like that type?"

"No—he would want his own way too much. We should quarrel."

"Do you often quarrel with men?"

"Often—always, I think, in the end. If they are my friends."

"Don't quarrel with me!" said Crayshaw with a swift

smile. He looked like a coaxing boy. "I should be so miserable that I should promise anything to make it up."

She laughed outright in her surprise. "Then do not try to become a friend of mine, Leander!" she said mockingly. "You have been warned."

"You know that no man would heed that warning!" In a moment Crayshaw had almost lost his head. Her beauty seen nearer drove him half mad, and the unspoken confession between them when their eyes met made this idle talking irksome. It was like sword-play between opponents who wanted to rush upon each other with a death-stroke. He was a past-master of flirtation, but he could not flirt with this woman. His passion was becoming too real, and she was torturing him with preliminaries.

"If you do not mean to know me better let me go!" he almost cried out in his excitement.

Some reflection of the heat in him seemed to reach Madame, for her face warmed as if with an inward glow. Their eyes met again, and she said: "I have a house here—at Roquebrune—the Casa Caralyn—you may come and see me." She spoke in short sentences and almost panted.

"When? Now? This evening?" he stammered in response.

"No—no—to-morrow."

"Why not to-day?"

"I have engagements."

"That man who was with you just now—does he visit you? Who is he?"

"Comte de Chalis. But you must not ask questions. I warned you we should quarrel!"

"I can't help it. You are driving me mad. If I may not come this evening, I shall know he is with you! You *must* let me come." The distress in his voice was so real that she looked at him as if startled for once. She had known the Latin races inflammable as this, but no Englishman had ever looked at her with such eyes. They were full of tears, and it touched her.

"Why, you are like a boy!" she said, half scolding him and half caressing. "It is not the Comte—I do not like Frenchmen. But I have promised to dine out with some neighbors of mine. I should be late."

"I can come late—at any hour."

"No," she said, and her tone was final. "You may lunch with me to-morrow. If that does not suit you, do not come at all."

"You know I shall come. But you are very cruel. Shall I see you to-morrow—before I come to your house?"

"I don't know—I may be at the tables, or I may go to Mont Agel."

"I saw you there yesterday! Did I see you there?"

"I was there. I do not know if you saw me."

"At a distance—with a lady and gentleman?"

"Those are the people I am dining with—they are Italians."

She turned without further farewell, and walked rather slowly back to the Casino with Crayshaw beside her. He was exultant and despairing at the same time, for he did not believe that it was not the Comte de Chalis for whom she shut him out. But he had her permission to go and see her at her villa, which was more than he could have hoped in such a short time. This was, to Crayshaw, the most important thing in the world and in his life, at the moment. It wiped out all nearer associations in England, all the ordinary surroundings of the hotel. He hardly thought of himself as having any existence beyond the fact that he might be her lover within twenty-four hours.

As she entered the Casino she paused and looked back at him with a slight smile.

"Perhaps we had better know each other's names," she said carelessly. "I am Madame Da Costa."

"May I know your Christian name?"

"Caralyn, or Cara."

"I am Hugh Curton. I am staying at the Hotel Beausite. A note there would find me at any time."

"Thank you," she said quietly. "I am going to play for a little while."

When she left him he stood for a minute as if in a dream. He had not hesitated for an instant in the lie about Curton's name, it had come so naturally that while he spoke he had felt that he *was* Curton. But as his eyes followed Madame in her slow progress to the Privée, for the crowd was thick, he wondered vaguely where she was leading him, and what would happen to them both. He felt no fear, he did not dream of retreating while there was time, though he knew nothing about her except her obvious notoriety in the Casino and the shadow of that ugly story that Curton had told him. But for a minute he had a curious premonition that this woman was his fate, and that he could not escape it if he would.

## CHAPTER IV

THE Casa Caralyn was not so far away as Crayshaw
had imagined, not indeed actually at Cap Martin
though on the road to it. He could have gone by train to
Roquebrune and walked back half a mile to his destina-
tion, but this he did not know. And so he took a taxi,
secure in his winnings at *trente-et-quarante*, and drove out
along the road that enters French territory over the bridge,
past other villas and a few small shops with glimpses of
the coast line like a colored picture amongst black and
white prints.

There was a cold wind, but the sun shone bravely, and
he was too excited to notice the weather. His headlong
fancy had entered the Casa and found Madame awaiting
him long before the cab stopped at a great pair of wrought-
iron gates, and a porter came out of the lodge to let them
pass. He did it with something of a flourish, and Crayshaw had time to see that he was dark-skinned like
Madame's female attendant, and also dressed in dark
livery that made his figure stand out somberly against the
gleaming white of the house and lodge.

For the Casa Caralyn was built of white stone and marble, and shone like some fairy palace against the rich green
of its trees and gardens. The taxi drove through the gates
and along a drive to the front of the house where Crayshaw paid and dismissed it. He had no idea of limiting his
visit by a waiting taxi, and the means of returning to
Monte Carlo could wait on the other side of a stretch of
hours that he saw in rainbow fancy before him.

The pillars and the steps of the entrance were of marble, and he walked up them as if he were really the prince in the fairy tale. Not a bad semblance of a prince either with his roving long-lashed eyes and handsome face, though his dress was that of the modern Englishman. To have suited the Casa he should have been dressed as a Spanish Toreador or some rich Eastern potentate, and a gasping sense of this brought a laugh to his lips as he was admitted into the vast entrance hall. What a hall! It was so white that it was not gloomy, though the window above the fireplace was of tinted glasses, and the columns supporting the gallery above were of different colored marbles. The butler who had opened the door to him was as dark and silent as the porter had been, and dressed in the same livery. Crayshaw remembered that Da Costa had lived in South America, and guessed that his servants had come from Chile. A second man took his hat and stick, and the butler ushered him silently across the great hall and through glass doors into what was evidently the salon of the house, and left him there without asking his name. He was so evidently expected that it sent his spirits up with a bound though there was as yet no sign of Madame.

Something in the sumptuousness of the Casa suited a need in Horace Crayshaw and gave him instant pleasure. He did not find it too luxurious for good taste, and he really liked the prodigal display of riches. The salon was so large that though it was crowded with valuable things he found room to admire them, and the lavishness of its upholsteries and furnishings seemed nothing but a suitable background for Madame's beauty. A less sensuous mind might have felt a little stifled by the display of wealth— might have wished that the parquet floor was not quite so covered with Persian rugs, that the walls were not

paneled with silk tapestry, that the room was content to
be a frame to the great view from the long windows opening upon the gardens and the blue sea, instead of asserting
its own claim to attention. But Crayshaw liked the very
smell of wealth, and could never have enough. He walked
over to the open windows and looked across the marble
terrace that ran the length of the Casa, to the vista of green
lawns and flower-beds and waving palms below him, and
what he said was, "What a place! It ought to be kept for
honeymooners. It must take about six gardeners too, to
keep it up like this."

Quite possibly it did, for it was ten times the size of the
Casino gardens and much more elaborately cultivated.
The roses were in bloom already over the balustrade of
the terrace, and the oranges and lemons made bright
blobs of color amongst the green. There were flowers
growing down there that were not all planted in pots and
renewed every fortnight, and their naturalness made it
seem as if summer were eternal in this one spot on earth
at least.

The sunny, blossoming garden was not even desecrated
by the presence of a gardener; it might have belonged to
the Sleeping Beauty or the White Cat, or some other
enchanted princess, so silent and secluded was it. And this
struck Crayshaw the more for the crowded houses and
flats in Monte Carlo, where everybody seems to be looking into the concerns of his next-door neighbor. Even the
villas along the shore, or just outside the Principality, had
little or no privacy, and a strip of ground the size of a
dining-room table was proudly spoken of as "a garden."
In contrast, the Casa Caralyn was a château in its own
grounds, and there must certainly be some hundreds of
feet of foreshore attached to it. He felt the advantage of

this seclusion in an *affaire du cœur,* even though the lady
was so conveniently a widow. But there were no doubt
servants, both indoors and out, invisible and discreet
though they might be, still to be avoided. Intrigue was so
familiar to him that he mechanically calculated the chances
of two or more exits to the grounds, and how easily a
stealthy step might lose itself amongst those far shrub-
beries into which he could not see.

Then, suddenly, three figures came into view, approaching the house from the right. One was unmistakably
Madame Da Costa, the other two a lady and gentleman
who walked one on either side of her. They paused at the
foot of the double marble stairway that united with the
single flight leading up to the terrace, and made some ges-
ture of admiration or inquiry which Madame appeared to
answer. Then they all slowly ascended the stairs to the
terrace.

All Crayshaw's rosy dreams of a *tête-à-tête* dissolved in
chagrin at this unexpected party. He had calculated too
soon on an easy rapture, and that mutual passion in
Madame's eyes as they met his own was nothing but a
snare. It seemed he must approach her on probation, and
his impatience made him want to walk out of the beautiful hateful house, and go back to Monte Carlo like a
spoiled child. He was so upset by the frustration of his
plans that for a minute he could not recover his usual
charm of manner, and when Madame and her other guests
approached the open window where he stood he was almost
formal in returning her greeting.

"I hope you have not been here long," she said half carelessly. "I suppose the servants did not know where to find
us. Signora and Signor Gazzi—Mr. Curton."

"I was lost in admiration of your garden," said Crayshaw, trying for an indifference to equal hers. "What a view!"

"Ah, is it not most wonderful!" the Signora broke out, using her hands as much as her tongue to express her feeling. "I never come here but it seems to me more lovely. Is this the first time you see it, then?"

"Yes," Crayshaw admitted, wishing that he could have claimed a knowledge of the house and garden equal to hers. He felt jealous of the Italians, who knew Madame so much better than he did, and hated their company, though the man was not attractive, being sallow and heavy in build and with no trace of youth left in him.

"It is too cold to-day to be pleasant in the garden," said Madame Da Costa. "As a rule one can sit out in the sun-loggia down there even after lunch; but to-day the wind is too rough."

She had been walking with a Japanese parasol held over her head, the gay colors making a contrast to the dull white of her cloth coat and dress. It was the first time that Crayshaw had seen her without a hat, for even at night in the Casino she had worn one with her dinner-gown. It made her seem more intimate, more accessible, and yet she seemed to hold him at a distance as she chose, without more return of his urgent feeling than she might have given to a complete stranger. Her hair was really beautiful, both in color and texture, with an obviously natural wave and undyed. When the sun caught it the chestnut turned to burnished bronze, and the looser waves over her forehead were touched as if with red gold. He saw also that she was younger than he had thought, probably not much over thirty, and it made him anxious not to betray his own age. He was generally taken for thirty-five at first sight, particularly by people who did not know

that he was married. Val was growing a confoundedly
big boy, and his father sometimes felt his vanity wounded
when they were seen together as father and son. That,
however, was not often, and certainly it could not betray
him to Madame.

Lunch was served in the room adjoining the salon, which
had the same fine view. This room was nearly as large as
the first, and the four people at the long table seemed far
away from each other with a wilderness of polished wood
reflecting glass and silver between them, and a mass of
exotics in the center. There was almost too much of this
house, even as a background to Madame. The voices
seemed to echo in its spaces, and the feet of the servants
passing to and fro were hardly muffled in the thick car-
pets. It was an excellent lunch, and the two Italians took
it as seriously as a ceremony. Signor Gazzi ate and chewed
and devoted himself to his plate almost to the neglect of
talking to Madame, and his wife combined her conversation with little signs of enjoyment.

"My dearest Cara, how do you contrive to get such fish
out here? (What perfect cooking!) We are always afraid
that it will not be fresh."

"I think there is a local fisherman who supplies us,"
said Madame carelessly. "I do not trouble about it."

The Signora turned to include Crayshaw in her eulogy.
"Are you well fed in Monte Carlo, Mr. Curton? You
cannot get anything like this at the Hôtel de Paris or the
Metropole!"

"I am at neither of those hotels," said Crayshaw dryly.
"The food is much like other smaller places—indifferent."

"It must be a treat to you to come out here!"

"It would be that, in any case."

The Signora nodded, smiling on him. Her English was

voluble, but not very intelligible owing to her accent. Every now and then she lapsed into French when speaking to Madame, and Crayshaw, who was no linguist, felt that he hated her. He knew that he was not at his best, for his ready laugh and quick uptake in conversation were two of his assets, and he could use neither. Madame only spoke to him in the general conversation, and the lunch dragged out to an hour while Signor Gazzi ate his way seriously through six or seven courses.

"I shall get out of this as soon as the beastly pigs have done gorging," Crayshaw thought, and then stole a glance at Madame and felt his heart fail him. If he outstayed the Gazzis he might after all have a few minutes with her alone. For that he would have sat out a school-treat or a service at the Cathedral of St. Nicholas.

"Have you heard that there is to be a revolution in April?" he asked the Signora languidly, with an effort after his usual manner. "The English papers have it all planned. Something to do with the Prince of Monaco, I think."

"We hear nothing of that. The Monacists are always agitating for one. I expect it will come to nothing."

"It would not affect you on French territory, I suppose."

"It would be a welcome distraction," said Madame Da Costa with a little shrug. "And if they blew up the Palace and made Monaco a Republic it might be a little livelier."

Something in her manner, some secret resentment, caught Crayshaw's ear, and made him guess that Madame had never been amongst the favored few who had been invited to the Palace. He had a vague idea that the etiquette there was almost Victorian in its vogue, and the company most carefully select. Even as the widow of a millionaire Madame Da Costa was probably too notorious to have the *entrée* to such circles. Her chagrin was of no immediate value to him, but he put the little thought into the background of his mind for future use. In dealing with women, Horace Crayshaw had found that odds and ends of knowledge came in usefully at unexpected moments. And everything that betrayed something they wished to conceal was like a secret key to unlock a guarded citadel.

It was past one o'clock when even the dessert was finished, and Signor Gazzi was dipping his fingers in a bowl to cleanse them of juices. "He might just as well have sucked them!" thought Crayshaw to whom everything the unwelcome Italians did was revolting.

"Let us smoke on the terrace," said Madame. "It is still sunny there. And you will sing to us, Anita——"

"Oh, but dearest Cara, you cannot want to hear me! My poor songs are nothing, and I have eaten too much!"

"You will sing to please me, in spite of that." There was the faintest contraction of Madame's fine brows to add to her imperious words. It was evident that these friends of hers were satellites as well as friends, and expected to pay a certain homage for their entertainment. She beckoned to the footman very much as she had disallowed the protest of her guest—as one who had a right to give orders. "Manoel, bring the Signora's guitar."

The lunch party trailed back on to the marble terrace where the servants had already placed lounging chairs and little tables with cigarettes and liqueurs. Crayshaw made up his mind to be further bored, but to sit it out doggedly till these people should leave; but the Signora's performance was an unexpected pleasure and made him almost

ashamed of having hated her. She had so fine a contralto
that he suspected her of having been in Opera, and though
she sang nothing but simple songs to the guitar, she held
her audience as by a spell. He was quite genuine when he
said "Another and another if we do not weary you!"—
and the boyish charm had come back to his face and
manner.

"I will sing something English, but you must not mind
my funny words!" said the Italian good-naturedly. She
played a simple little accompaniment on the strings of her
instrument, unlike the thrumming which had made her
Neapolitan songs so gay, and despite her accent the words
were quite distinct.

> "You are my dream come true,
>  You are my Paradise!
> All of Heaven I ever knew
>  I find in your dear eyes."

Crayshaw raised his head suddenly and looked at
Madame Da Costa. She turned her face as if compelled,
and once more they spoke to each other with that naked
passion that needed no words. The conventionalities—of
the other visitors, the luncheon, the formal servants of the
Casa—were wiped out for that one minute and did not
exist:

> "The lonely days are drear,
>  I sleep to dream of you;
> O let me wake and find you near—
>  You are my dream come true!"

The Signora dropped her voice on a sighing note, and drew
her hand across the strings of the guitar. Her method was
perfect, and her voice rich and round in spite of her age.

"And now we really must go, dearest Cara, for we have to meet some friends in Monte Carlo at three o'clock"— her voice ran on through the murmured thanks of her audience, and she rose, holding Madame's hands in an affectionate clasp. But when it came to Crayshaw's turn to say good-bye he paid her a better compliment than his faltering words, for his large liquid eyes were full of tears. Many women had brought strange emotions up from those shallow pools, but it was an impulse of genius that made him give his feelings full play under the spell of the little song.

"Ah! but you have a heart, Mr. Curton!" The Italian was delighted, and her hand pressed his with fervor. "My singing has touched you? You please me more than any great audience crying Encore! Bravissima!"

"I am a fool!" said Crayshaw, and the tears hung upon his thick eyelashes and made his face almost spiritual.

"Never say it, if it is music that makes you cry! Ah, if all your countrymen had that beautiful sympathy, you would not be accused of caring little for Art!"

"I am Celtic, not Anglo-Saxon," said Crayshaw with a smile. His tears were the real success of the afternoon, as he half recognized. The Signora kissed Cara Da Costa again with a reflection of Crayshaw's emotion, and whispered to her, "He has charm, this new friend—he has beauty! I could love him, myself!" and even the Signor shook hands with such ardor that Horace found himself sufficiently English after all to fear that the Italian might kiss him!

Madame Da Costa had said very little, and after that revealing look her eyes had not met Crayshaw's again. She went out into the hall with her guests, leaving Crayshaw in the salon, and her step as she returned to the room

was so slow that for a minute he—waiting for her—
thought that she was going to pass the door and treat him
with the indignity he deserved for his persistent lingering.

He was standing by the Adams mantelpiece as she at
last re-entered, leaning his hand upon the cold marble as
if to steady himself. She came deliberately into the room
and stood looking at him with stormy eyes, while still yards
away.

"Well?" she said sharply.

She was evidently angry. He had outstayed his welcome.
It was so different from what he had planned that he
looked at her with a feeling little short of grief.

"You knew I couldn't leave without seeing you alone!"
he pleaded, and he held out hands that actually trembled
in his excitement.

She made a movement of impatience that was as uncontrolled as his. "I warn you," she said, as if she were fighting
for breath. "I tried to warn you when you spoke to me in
the Casino. I take men as I find them—they are all alike.
But you—it is like taking advantage of a child——"

She stood there in her splendid beauty, struggling with
herself. Then with an indrawing of the breath she almost
rushed across the great room into his outstretched arms.

"You are my dream come true!"

murmured Crayshaw as his lips left hers. He was too carried away by his own passion to wonder why she had
warned him, why she had hesitated. Her head was a little
thrown back, with closed eyes, and lips still parted as if
thirsting for his own, and her loveliness seemed to him
like some intoxicating flower. He kissed her throat raven-
ously, and strained her body to him with a foretaste of
possession. They were both so unbridled with the passion

of the moment that they were beyond words. To any one entering the room it might have looked like a love scene in some scenic drama, overdrawn to satiety. But they were unaware of being theatrical because sensation was natural to them both. Even sentimental emotion no longer prompted Crayshaw to woo as he had done in the words of the Signora's song. When he could speak he only did so baldly for his ardent desire:

"Take me somewhere where we can be alone!"

She murmured something that sounded like, "You will not be warned!"

"Let me come with you—let me make you mine. This is cruel—you must! . . ."

A sudden silence seemed to have fallen on the house with the departure of the Italians. The servants had disappeared as quickly as if they had dropped into the earth. The great hall was empty as Crayshaw stole across it with the woman half encircled with his arm. They climbed the wide marble stairs like this, their steps muffled in the thick pile of the carpet, and the shadows of the gallery engulfed them. . . .

A door opened and closed. There was a faint scent and a dim vastness of tapestries and inlaid wood and more marble. A couch, spread with silks that were stiff with gold, in the semblance of a royal bed. Long mirrors reflecting two figures. Then a man's hand drawing the curtains to shut out the sunlight for a purpose that had no shame in Eden till the day of recompense.

## CHAPTER V

CRAYSHAW walked up to the counter from which the hotel concierge dispensed stamps and good advice to visitors, and asked for letters. There were none for himself, but as it happened two or three for Hugh Curton.

"I'll take Mr. Curton's," he said. "He asked me to forward them."

He saw, as he took them, that two had come from England, but the third had the local postmark. He had been expecting this last from Madame Da Costa. When they parted at the Casa Caralyn (that visit that was so disappointing at the beginning, and so full of tardy bliss at last!) she had told him to wait until he heard from her. He would have been in a difficulty but for the arrangement between him and Curton about the letters, but all he had to do was to keep a sharp look-out that the concierge should not lock up Curton's correspondence until he could get his address. Curton had not troubled to give it, as he had left Crayshaw to send on his letters, but by some misadventure the concierge might have got it from a former reference. Crayshaw could not remember if Curton had stayed in the hotel before or not.

He re-addressed the two business letters to Curton in England, and put the third in his pocket. Then he went up to his room with a smile in his eyes that made the valet and the chambermaid on his floor nod to each other in admiration of "Ce beau Monsieur!" He was the first Englishman they had seen who looked really happy.

The letter was brief and to the point, and changed Crayshaw's smile into a little laugh.

"LEANDER.—I want you for the week-end. Come on Friday.                                   HERO."

Crayshaw looked round for a means of destroying the letter, and still more the envelope; but as the hotel had central heating and the fireplace was closed with the usual shutter over the grate, he found none. His mind, however, was ingenious. He cut the one word "Hero" from the letter and put it in his pocket-book, folding the rest of the sheet into an old-fashioned spill. He lit his pipe with it, and prodded the burning paper into his empty lavatory basin until it had burnt itself into a little black ash. Then he washed it carefully down the waste, and treated the envelope in the same way. The pipe, he thought sentimentally, smoked all the better for the burnt offering, and the faint perfume that had hung about it—Cara's own scent—reminded him as only scent can do of the rapture of her flawless body in his arms.

He wrote in answer:

"Hero, how can I thank you for this? I will try, on Friday. I am starving for you. The days between are like years." (It was Wednesday already.) "Think of me sometimes. 'You are my dream come true.'—Yours always and only,                                   LEANDER."

As he sealed the letter he wondered what the real Hugh Curton would have said in the same case. He could not fancy him anything more than commonplace, like this: "My dear Cara,—Yes, of course I will come on Friday. Thanks very much for the chance.—Yours, Hugh Curton."

For Curton would always be afraid of incriminating himself, even to his mistress, and would reserve the natural warmth of man to woman until they were safely private. Crayshaw loved his own reckless extravagance in contrast. He felt as young as Romeo risking the whole tribe of Capulets under Juliet's balcony.

The morning was dull and threatened rain, and as one must do something in Monte Carlo he strolled down the hill to the Casino, thinking that he might look at the gamblers if he did not play himself; and, possibly, that his lady might be present. She had told him that she came in to play as the mood seized her, but she did not go to the Casino daily. As he crossed the square, a gentleman came out of the Hôtel de Paris, and pausing on the steps suddenly hailed him. Crayshaw dodged a huge bus that took people to Nice, and was nearly cut down by a private car coming in the other direction. But he was laughing as he ran up the steps to greet the acquaintance who was paralyzed with dismay at the accident he had nearly caused.

"My dear Crayshaw, I am damned sorry!" he explained. "I never dreamed of your running across like that. I did not know you were in Monte, and I shouted out to you on impulse. What a sport you are!" he added, looking at Crayshaw's splendid, careless face. "You take the risk as a joke—but it was a narrow shave!"

"I love the Bright Eyes of Danger!" Crayshaw quoted lightly. "How are you, Vanstead?"

"I've been staying at Cannes, and got bored stiff with titles. Upon my word, I think half the British peerage is in the town. It's so common to have a title that it's more distinguished to be without one! I came over to Monte for a few days' change."

"Anything doing, or are you on holiday?"

"Oh, I'm always a business man, and ready for a deal, but I don't come to the Riviera for that. It's amazing, though, how people come to me. I don't ask them. Look here, Crayshaw, will you dine with me to-night? I must go back to Cannes on Friday."

Again Crayshaw's luck was in the ascendant. It was almost uncanny. He knew Percy Vanstead only slightly, having met him at the houses of one or two monied men in London, generally at bachelor parties. He knew *of* him, however, rather better. Vanstead was reported a very clever financier, and the promoter of several Companies which were paying substantial dividends. He was not prodigal of advice, but (as he said) people came to him in the hope of making money rather than he to them to persuade them to invest. He was a business man, and showed an objection to the ordinary social functions where ladies were present—hence the exclusively male element where he accepted invitations. He seemed to have been attracted by Crayshaw on the few occasions when they had met, perhaps because he lacked the very advantages that Crayshaw's manner and appearance gave him. The financier was a man of middle height and sturdy build, always so well dressed that he had an air of quiet prosperity. His face was shrewd, but he looked young for the position he had already gained in the City, perhaps because he was very fair with pale hair and skin and light eyes. He spoke rather off-handedly and certainly did not ingratiate himself with people. It was his reputation that brought him into the limelight and gained him attention, the success with which he had financed small undertakings until they had grown into big ones, the judgment that made even insecurity safe.

Crayshaw was eager to pursue the acquaintance and hoped that it might ripen into friendship on Vanstead's part. He could find many uses for Vanstead. But in London the man was too big to be courted, too engulfed in business to be found unless he himself willed it. It was a farce to ask Vanstead to come and play a game of golf, as Crayshaw might have done a lesser man. But this chance encounter was a different thing, and the opening he wanted. He would not have missed dining with Vanstead for any consideration—except Madame Da Costa. But there again he was lucky. Vanstead was leaving on Friday, the very day that Crayshaw was summoned to the Casa. And there was the whole of Thursday to cultivate his good will.

The two men walked over to the Casino together, and Vanstead sat down to play *chemin de fer* while Crayshaw—who did not know the game—stood and watched him for a while. Vanstead played in the perfectly business-like manner in which he did most things, even dining or sleeping. He was expert at *chemin de fer,* and he won steadily. Later in the day, as he told Crayshaw, he would go to the Sporting Club, and they could dine together at the Hôtel de Paris at eight. Crayshaw excused himself from going to the Club. He was not a member, and he said with a charming air of frankness that he could not afford to play so high.

He was too wise to attach himself to Vanstead on this occasion of meeting him, until they had dined together and grown more social over the menu of the Hôtel de Paris. Crayshaw knew the influence of food and drink in such a place, and his own value as a companion. He was at his best when being luxuriously entertained. A little careless-ness of Vanstead, an air of having other interests and occupations, became him very well, and made him independent of the richer man's importance. People usually courted Vanstead for what he could do for them. Crayshaw quietly left him to his game of *chemin de fer*, and slipped out of the Privée without speaking to him again.

The record of a man like Horace Crayshaw is chiefly of meals and games. He played at life, and seldom took anything seriously unless his passions were involved. Somebody was always asking him to lunch or dinner because he lunched and dined well and made other people enjoy it as well as himself. He was asked to play golf and bridge for the same reason, not because he was a particularly good player but because he diffused an atmosphere of enjoyment into games to temper the strenuousness of more earnest players. It was his gift, and one that cannot be overrated in a world given up to sociality such as he inhabited. Even in business his success was mainly due to his engaging personality. In writing of him I find it hard to get him away from a table spread for eating and drinking, and yet he was as little of a *gourmet* or an epicure as any athlete. He dressed well and looked well, and talked well without saying anything that was worth remembering. But such men as Hugh Curton and Percy Vanstead would always choose him as a companion though they had better brains and more purpose in life.

Vanstead, at any rate, did not undervalue Crayshaw's social gift. He knew the worth of it as well as he knew the worth of his own flair for finance. The dinner at the Hôtel de Paris was good, and the wine well chosen. Crayshaw was radiant, and his host was quietly aware that his guest's good looks and good manners drew the attention of other diners who would hardly have looked at himself

if he had not been a marked man even in such a hetero-
geneous place as Monte Carlo.

"That is Percy Vanstead, the financial genius," they
said: but they would never have taken the trouble to ask
"Who is he?" as they did about Horace Crayshaw, if he
had not been successful in making money for himself and
other people.

When Vanstead went off to the Sporting Club the two
men had arranged to meet the next day and lunch at the
Metropole (as being quieter than the Paris) still at Vanstead's expense.

"I should like to have a business talk with you," he
said, and Crayshaw's heart throbbed with excitement more
than it had done at the roulette table when he had won
his five hundred pounds. "I might be able to put something in your way. You were with Lowland Brothers at
one time, were you not?"

"Yes. It was like my luck that they amalgamated with
Small's and had no further use for me." Crayshaw wondered how Vanstead had got his knowledge of the connection with Lowland's, and still more that he should
remember. It was a small detail to bear in mind for a
man with such big interest. He was a little flattered.

"You worked on commission, I suppose."

"Yes. I did."

"Well, it's not a bad training. Makes you quick on the
chances."

"Oh, nothing comes amiss to me," said Crayshaw lightly.
"Good night, Vanstead. Thanks for a gorgeous tuckin."
He lit the cigar that Vanstead had given to him, and
smoked it walking back to his modest hotel. A pleasurable
anticipation made him look forward to the morrow, and
he wondered what Vanstead had got in his head. The

good-will of such a man might mean a lot to him, and it was particularly fortunate that he had met him just now as it gave him the excuse he wanted for remaining longer out of England. He could write and explain to Noel how important it was to cultivate Vanstead, and that he hoped to see more of him. She could not know that Vanstead was leaving Monte Carlo on Friday and going back to Cannes, and as long as he could play Vanstead as a trump card he could spend his time at the Casa Caralyn without having to account for it. Moreover Noel would not know that the "treating" was all on one side, and would be less likely to ask him for money if he carelessly deprecated the expense that Vanstead's friendship entailed on him.

It was a peculiarity of Crayshaw's mentality that he would always rather lie than tell the truth. He really enjoyed lying, though not always consciously. When it happened that there was no advantage in lying, but rather in speaking the truth, he spoke it; but he always embroidered it to save dullness. His wife, who had learned his character with painful experience, allowed for this. Possibly she ascribed it to a Celtic origin, and she may have been right, for the imagination of the Celt is an acknowledged marvel.

What Vanstead had got in his head exceeded Crayshaw's widest hope when it was laid before him on the morrow. The man of business came to the point with a brevity that suggested how little time he had to spare on preliminaries, though he had chatted through the lunch on ordinary topics.

"I want another secretary. I think you are the man I'm looking for," he said, with his light eyes fixed on Crayshaw's face. "I've got two already, stenographers, good at their job. But I want a man who can see people for me, and put them off if necessary without offending them. My young men are no good at that. They haven't the manner. I'm simply getting crowded out with people. I don't know what your own jobs are worth. Mine is six hundred. If you like to take it, it's there."

Crayshaw hoped he kept his face under control. "My dear Vanstead, of course I'm only too glad," he said quietly. "It's not a chance a man like me throws away. But I should like to be sure you want me?"

"You needn't worry about that. When I take a man into business I know what I am doing. It's not a trial trip—it's because he suits. I've had my eyes on you for some time—since I met you at Sir Joseph Jennings."

Crayshaw remembered that lunch party. It stood out in his mind for the very reason that it was the first time he met Vanstead, and most needy men wanted to meet Vanstead only to find that he brushed them on one side like flies. Crayshaw knew, of course, that the financier had not entirely overlooked him like others. His personality had had its usual effect. But he had never dreamed that it would end in his being offered a job with Vanstead. To be so successful in oneself, almost without effort, was enough to make any man lose his head a little. It says something for Crayshaw that he kept his.

"And when should you want me?" he said, as easily as if jobs at six hundred a year were a weekly offer to his necessity.

"Oh, not before I go back—some time in April. I want to show you round myself. There's bound to be some jealousy amongst the staff. You understand?"

"I think I can manage that," said Crayshaw with his happy smile. "People never are jealous of me for long, somehow."

Vanstead studied him quietly with a look that gave nothing of his own thoughts away. "You have the knack of making yourself liked. I want that. When you refuse to let a man see me, I want him to go away satisfied with having seen you. You will want a general grasp of the business, but you need not *be* the business—as I am." He laughed a little, himself, a laugh with little merriment in it, as if it had dried in the making. "I will write to you from Cannes in good time before I go home."

There the matter rested, and Crayshaw was well content to let it rest. The offer of a settled salary at six hundred a year, to a man whose income had been generally precarious, was as satisfying as a good dinner to one always hungry. His private means were only two or three hundred, supplemented by such commission agencies as he could get, and he had found it difficult to keep up appearances and live amongst the people he had to cultivate. Certainly he had lived on them as well as amongst them, or he could not have done it. Vanstead's offer would make life very much more comfortable for him. Incidentally, it would enable him to take a holiday every now and then to Monte Carlo if the attraction at the Casa Caralyn remained and did not burn itself out as such things usually did. He could explain it so easily to Noel as part of his job, and invent a branch in Paris for Vanstead, if not actually at Monte Carlo. In his exuberance of spirits he even thought of making an extra allowance for his wife and child; but on thinking it over he decided against this. He would not, at any rate, give Noel any extra money as a settled thing—he would simply pose as more generous at his own expense. If he once let her know what he was making in Vanstead's offices, she might urge expenses on him about Valentine's education and health which would seriously detract from the benefit to himself. It would be like throwing the money away. He decided to represent himself as still taking small commissions on some work done for Vanstead. Noel did not expect much from commission agencies. She had had to live with them all her married life. And on the whole she and the boy did very well. She did not have to take office work herself, as many women did. He knew several wives who drew their private incomes from their own exertions. Noel was not independent, and she could not expect to do more than share in the living made entirely by her husband. He wrote to her, however, the next day, telling her that he had been lucky enough to meet a man with influence in the City, who might help him, and that he should stay on a bit to keep in touch with him. After which he strolled down to the station to see Vanstead off to Cannes, and nodded his care-free farewell to him much as he had done to Curton.

The last thing that Vanstead said from the train was, "I'll write to you as soon as I fix a date to return, and confirm my offer. It's always well to have these things in writing. Good-bye, Crayshaw. Very glad to have met you."

"Oh, the luck is on my side!" said Horace lightly.

# CHAPTER VI

THE garden of the Casa was bounded by a terrace above the foreshore, to which a private flight of steps led on to the beach. Bathing in Monte Carlo begins—officially—in May; but at eleven o'clock the sun was hot enough to take the chill off the March sea, or so it seemed to bathers from the Casa who took the plunge and then fancied that the warmth on their faces permeated their whole bodies. At any rate it was bracing. Crayshaw came up from his morning dip with a wet black head shining like a retriever's, and his skin faintly bronzed. He wore his bath-wrap over his sleek, saturated body and dripping bathing-dress, but no shoes, and the marble steps to the terrace felt almost warm to his bare feet. Crayshaw was proud of his feet. They were as shapely as a child's—much more so than most women's.

He paused before mounting to the house terrace, and looked at the lily pond at the foot of the double stairway. All round it grew white arums in bloom, and in the center a white marble figure of Leda caressing her swan. It was all most beautiful in the fickle sunshine that had come back to Monte Carlo in the nick of time. Yesterday had been dull, but to-day was supremely fine. The Casa gleamed before him, more than ever like a fairy palace, and on the balcony of the upper floor he could see a filmy white figure, standing at the open window of the room next to his own—the enchanted Princess of the tale.

He had been two days at the Casa in Cara's unmitigated

society, and had learned a great deal about her. She was a woman who liked to talk about herself, and though she represented her own life as she wished it to appear, Crayshaw had no difficulty in supplying certain details in it which she ignored, or in judging her pretty fairly despite his infatuation.

She did not, strictly speaking, know her own parentage, but she stated as facts what she only surmised. She had both Spanish and Irish blood in her veins—a combination which is said to produce the most perfect beauty in all the world: but the Sisters of Mercy who had taken charge of her as an infant either could not or would not disclose how she came into their charge. She was certainly not legitimate, but had been "adopted" by strict Catholics when she was three years old and brought up by them until she was fourteen. They were middle-class, narrow-minded people, with so strict a disapproval of Cara's origin that they never permitted her to discuss it or to ask questions about it; and they were continually shocked and shamed by the rebellious child who seemed to have inherited—to them— all her parents' vices. Nevertheless, this was the most beneficial period of Cara's life, since it had given her some sort of education despite idleness and revolt and love of pleasure. She had a passionate temper and was constantly in disgrace both at home and in her convent school. But she was very early aware of her beauty and its value. She walked with young men, met at haphazard, when she could circumvent her teachers and guardians, until her adopted parents discovered it and there was a furious outburst on both sides that ended in the girl running away.

She joined a traveling circus, partly to hide her tracks, and it was then, as Crayshaw divined, that she first lost her maidenhood. Up till then, as by a miracle, her religion and upbringing had saved her from seduction, but it was bound to come sooner or later, and probably sooner. She might have remained with the circus if she had been active, or anxious enough, to learn to ride; but she was of no use except to appear in processions through the towns as an advertisement, and the training and refinement forced upon her at school and in her former home, made her fastidious about her surroundings. She was unpopular, even with the hard-working men of the troupe, and she left the circus and went into a provincial theater whose manager had seen and marked her amongst the circus crowd. For a time she did better on the stage, because she could look some parts if she could not act them, but she had no dramatic gift and again she hated the hard work that she must undertake if she were to get any farther in a much under-valued profession.

At sixteen, however, she married an actor, and continued to work and starve with him until the Cinema boom. They were probably neither of them faithful to each other, but for some odd reason they stayed together and kept up the semblance of married life.

"I liked Jim," she told Crayshaw in one of her confidences. "He was a rotter, of course, and he treated me vilely. But I was very good to him, and when you are good to people you get fond of them. I ought to have thrown him over a dozen times, but I knew he would have gone straight to the devil without me. We pigged it with one filthy crowd after another until I was sick of it. We neither of us ever got a chance—there was so much jealousy, particularly of me. I wasn't very strong, and Jim had rotten health. He died when I was twenty—worn out, poor devil. I cry over him still, sometimes.

Her wonderful eyes were magnified through tears as she spoke, and Crayshaw held her hands and kissed them.

"You have had a rough time, Carissima. I feel that I want to make you so happy now that you shall forget it all. I want to make up to you for it with all my love. Do I make you happy, darling?"

"Yes, Hugh. I knew that I could be happy with you when I first saw you at the Casino. I wanted you. Am I the only woman in your life now? I don't ask you for your past—you are a man, and I'm no fool about men—but you must be true to me in your present life and your future. I know you are not married, but is there any other woman with a claim on you?"

"None! I swear it!" said Crayshaw, lying luxuriously. He was growing so used to being Hugh Curton that he almost believed himself, though had he paused to think he would have been cynical of the real Hugh Curton's virtue, even as a bachelor.

The remainder of Cara's story was not so fluently told. It had many a hiatus in it that Crayshaw filled in from his own unelevated knowledge of life. He knew, however, that after Jim's death she left the company with which they had been playing, and went on to the cinema stage. Even here she was not such a success as she might have been if she had had talent or ambition. Her beauty had been her bane. She was apt to consider it so much of an asset that she resented having to use it as an accessory: she could only play in scenarios written round her, and in which she had no strong emotional or dramatic part to play. And the drilling that she received at the hands of her exasperated Directors ended in tantrums of anger or sullen resentment. As long, however, as the film plays were silent she did fairly well, and it was in one with a Mexican set-

ting that she went to South America. There she met
Da Costa, who—eventually—married her for her beauty,
exhibited it for the envy of other men, and then became
maniacally jealous of their admiration. That the husband
and wife quarreled furiously was inevitable. Cara was only
telling the unhappy truth when she said that she always
quarreled with those who loved her or whom she loved.

The marriage, like Cara's first venture, had dragged on
for some years, punctuated by such scenes as had made
them notorious in Santiago, where they had lived for a
time. At last the scandal had ended in Da Costa nearly
killing a man and being murdered in his turn. And here
the hiatus in Cara's tale became a wide blank. She did not
discuss her own part in the affair, but burst into vitupera-
tion of her husband's brutality. He had left her a wealthy
widow; but his vengeance for the infidelity he suspected,
pursued her beyond his life, for if she married again she
forfeited the whole of his huge fortune. Unfortunately for
Cara, José Da Costa was an American by birth and nation-
ality though of Spanish descent, and so could control his
own property. Had he been a Chilean or Argentine, one
half of his fortune must have been his wife's at his death,
without restriction. He had, however, left it in her power
to will as she pleased. His jealousy was a personal one of
Cara. He could not bear to think of her enjoying his
wealth with another husband. Lovers he knew she would
always have. She had had them in his lifetime despite his
physical violence to her. But he knew that Cara loved
luxury. It was the power of reckless extravagance that had
prevented her leaving Da Costa when he was alive and
prevented her reinstating herself with the world when he
was dead. She had had too many lovers even for the morals
of Chile, and she found herself taboo in the social life of

the place. She had not become more chaste since her husband's death, and yet she resented not being accepted in the Principality of Monaco or on French territory. Da Costa had built the Casa Caralyn at Roquebrune as a plaything for his wife when they came to Europe, and in some sort a prison. His suspicions had kept her as solitary as an Eastern woman, and even when his death had freed her of supervision, she had not found it easy to retrieve her position. Crayshaw had discovered that Madame Da Costa knew practically none of the English residents in Monte Carlo. Her acquaintance was limited to people she had met at hotels along the Italian Riviera, and to the class of Americans whose curiosity will take them anywhere. She had the most beautiful house on the Côte D'Azur, but it had not brought her a circle of friends. Her indiscretions were too notorious, and her life had been too violent in all its phases. There was something sinister even in the staff of South American servants that she kept, and over whom she seemed to have implicit power. The household was too decorous for safety. As Crayshaw came up from his morning dip, this perfect morning, no gardener was at work in the grounds, and no one seemed to be on the watch as he went in by the side entrance and up the great staircase to his room. It was more than ever like the attendance in an enchanted castle, the "service by invisible people" of a fairy tale. Like all such houses the servants' quarters were of course in the basement, so that the staff lived practically underground; but even allowing for this, Madame Da Costa must have them in very strict training to account for the absence of prying eyes.

As soon as Crayshaw had rubbed himself into a glow and changed his bathing dress for silk pajamas he walked out on to the balcony to look for that white figure he had seen at the window next his own, and greeted his hostess.

"How beautiful you look! Are you rested? You might be about seventeen this morning!"

She smiled back at his glowing face, and put up her white hands caressingly to his wet dark head.

"Did you enjoy your swim?"

"It was splendid. I wished you had been there, that was the only drawback."

"It was too cold for me. I can only bathe when the water is really warm, and then the sun is too hot."

"You are not really delicate, are you, Cara? You look as perfect in health as a child!"

"It is nothing," she said carelessly. "But my chest is weak. I catch cold too easily. It was all those wretched years of hard work and poverty when I was on the stage. Even if I go to Paris I generally come back ill, and England kills me. But I hate it so much that I never want to go back."

There was something more here than mere climate, Crayshaw thought. She had reasons why she did not care to be seen in England, as well as not seeing England herself. It was a peculiarity of his mind, like a twist in it, that he could never accept a simple statement as truth if he could by any means suspect it of being an untruth. Perhaps it was because he could not tell the truth himself but preferred it perverted, that he looked for the same thing in others. In Cara's case he was convinced that it was not her health that made England a place to be shunned. She looked as if she had a body as sound as it was perfect in outward form. But he was ready to believe that she had done something, not exactly criminal, but shady enough to make it convenient not to be able to return to the country where she had been born and brought up whatever her parentage. It did not matter to him in his present relations to her; indeed he welcomed it as an advantage to his own duplicity. It might have been awkward if she had seen fit to summons him to meet her in London under the name of Hugh Curton, and he knew already that her imperious demand would have brooked no excuses. He would have had to go to her, or she would have become furious with suspicion and jealousy and set herself to find out the whole fabric of lies that he was weaving thicker round himself with every hour they spent together. No, it was much better for him that she should not come north, even as far as Paris. And even as he thought it he drew her back to the privacy of her room, and held her in his arms with a mixture of tenderness and concern.

"You are not really *ill*, my darling? You must take more care of your precious self. I ought not to have let you stay out so late in the garden yesterday. What brutes men are! We only think of ourselves. I wish I could be with you always to take care of you—you should never have a rough wind touch you!"

She looked up at him with eyes whose color seemed to deepen and glow, and she returned his clasp with her perfect bare arms round his neck.

"You talk like a boy of eighteen—a great big schoolboy in love for the first time! I never knew another man who was so young, and seemed so happy and jolly. Well? What is it now?"

For he had suddenly flung up his dark head and gave his great hearty laugh, like a schoolboy as she said. Her smile faded, and she looked half offended, the frown drawing her brows together like a cloud crossing a fair landscape.

"Don't be cross with me!" he said coaxingly. "I'll tell you why I laughed. I have an old aunt who disapproves of me so thoroughly that she calls me 'The Miserable Sinner'! I believe she always refers to me in that loving fashion to all my relations. It struck me as such a contrast to your own kind description—but then I suppose I am at my best to *you,* just because I worship you!"

The frown faded in turn from her face, and the smile came back. "Your aunt is an old fool!" she said contemptuously. "Even if you are a sinner, you will never be miserable, Hugh. I don't think anyone would make you unhappy or rebellious as I am."

"You could!"

"Could I?" She was delighted, and showed that she loved her power. "Perhaps I could. I told you that I always quarrel with the people who love me, and I bring them ill-luck." She really shivered in the warm morning. "An old gypsy woman said it of me as a child, and it has come true—not once but many times."

"Never mind the ill-luck— 'You are my dream come true!' But don't quarrel with me, my beauty! Let me be the exception to your rule. You don't know how easily I can be hurt by the few people I really love. I am Celtic, you know. We are not so phlegmatic as the ordinary run. You have some of the Celt in you too, you lovely, passionate thing!"

Her breast rose in a long sigh, half of pleasure and half of pain. "No man has ever satisfied me as you do!" she whispered. "You have a man's strength and a boy's ardor. You seem to me so young. You can make love at morning as well as at night. Most men are as bright as gold at night and as dull as lead in the morning. But you are my daylight lover!"

"I could make love to you at any time—in any place—
in heaven or in hell!" said Crayshaw, and believed himself
with the spell of her beauty upon him.

    .     .     .     .     .     .     .

It could not last, of course. People whose feeling for each
other is all passion and not love must either weary or
suffer from something like revulsion. Their first quarrel
occurred when Crayshaw's week-end was over, and he
found that Cara was willing that he should leave her. He
did not really wish to stay—he was, for the moment, at
the end of his tether with her demands upon him, body
and soul, her exactions and unreason. But the realization
that she also was on the verge of a reaction made him
suspicious. He had reason to know that she was univer-
sally unfaithful to her lovers from her own confessions,
and he guessed at a rival. His reproaches annoyed her, and
she told him he might go if he pleased and never return,
with a blatancy that a more disciplined nature would have
avoided. They parted with furious anger in the dawn of
the day on which he was to leave—but only for Crayshaw
to rush back to her and beg forgiveness with his tears on
her stormy breast. They were reconciled, and when he
really left her some hours later it was with mutual protes-
tations that they must meet again in a day or so.

But as he was driven out of the Casa's great iron gates,
and along the hot bright road to Monte Carlo, his doubts
returned. She was not coming to the Casino to-day, nor
to-morrow. She expected her Italian friends, with some
American visitors who wanted to see the Casa. The excuse
of the Gazzis and their American friends was plausible,
but perhaps for that very reason Crayshaw did not believe
her. He began to torture himself with his physical jealousy,

and to picture another man taking his place almost before the sound of his departure had died away.

At his hotel he was unusually silent and *distrait,* so that the people who would have welcomed his return wondered what had happened to him, and as usual ascribed it to losses at the tables. He was too pettish to rouse himself, and let them think as they would.

"Everybody has their bad days," was all he said to a lady who rallied him on his absent-mindedness. "I am getting tired of Monte Carlo."

It was certainly a bad day for him. There was a letter from his wife, not exactly reproaching him—Noel Crayshaw never did that now—but asking quite plainly for money to take their boy to the seaside for Easter. He did not want to send more money home, and as she had not heard of his luck the week before he saw no reason to be generous. She was always asking for something. But it was disagreeable to refuse. He felt that it showed him in a less attractive light than usual, and blamed Noel for forcing him to such a position, even between them and in private.

After lunch he fell asleep in his room, and did not wake till the chill of the setting sun. His nights had been broken of late. His body was rested, but his mind was still restless, and he put on an overcoat and walked through the town for exercise. His feet took him along the Boulevard and out in the direction of Cap Martin as if he moved mechanically. It was only a few miles to the Casa Caralyn, and he remembered that he could catch the car back to Monte Carlo. It was pleasant walking in the spring evening, though the wind was treacherous after the heat of the day, and the daylight still lingered when he came in sight of the iron gates, and with a sense of spying walked past them a little way, under the high wall of the Casa's grounds. He thought guiltily how angry Cara would have been if she had known that he had come back, but persuaded himself that it was half sentiment on his part. He had found the Casa so much to his taste that he almost felt as if it belonged to him and he to it. It was his right background. The luxury and the beauty and the absence of anything to worry or disturb life in its artificial seclusion, seemed to him ideal now that he had left it. At the end of the wall he turned, and began to walk back, planning to take the car at the next stopping-place on the coast road. As he once more neared the iron gates of the Casa, a private car coming from Monte Carlo slowed down and stopped there. Crayshaw caught a glimpse of a man with a small silky beard—a virgin beard—and shoulders too square to be natural under the padded coat. The Comte de Chalis! . . . The porter opened the gates as if he were on the watch, and the car passed in . . . Crayshaw had never halted in his steady walk, but he no longer saw the scene round him or even the Casa gates. He walked on and on far past the car halt, the fury in him making the miles seem less than as he came. He made his way back to the hotel mechanically, and until he found himself in his bedroom again, he did not know that he was tired, for his brain was following the same course as the reckless anger in his heart. Duped—betrayed—so soon! A vile woman. A harlot. He forgot that it was in the hope of her being of this type that he had pursued her first. His manhood and his vanity were alike outraged.

He had no plan of action save to give back some of the pain that she had given. And as the loss of her had torn him, so the loss of him as her latest conquest might revenge itself on her. He decided, on the moment, to go back to England as soon as he could get a seat on the train (they were becoming crowded as he knew) and actually began to collect his scattered belongings, and pack his suit-cases. If he left the day after to-morrow, he would be in England by the Saturday. He could wire to Noel to-morrow to expect him, and would write to Hugh Curton to come out and see him and arrange a game of golf. The hurry of plans was the only thing that seemed to quiet his anger and chagrin. He did not himself know why he wanted to see Curton, except for his association with Monte Carlo. Crayshaw hated Monte Carlo at the minute—but he knew that he would want to talk of it to somebody who had been there—who had seen Madame Da Costa. He could tear her reputation to more rags before Curton's cynical eyes. "That woman—the Da Costa—you didn't tell me half! After you had gone I heard a lot about her. One can hardly credit it. I wonder the police don't raid the villa where she lives. . . ."

He wrote to Curton that same night. It was something to do after dinner. He had thought, in his savage reckless-ness, of going down to the Casino and gambling with the remainder of his five hundred pounds until he lost it all and more; but he found suddenly that he was so intensely tired, mentally and physically, that even gambling had lost its zest. The unbridled emotion of the last few days— and nights—his walk, and then his fury of rage, had worn him out. He wanted nothing but to lie down and sleep like a healthy animal. He was, on the whole, very healthy, and rarely taxed his mind as he did his body. When he had finished his letter to Curton and the telegram to his wife to expect him, he wrote a brief and sarcastic note to Cara Da Costa to say good-bye, and carried the letters him-self down to the concierge whom he instructed to send the wire first thing in the morning.

As he got into bed he wondered whether Cara would be angry. He hoped so. He had been almost rude, and quite plain-spoken. He would like to rouse her to one of her tempests of passion in which she admitted that she was barely sane. He had told her that he had seen De Chalis entering her gates and what it meant with such a woman as herself. He thought he had been sarcastic, but he did not realize that the chagrin of being so easily supplanted and betrayed was as plain to read as his handwriting. He did not expect to sleep, though he had felt so tired; but as soon as he lay down he dropped off, and neither dreamed nor wakened until the morning. The blessed oblivion came to him as easily as to a child.

The next morning he wakened with a sense of discomfort that quickly resolved itself into remembrance. Nevertheless his mood was different. He was rested, and his resentment took the form of wishing to be revenged. He wished that he had said more rather than less in his letter to Cara, and flung a flirting glance across the lounge at the first good-looking woman he saw on his way out of the hotel. She was ready to oblige him, and quick in the uptake. After a few minutes' laughing conversation she agreed to walk down with him to Cook's where he was going to book a seat on the train on Friday, if he could get one.

"But why must you go?" said the lady, as they strolled down the hill to the gardens. "It will be horrible in England! We—my husband and I—thought you were staying until April, as we are."

"Are you sorry?" said Crayshaw, half closing his long gray eyes so that the lashes seemed entangled. "Ah! you should have said so before, instead of ignoring me all last week."

"You were away for the week-end!"

"Of course I was. There was no one to speak to me in the hotel. My friend had gone, and you were taken up with that long fellow who played bridge with you."

"Captain Carlton? He talked racing with my husband all the time! I was bored to tears. I nearly sent you an S.O.S."

"Why not quite? I should have come on top gear."

"Mr. Crayshaw, you are the most awful hypocrite I ever met. But *must* you go on Friday?"

"I've wired to my wife to expect me."

"Then probably she won't!"

They both laughed, and Crayshaw looked down at his companion's face with a smile that was half sad and that lifted the corners of his full, sensitive lips. "Why do we always miss the good times we might have had?" he said. "Is it cowardice or shyness? You and I—both bored—looking at each other across the lounge and saying 'She likes that ass Carlton!'—'He is only interested in the Casino'—and all the time——"

He was an adept at leaving a sentence unfinished. Nevertheless he went to Cook's and got his seat on the train and changed some French money for English. And then they strolled back to the terrace and sat in the sun and listened to the quick dropping deaths of many pigeons trying to flutter out to safety. Crayshaw had hoped that Madame Da Costa might be there by chance and see him with another woman, but if she were he did not catch sight of her. He walked back to the hotel with his new friend on more intimate terms than when they had come out together, but the flirtation was nothing to him. He was still enslaved by the memory of Cara Da Costa for all his rage against her, and she made another woman seem pallid and unreal.

As he went to leave his hat and cane with the concierge, that functionary handed him a letter which had come by hand.

"It is for Monsieur Curton," he said. "Will you still forward his letters, Monsieur, or will you give me his address as you are leaving on Friday?"

"I'll take this with me—it will reach him quicker," said Crayshaw with a beating heart. The rough square envelope had that faint scent about it that brought Cara most vividly to his mind, and in a moment his anger was gone, and the glory of her, the infatuation of her beauty, seemed to flood all his senses. Instead of going into the coffee-room he took the lift up to his own bedroom and opened the letter. It was nearly as brief as his own had been.

"I have had your insulting letter, and I demand that you come to me at once and explain. Or you can go to hell and never see me again."

There was no signature. But on the inner page was something written in pencil as if her anger had been suddenly quenched in tears no less stormy:

"Oh Hugh—Hugh—Hugh——"

Crayshaw's hands trembled as he held the faintly scented sheets. He looked at them almost ashamed of his own weakness. This woman claimed him, body and soul, and he had no power to throw her aside as he had expected to do. She had said that he was like a boy in his impetuosity and the impulses that swayed him, and it was true. He crushed the letter to his lips where she had written his name—Curton's name, and not his, but that he entirely forgot in his excitement—and his hands were still unsteady as he placed it in his pocket-book and ran out of his room and down the stairs without waiting for the lift this time. The concierge had gone to his own lunch, but the lift boy was in the lounge.

"Give me my hat and coat, and call a car," said Crayshaw breathlessly. "Be quick—I've forgotten an important appointment."

He could barely wait till the car came, he forgot that he was hungry and had forgone his lunch, or that his new friend of this morning was looking out for him in the coffee-room. He remembered nothing but the woman who had called him back as the car took him out to the Casa Caralyn, through the iron gates, up to the dazzling white entrance of the fairylike place. Was it only twenty-four hours since he left it? The inscrutable butler led him in across the great hall to a smaller room than the formal salon, a room used as a library and writing-room, and there left him, closing the door with a soft deference as if this guest had gained his footing in the Casa.

The man had not announced him, and Crayshaw's dazed eyes did not at first see that he was not alone: until Cara's voice, angry, shaken, but with no pretense of indifference, fell on his ears.

"You damned fool! De Chalis never entered the house. If you had waited three minutes you would have seen him drive away again. What have you to say to me?"

They looked at each other across the room. Whether he believed her or not he did not care to think in the magnetism of her presence. As once before they hesitated, like combatants who hope for each other's death, and then closed and held each other tightly enough to bruise, their pulses hammering from breast to breast, their lips sore with kissing.

.    .    .    .    .    .    .

"I shall have to go to Cook's and get the date of my ticket altered," said Crayshaw, laughing, as they took their delayed lunch together. "I booked a seat on the Blue to-morrow. I really meant it, Cara!"

He remembered also that he must send another wire to Noel to say that he was detained.

But of his letter to Curton he never thought again.

# CHAPTER VII

HUGH CURTON'S clerk had sorted the letters before his chief arrived, and laid the important ones on his table, keeping those that belonged to the ordinary routine of the office for the other clerks who dealt with them. Mr. Staine, the senior partner, rarely came to the office of late, and was expected to become a "sleeping partner" very shortly, owing to his ill-health; but Curton was on a friendly footing at his house and frequently there, whereby Mr. Staine kept in touch with the developments of the business and discussed them with the younger man. Incidentally, Mr. Staine had married late in life, a lady a good deal younger than himself and very well-appearanced. Mrs. Staine dressed well, looked well, danced well, did everything well that she attempted, and was clever enough not to attempt what she could not do. Hugh Curton was her most frequent dancing partner and companion when she went about without her husband, and she had set up a standard in his mind whereby he judged other women. There was no scandal about their friendship, but the clerks in Staine & Curton regarded it as a "sure thing" that when old Staine dropped off Curton would marry the widow.

Curton's own nephew had been articled to the firm after he left Cambridge (as Crayshaw had told Cara Da Costa), and was an old-young man of six-and-twenty, already responsible enough to attend to a good deal of the business when Hugh was away on holiday. He was in reality the son of a stepsister a good many years older than Curton,

and his name was Stephen Gould. Crayshaw's conclusion
that it was Curton, like his uncle's, was a natural slip, but
a little more thought would have told him that it was
impossible that Hugh Curton could have a nephew old
enough to be in the business unless there were an unusual
and extensive family before him.

The only private letter amongst Curton's mail this
morning was marked "Personal" and was from Monte
Carlo. The clerk put it on one side from the others, and
when Curton came in a few minutes later he saw it at
once. He felt pleased that Crayshaw had written to him,
for, beyond forwarding one or two business letters that
had arrived after he left, he had not heard from his late
companion, and had supposed (cynically) that he was
engrossed with the affair which he had seen begun in the
Casino. Curton saw much more than he appeared to do,
and had been faintly amused at Crayshaw's transparent
disguise to his infatuation.

"I suppose he's been shelved for one of the Foreign
Legion who attend upon the lady," he thought, "and has
time to take a look round and think of his golf again. He
played a rotten game at Mont Agel that last morning up
to the last half."

He did not open Crayshaw's letter until he had practically finished his morning's work, and was going out to
lunch. Then he glanced through it before consigning it to
his pocket-book, and learned with some surprise that Crayshaw was coming home—must be in England by now, and
asked him to call and be introduced to his wife and the
boy to-morrow. The short, easy-going sentences recalled
Crayshaw's personality with sudden vividness to his mind,
and gave him a renewed liking for the man as almost invariably happened to more constant natures when brought

in contact with Crayshaw's shallow attraction. Curton remembered with satisfaction that he had no engagement for the next afternoon, and wrote a short note to the address given him, saying that he should be delighted and he hoped to have a yarn about Monte, and that Crayshaw would play golf with him at Roehampton at the week-end.

That evening he dined with Mr. and Mrs. Staine and took his hostess to the theater, leaving John Staine to his massage and treatment for neuritis. Mrs. Staine wore a new gown that was extremely effective. "Tell me the truth, Hugh," she said as she slipped off her dinner-coat and looked at herself in a long glass, "do you like it? I am not over-gowned, am I? The outline seems to me hard."

"Your figure is too perfect to be spoiled by a straight line, if that is what you mean," said Curton. "Turn round this way—yes, it suits you. Not one woman in ten could wear it, but it suits you. I have never seen a woman carry her gowns better than you do, Sybil."

"I am thankful they are longer. That short vogue was very trying—it made me look like a little girl!"

He came and stood beside her, his rather massive build dwarfing her still more. She was small and exquisitely proportioned. He thought that he could never admire tall women. Even Madame Da Costa, whom he had acknowledged to be beautiful, was on too large a scale. She flashed into his mind in connection with Crayshaw's letter to-day, and he recalled her critically as compared to Sybil Staine.

"She had not the smartness," he told himself. "She was too pretty to be quite well bred."

As they drove to the theater in Mr. Staine's own car it was impossible to talk freely or to do more than touch each other's hands under the rug. They had done a great deal more on one occasion, but their chances were singularly few since neither of them wished for discovery. Their relations to each other were such that the chauffeur's back did not make them conscious either of him or themselves. They behaved as perfectly as if nothing had ever happened to make disclosure possible. Well, it had only happened once.

"I'm afraid your husband suffers a good deal," said Curton with just the right amount of concern. He really liked his senior partner, though this had not prevented his taking advantage of his illness, with a young wife.

"Do you think he looks worse or better for his treatment? I feel anxious sometimes—but the specialist is clever, and one hardly knows what to do."

"My dear Sybil, you need not reproach yourself. You have always done the right thing, and considered him before yourself."

"I should hope so! I should be a very heartless woman if I did not."

Sybil was not in the least conscious of hypocrisy, nor was Curton. They were really very respectable people, and would have preferred a legal right to the discomfort of a secret claim on each other. Neither of them had quite intended it, and the fact that passion had taken them by surprise and proved stronger than their ordinary, measured ways, was disconcerting. Sybil was too clever to think that she could hold Curton by having him as her lover. Unless he could eventually marry her he would gradually slip away and make other ties, not necessarily more lasting, but more accommodating and newer. He was not sentimental, and if he had not compromised her he would see no reason for faithfulness once his inclination faded. Her hold upon him was her appearance, and her companionship which was always pleasant and tactful.

Curton enjoyed the play, and was pleased with Sybil. She was very good company, and so much *en rapport* with him that they sometimes divined each other's thoughts before they were spoken. As they were driving home she startled him by saying, "Has that man come back yet who was with you at Monte Carlo? What was his name? Crawshay?"

"Crayshaw—like the poet, only spelled with a y. He sometimes claims descent from the author of "That not Impossible She," but I very much doubt it. What made you think of him, I wonder? I had a letter from him this morning saying he was back and asking me to go and see him and meet his wife."

"Is he married? I had the impression he was a bachelor."

"So had I till this year. He is not only married, but he has a boy of twelve who is crippled, poor little chap. Crayshaw seems awfully cut up over it."

"Oh Hugh, how sad! Was it an accident, or from birth?"

"I don't know. Crayshaw did not say, and I could not ask as he does not like to talk of it. The boy seems to be clever, but of course very handicapped for doing anything in life."

"I wonder what the wife is like. You have not seen her?"

"I have an impression somehow that she is not quite in the same class as her husband. Crayshaw did not say so, of course—he's too much of a gentleman for that. But he never takes her about with him. I've met him at quite good houses, always alone. And they live out at Daisy Hill."

"Well, that is rather off the map. But she may have her

own friends, and they go their separate ways. I hope she is a good mother to that poor child. Can't you do something for him? Take him to the Pictures, or for a run in your car?"

"I thought of that. But I must see how the land lies. I am going out there to-morrow afternoon."

"Come and dine with us, and tell me all about it."

"I will if I can get back in time to dress. But Crayshaw has no idea of time or of engagements. Once he gets hold of you he is hopeless. He is the only person I know who can make me late."

"The next day, then. Is Mr. Crayshaw an Irishman? He sounds rather like that."

"No, I don't think so. But he is certainly a Celt. He admits it, particularly when his golf is most erratic!"

They both laughed, but Sybil's thoughts were really on the lame son rather than the undependable father. She had a passion for children, and the only real grief of her life had been that she had none. If Mrs. Crayshaw were not utterly impossible she had a vague thought of getting acquainted with her through Curton in order to do something, herself, for the clever, crippled child.

.  .  .  .  .  .  .

The weather was intensely cold for March when Curton drove himself to Daisy Hill. A white frost had all London in its grip and had made the morning foggy in St. Clements, but as the car rolled north the light became better and in the suburbs it was merely white and misty. He knew Daisy Hill as a new Garden City, but there were some good substantial houses left from the time when it was still outside the radius, as he knew from several mortgages that he had had in his hands; and he naturally thought that the Crayshaws lived in one of these. The address given him was Lordside, North Road, and he was obliged to stop and ask a policeman to direct him. Then, somewhat to his dismay, he found that it was in the newest part of the suburb, and drove through rows and rows of bungalows before he found himself outside a tiny front garden with a little house set down in it like an advertisement picture on the district railway. It was so small and so sham in all its detail of imitation tiles and painted porch that he felt its cheapness strike him with a chill worse than the weather, and his large car had an opulent and incongruous air drawn up at the tiny gate.

He rugged the engine, for the frost was cruel. As he walked gingerly up the path between the perky grass plots and miniature beds, he saw that each blade of grass was delicately frosted, and some rash bulbs that had begun to push up weeks ago had become crystallized. It was all rather like a sugar cake, he meditated, and as tawdry. He could not associate it with Crayshaw as he knew him—Crayshaw dining at the most expensive if not the most exclusive clubs in town, Crayshaw taking a holiday on the Riviera and playing golf and gambling light-heartedly at the tables, Crayshaw, well-dressed and well-groomed and superbly handsome! The cheap little bungalow in the Garden City was such a revelation that it seemed like an intrusion on a man's poverty to have gone there, even on his own invitation. But it was like Crayshaw not to be ashamed of his surroundings, and to pass it off with a light laugh and perfect frankness. Curton could expect him to do that, and to admire him for it. Perhaps it was the man's way of admitting his circumstances and his drawbacks, that he had offered to introduce his friend to the wife and child in a *milieu* suited to them. That was, perhaps, like Crayshaw also, revealing the skeleton in his cupboard with a shrug of his shoulders. Curton found himself nonplused.

There was a horrible little bronze chain with a handle to it for a bell, at which Curton pulled with a fear that it would come off in his hand. Everything seemed of the same gimcrack quality in the tiny house, even the little brown door with a bottle-glass lighting above it. He felt so large in his leather coat, standing on the step (which at least was very clean), that he wondered if he would ever get through the doorway.

The door was opened at last by the working-housekeeper, or cook-general, in an apron over her gown which was not even the regulation black. She was a youngish woman with a face that might have been bright if it had not been tired, and a tall figure. Her mouth was too wide for beauty, but it looked as if it were often smiling; and she seemed taken by surprise at the sight of him.

"Is Mr. Crayshaw at home?" said Curton in the pleasant tone of a man who is making the best of things. "I think he is expecting me—Mr. Curton."

He did not quite know how to place the woman in the doorway. She might be a "lady-help" and consider herself one of the family, or some sort of attendant for the invalid boy. When she spoke her voice was not of the actual working class to which he had first consigned her.

"I am so very sorry—Mr. Crayshaw is still abroad. We had a wire yesterday to say he was not coming. I am afraid he forgot to let you know." She added tranquilly, "Will you come in? I am Mrs. Crayshaw."

The shock of her announcement drove even Curton's self-possession and good manners away for the moment. He raised his hat and stepped into a narrow hall-passage, feeling that he must gasp. Mrs. Crayshaw retained her composure though he had lost his. She opened a door on the right and showed him a vista of a small comfortable room with rather shabby furniture and a bright fire before which was sitting an elderly woman making toast. Drawn up on the other side of the fireplace was a spinal couch on which a boy of twelve was half lying and half sitting. His surprised face was turned to the opening door, and Curton saw at once that he had inherited his father's beauty. The traces of his ill-health had made him too thin and white for normal boyhood, but the features were fine and the large dark eyes were full of intelligence.

"This is Mr. Curton, Horace's friend, Aunt Anstice—Mr. Curton, Miss York—and my boy, Valentine." Mrs. Crayshaw's introduction was made almost from the doorway as she ushered Curton in, and he bowed to the elder lady and shook hands with the boy to regain his self-possession before speaking. "Mr. Curton expected to find Horace, who told him that he was coming home and then forgot to wire as he did to us," Mrs. Crayshaw added in explanation.

Curton was aware of a swift glance between Miss York and the boy as the elderly lady drew forward a seat for him with her free hand. All the chairs and most of the furniture he noticed were basketwork or bamboo—the sort of chairs and tables that one would expect to find in seaside lodgings in the summer. He wondered if it were a furnished house, taken for some obscure reason, and only a temporary abode. There was hardly anything of value in the room except the couch which he knew must have cost money. Even the tea-service on one of the bamboo tables was of plain china without even a silver teapot or hot-water jug.

"How like father!" said the boy with a comical raising

of his brows. "The wonder was that he remembered to wire to anybody when he changed his mind. Won't you sit down, Mr. Curton?"

"I was waiting to see where your mother would sit." The little lesson in good manners was perfectly obvious to every one present, but the boy did not appear to resent it. He transferred that slightly ironic smile to his mother, that was all, and the same subtle intelligence passed between them as between him and Miss York.

"I was just going to make the tea, if you will excuse me," said Mrs. Crayshaw without the least effort or self-consciousness. She did not add, as almost all women would have done, "My maid is out, and I am looking after the kitchen fire for her."

"But I hope you are not taking the trouble for me?" said Curton with far more embarrassment than his hostess. "I assure you I——"

"We must *have* tea," Miss York put in quietly. "We should all die if we didn't, all over the furniture! You may as well share it, and I feel sure you will like my toast."

"I adore toast newly made!" said Curton, trying to laugh it off. "And one's own cook never makes it properly. But I wish you would let me be of some use—may I hold the rack for you?"

"It is on the mantelpiece. You can reach it down if you like, and cut the slices in half. There is a knife on the table somewhere."

"Here it is!" said Valentine quickly, getting off the couch and going to the table. Then Curton saw the extent of his lameness, for he walked with a heavy halt, and one leg was obviously shorter than the other. He did not, however, use any support, though there was a stick leaning against the couch.

Mrs. Crayshaw came back with the tea before the toast was finished and pushed the table up to the couch. She had taken off her apron, and revealed the fact that she was wearing a knitted woolen dress that clung to her tall figure. She was too tall for Curton's approval, but he admitted that she had fine sloping shoulders and a straight back. Her hands were strong and clean but roughened, like a working woman's. She sat down beside Curton and folded these hands loosely in her lap as if glad to be at rest.

"Val generally pours out the tea—he does it better than any of us," she explained.

They all seemed singularly simple in their manners, and under no obligation to conceal anything. Valentine poured out the tea, as she said, as carefully as any woman could have done with a courteous attention to individual taste. Curton moved about the room handing toast and teacups, but it was so small in space that they could really all sit still in their chairs and reach one another.

"When did you hear from my husband?" Mrs. Crayshaw asked as she buttered the crisp toast.

"The day before yesterday. I understood that he would be in England almost before the letter reached me."

"Yes, we heard the same day. I think he quite meant to come, but he wired to us this morning that he had decided to stay."

"I expect he had a run of luck at the Casino!" said Val with Crayshaw's own flashing smile. How like his father he was! "It must be jolly fun!"

"Until the luck turns," said Curton. "He won rather heavily the night before I left, but he did not mention the tables when he wrote to me. He was playing a good deal of golf."

"How much did he win, Mr. Curton?" asked Valentine with interest. "He never told us about that."

"I think he won about five hundred pounds."

The two women looked at him in some surprise, and the boy exclaimed in a fashion of his own.

"Lord-love-a-duck! How long did it take him?"

"It was all done in about an hour. But big winnings are almost always like that. The luck seems to come in a rush. Nothing that you can stake is wrong. Then it changes, and nothing is right. Your father had the sense to leave off a winner."

"I don't suppose there was much of it left though when he decided to come home!" said Valentine with the shrewdness of an old man. "I know there wouldn't have been if it had been mine. I should love to gamble! I should go on for the sake of the play, even if the luck turned."

"So should I," Miss York agreed, quite unexpectedly to Curton. "But I should buy something first, just as a souvenir of the luck."

"I should put by enough to have a topping time," Valentine agreed, "doing everything and going about, and then gamble with the rest."

"It is obvious that we are amongst very imprudent people, Mrs. Crayshaw!" said Curton, smiling. "The members of some gang, I believe."

She had not spoken, nor suggested what her own use of the money would have been, but she suddenly smiled back at the boy, and he saw her mouth widen to show a good set of teeth. It was fortunate that she had good teeth, he thought, for her mouth was certainly very wide. Her smile was rather pretty in spite of its drawback, because it was without bitterness.

"Let us hope Horace has another run of luck!" she said.

"How much can you win in a night, Mr. Curton?" said Val with unabated interest. "Thousands? Can you go on till you break the bank?"

"That depends on how much you stake, I suppose. The Casino does not close till two in the morning. But I heard of a man winning six thousand pounds in about half an hour one season."

"Six—thousand—pounds!" Valentine drew a long breath. His big eyes sparkled in his thin face and Curton noticed that their beauty was intensified by the long curling lashes. The dark hair curled too, where it was long enough, or broke into crisp ripples. He was almost too good-looking for a boy.

"What is Monte Carlo like? Is it a big town? Is there a theater?" The questions came from Valentine, and threatened to absorb the conversation.

"Oh yes, quite a good theater in the Casino, and very good performances. French plays, mostly." Curton spoke as much to Miss York and Mrs. Crayshaw as to Valentine. He did not quite approve of the boy doing all the talking, though it seemed that Miss York would not, and Mrs. Crayshaw could not, take the lead out of his hands. Mrs. Crayshaw was rather a dull woman, it seemed, and slow in the uptake.

"Sooner or later Val always asks if there is a theater in a town if one is mentioned," Miss York remarked in answer to Curton's glance at her. "He is so interested in the Stage that it cannot be kept out of the conversation."

"The cinema stage, or real drama?"

"Both," Valentine answered for himself. "But real drama for choice, of course. The cinema is only getting there, as far as real acting goes. It used to be all show and spectacle, and they had to use so much expression that they made faces at you. But the new Talkies are getting rid of all that."

"We went to see 'Disraeli,'" Mrs. Crayshaw said quietly. "And we all thought George Arliss wonderful."

"He's real!" said Valentine breathlessly. "I should love to write a play for him."

"You must come and do a theater with me, and then you can tell me what to admire!" said Curton with a certain tolerant patronage of which he was not conscious. "Will you bring him, Mrs. Crayshaw? We needn't wait for your husband's return, as he is such an uncertain fellow. Come to a matinée, and then you can get back before it is dark."

He saw her glance swiftly at the boy before she answered, and saw that his face was radiant with excitement. The invitation had of course been prompted by his conversation with Sybil Staine the night before, and her suggestion that he might do something for the lame child to give him a treat; but he was pleased with the instant success of his good nature. The boy was almost quivering with eagerness, and was more boylike—more childlike perhaps—than he had yet shown himself.

"Oh Mother, don't say it's too cold!" he said despairingly as she hesitated.

"We shall love to come! It is very kind of you," she said at last. "And perhaps the weather will have changed in a day or so."

"Shall we say Saturday? I'm afraid I'm engaged up till then. And I must see if I can get seats so soon. What play do you want to see, Val?"

"*Thebos.* Can you take us to *Thebos?*"

"I will do my best at any rate. Will you come and lunch with me somewhere first, Mrs. Crayshaw?" Again that hesitation on the woman's part, until, this time, Miss York put in quietly, "The Criterion is nearly next door."

"Yes. Would that suit you?"

"Thank you," she said again, this time with a direct look at him that he found rather touching in its gratitude. It was so plainly on the boy's behalf that it seemed worth while to Curton to take a dowdy woman and an invalid child to a crowded restaurant and then pilot them to a more crowded theater instead of running out of town for a game of golf as he usually did on Saturday. It was rather a bore, but Sybil would be pleased, and Crayshaw's unfortunate wife had obviously been on her knees to him for his kindness to her crippled son.

He took his leave soon after, having arranged the time and spot for their meeting on Saturday, provided he could get the tickets. As his great car rolled away from the mean little house he thought with definite pity not only of Valentine and his misfortune, but of Crayshaw's dull, unattractive wife and the blazing contrast to her of Madame Da Costa. What chance had any ordinary woman against such as she? Hampered by the familiarity of years of intercourse, no longer in her first youth (he judged Mrs. Crayshaw to be older than her husband) with no marked personality to help her, how could she hope to hold a man as erratic and as attractive himself as Horace Crayshaw? The mystery was how he had ever come to marry her. But Curton was really very sorry for Mrs. Crayshaw as he drove back to his comfortable bachelor flat in Whitehall.

"The boy, of course, is exactly like his father, mentally as well as physically," he decided. "Precocious youngster, spoiled by not going to school. And the woman dotes on them both, no doubt. A pair of rather charming rascals—but I hope she doesn't realize it."

# CHAPTER VIII

WHEN the visitor had departed, the three friends naturally began to discuss him.

"What a great whopping car!" said Val, peering out of the window after the monster with her flashing lights. "It was rather like its owner, somehow, wasn't it? He reminded me of a Big Six all the time!"

"I don't think we were quite what he had expected," said Miss York dryly. "He gave me the impression of being rather uncomfortable. Like the Big Six, that Val says he resembles, in a garage too small for it. What did you think of him, Noel?"

Mrs. Crayshaw was slower to express herself, even in such intimate society as her son and her aunt. She seemed to be looking back at their late guest and considering him.

"What struck me most was that he was so unlike most of Horace's friends—those that I have met. I cannot find the connecting link between them."

"Golf, I suppose. But in anything else they must be always misleading each other."

"I wonder if he likes Horace! He was certainly not taken with us."

"He particularly disliked me!" said Valentine, with the shrewdness that made him seem thirty instead of twelve. "He was trying to snub me down all the while—only he was afraid of mother."

"*Afraid* of me? I don't think he is afraid of anything, except perhaps his dignity. That toppled a little in this small house."

"Oh come, Motherkin, I don't think he is a snob!"

"No," said Miss York critically. "He isn't, really. But he condescends to be good-natured, and it maddened me. It really was good-natured of him to come out here to see Horace, and when he found that Horace had sold him to try to be nice to us all instead."

"He seemed to be rather a good type of man." Mrs. Crayshaw spoke as if she were still trying to find that lost connection between her husband and Curton. "But you don't like him, Aunt Anstice?"

"No more than I do dressed crab. They both give me indigestion." She made a face that caused Val to chuckle.

"It is jolly decent of him to take us to see *Thebos*. I hope to goodness he gets those seats! But I wish he had offered us a run in that Big Six out into the country, instead. You'd have loved that, Mother!"

The genuine unselfishness of the wish lit up the boy's beauty like some inward radiance that was reflected in his mother's worn face. But she said quickly, "No, thank you! not in such weather. We should all be frozen. I would much rather have a good lunch and a matinée. I am building on it."

"How will you get there?" Miss York asked practically. "Don't go by bus if you can avoid it. They are like ice-houses. Can't you get on to the tube?"

"Leicester Square would be the nearest, and we should have to walk."

"A taxi would be only a shilling."

"We are almost on our beam ends," Val explained, without any fear of being misunderstood, or asking for help. "Father didn't send us any money because he was coming home, and when he changed his mind he probably forgot that some was due to us. I say, Mum! he never told you about that five hundred, did he? He might have sent us a tenner out of it."

"I expect it all went as soon as it came," said Mrs. Crayshaw with a patience that was not bitter because it expected nothing. "Or there is just the chance that he really did save it to come home."

Valentine and his aunt looked at each other with that quick comprehension that Curton had caught when he first entered. There was pity for Valentine's mother in it, and a mutual conviction that Horace Crayshaw would never bring any of the money to the little house in Daisy Hill except for his own exclusive comfort.

"Are you writing to Horace for money?" Miss York asked her niece.

"I must, of course. Unless he came at once."

"Can I lend you some till it comes? I have some of my salary left this week."

"If you could lend us a pound it would be useful!" said Mrs. Crayshaw with a smile that made Anstice York want to cry save that she was too angry. The heat of her rage at Horace Crayshaw frequently dried up her tears. "I shall write at once and tell Horace that he must send me funds to go on with. He has really been very regular, for him, up till now."

"I wish he would settle Captain Lewison's account," Val remarked, as he reached for his stick and got off the couch. "I hate poor old Lewy to have to wait. He has a dog's life of it as it is, cramming me as if I were going to a Public School!"

"How is he, poor man?" Miss York had an ironic way of speaking that delighted her great-nephew. "The last time I met him he told me that teaching you was a godsend to him. Well, we all have our own way of doing penitential duty!"

"He meant the occupation, Aunt Anstice—not the joy of a brilliant pupil, though, of course, he is devoted to me—and to mother!" he added slyly. "May I light the lamps, Mum? I've got some prep. for Lewy. Don't you move—I'll work in the kitchen till you are ready to wash up the tea-things."

"Don't bring the lamp in here, Val," Miss York amended. "I'm going to catch the 6.30 bus, and it isn't worth while."

The boy kissed his aunt heartily for farewell, and went out of the room whistling sweetly. They could hear his halting foot in the little passage and across the kitchen which was behind the sitting-room. Miss York looked at her niece with a new expression when they were alone.

"Noel, child," she said, "this is a respite for you—his not coming."

"Yes. But he must come, sometime, and we must have some money. I hate borrowing from you—but he cannot send us any for two or three days, and there are small things I must pay for as we go on."

"He must have meant to come, or he would not have asked that man here. What do you think kept him? A woman?"

"No, I think it was more likely the tables. If he had a run of luck before, and lost it, he might be gambling to get it back. Oh, if *only* he had sent some of it home! Twenty pounds would not have been much out of five hundred, and I could have taken Val away for a fortnight at Easter."

"Yes, he ought to go—he needs change," said Miss York fiercely. Her whole face seemed to grow thinner and drawn in with some suppressed passion, but her voice was under control. "I suppose—you couldn't go to Greatoaks?"

"The General is away. And he is more than good in having us for a month in the summer. We can't be always there."

"I don't believe he would mind if you were—but Horace would. He would make it a grievance, and build up a whole *cause célèbre* against you. Ha! ha! that would be funny—from Horace."

"He is only jealous of our being asked to Greatoaks and never himself. He would not dare to say anything else, even if the General were not father's friend, and yours. There is too much on the other side."

"Has he tried to have his women here lately?"

"I would not have it. Val was growing up too fast. He understood. And that common little girl Horace brought here ventured on impertinence. Otherwise he might have made the place a harem, as far as I cared—so long as he left me out." A shudder passed over Noel Crayshaw's long, active body and she swallowed her breath like a person trying not to be sick.

"How do you manage—when he is home?"

"I sleep down here, sometimes, or in the little attic. But I have to pass Val's room to do that. I don't want him to think—too much."

"You can't go on hiding it. He knows, Noel—he knows."

"Yes, and I can't go on bearing it—not that one thing. If you are in love it is heaven, and if you are not it is simply indecency. And the awful thing is that Horace thinks he is paying me a compliment when—when he wants to come to me. He thinks I should regard myself as neglected if he never lived with me as his wife. I suppose," she added simply, "that is the difference between a man's and a woman's point of view. The idea of being proud of any man's lust! It seems to me so childish that I can't disillusion him. I can only slam the door in his face. Then he thinks that I am jealous, and it always makes me want to laugh."

She was indeed smiling, and Miss York looked at her in wonder.

"Sometimes I think that you don't really hate him as much as I do, Noel!" she said.

"It is very difficult to hate any one consistently when you are living with him, unless you have a large house and can avoid him or never speak. Here we are packed like sardines, and I am obliged to talk about the things that happen every day. There are little jokes—one can't help it, and he has to tell me some of his plans and consult me. Horace is easy to live with, he does not nag, and he is not very cruel. All men are, a little. I don't hate him—except when I look at Val. Then I feel that I could kill him, and that he would be better dead."

She did not even speak in anger, but she spoke with conviction. Miss York was silent for a minute, and then her tightened lips found three words, with difficulty, as if they came of themselves against her intention.

"The miserable sinner!"

"He thinks that is a joke."

"I know—but he won't, some day."

Noel shook her head. "He can only feel things that affect himself, not other people. He said to me once about poor Captain Lewison that he couldn't bear to see him because it made him realize what he had himself escaped in the War. He wasn't sorry for Lewy, but it appalled him to think that he might have been maimed himself."

"Is Captain Lewison any better? He looks very ill."

"I am afraid he grows worse, but he is too plucky to admit it. He was gassed, and it has affected his lungs, and he had shrapnel poisoning. He ought to go to a warmer climate in the winter, but of course he can't afford it. He has only his pension, and he lives in one of these bleak little houses while people like Horace can go to Monte Carlo for the worst months. Horace never had a scratch on him. He rather enjoyed the War."

"Don't talk of him. Do you think Lewison is the best tutor for Val?"

"Not the best, but the best we can do. He is not a gentleman, but he was well educated and he can teach. He was a schoolmaster, you know, in one of the Secondary Schools. He always meant to get to Cambridge, and I think he might have done by sheer dogged hard work. But he seems to have lost heart."

"Yes, he has lost his heart," said Miss York thoughtfully. "It is so patent that even Val sees it."

"The only thing to do is to make a joke of it. Val likes him far too well to give it away to anybody but you and me."

"Well, I suppose it doesn't matter, really."

"I have so often said 'It doesn't matter' and then had to live with the results!" Noel's smile was half-humorous and half-deprecating, and both women laughed. "I'm afraid you ought to be going, Aunt Anstice, if you are to catch your bus, and I must wash up and get supper."

"The only good that Horace brings with him, that I can see, is that you are obliged to have a woman in to help. That takes some of the work off you, doesn't it?" Miss York put on her coat and gathered up the capacious bag and worn fur gloves peculiar to her age, while she was speaking.

"I shall try to get Mrs. Green again when he does come. It was so tiresome, I had to engage her yesterday, and she arrived before the wire so I could not send her away. However, she did some of the rough work for me."

"Does she make things any easier?"

"Not much. But I could not quite do it alone with Horace here. There is more cooking—much more—and more marketing. Good-bye, Aunt Anstice—I'm afraid it is awfully cold outside!"

"I'm getting used to it, and I had a good tea. I wish I could wait to wash up, but I should lose my dinner at the Club."

"You will be late as it is, I am afraid. Come out on Sunday if you can, and hear all about *Thebos* and the lunch. Thank Heaven, I shan't have to cook it!"

They parted laughing. The older woman went out into the fog and the frost to stand for some minutes before she began the tedious omnibus journey that would take her eventually to West Kensington; and the younger put on her apron again, rolled up her sleeves, and began the eternal washing up and preparation for meals that, with other housework, made up her life.

## CHAPTER IX

CURTON did not have an opportunity of telling Sybil Staine about his visit to Daisy Hill as they had planned. When he reached his flat, just in time to have dressed for dinner at Mr. Staine's house, he found a telephone message awaiting him. Mr. Staine had had a bad turn, and his illness appeared so much worse that Sybil had had to send for the specialist, who had asked for a second opinion.

Curton dined alone at his Club, and the next day went round to inquire for his partner before going to his office. He saw Sybil for a few minutes, but there was nothing spoken of save her husband and the complication that had set in, partly she feared from the specialist's treatment.

"I don't know *what* to think," she said, with real anxiety in her eyes. "Dr. Gurney believes that this may be a turning point. But the question is, which way? Would you advise me to assert my authority and insist on the old remedies, Hugh?"

"What does the last man say—this one that Gurney has called in?"

"They have not told me yet. They had a consultation this morning. Of course if he differed from Dr. Gurney it would be simple—and rather a relief, I must own. It seems like increasing the disease to get rid of it, this last week's treatment. But when you have given a case into the hands of a specialist like Gurney, it is difficult to say you are not satisfied."

"Was it your wish to try his treatment, or John's?"

"Oh, John's, all through. And he thought it was doing him so much good, until yesterday. Gurney thinks he caught a chill—you know how bitter the weather was—and that has complicated the case. And John is too ill to be asked to decide anything just now."

"I do not see that you can do anything, except show Gurney how anxious you are. The man must be doing his best, for his own sake as well as his patient's. Is John's strength maintained?"

"That is what worries me. I am afraid he will not be able to fight it. If he were a younger man it might be the turning point, as they say."

"Have you a nurse?"

"Two."

"Keep up your heart, Sybil, and don't neglect yourself or you will break down next. I will call round this afternoon, and if you want me before that, telephone to the office. I shall not go out before lunch."

"You are such a comfort, Hugh! I always feel I have you in the background."

Curton kissed her with real affection, and saw with approval that in spite of a disturbed night and all this worry she was still as fair and *soignée* as if she had been living her ordinary life. For a woman to look like that at a crisis was a very great tribute to her character, to his mind. But Sybil was always a satisfactory person who could hold her own even while she deferred to him. He thought of the woman with the jaded face who had brought in the tea-tray yesterday, and wondered how *she* would have looked if he had arrived at Daisy Hill to find Horace Crayshaw very ill. Probably her hair would have been roughened, and everything in confusion.

It did not occur to him that Sybil had two nurses to

attend to her husband and an excellent staff of servants.

They had not had time to speak of Mrs. Crayshaw and the lame boy when Curton left, and he did not tell her of the proposed theater party on Saturday. In fact he forgot it, both then and later in the day when he called again, but could not see Mrs. Staine. As he was driving home, however, he remembered Valentine Crayshaw's desire to see *Thebos* because he caught sight of a flaming poster of the play, and stopping at the first theater agency he passed, was lucky enough to get three seats for the matinée, which had been returned. He wired to Mrs. Crayshaw that he had the seats, and then wished that he had not got them. It was a nuisance having these people on his hands with Staine so ill and Sybil wanting him at any minute.

The weather on the Saturday was hardly less cold than it had been when he went to Daisy Hill, but it was rendered still more disagreeable by a rough wind. There was, in consequence, no fog, for which Curton was thankful. He did not want to have to pilot his guests out of the radius for fear they should not get home again. At one o'clock he stood on the steps outside the Criterion restaurant looking up and down the street with vexed eyes, and wondering if they had missed a train or a bus from their outlandish place of residence, and would be late. He hated hurrying through his lunch, and the boy would be on tenterhooks if they did not see the curtain rise.

Curton was a sufficiently imposing figure in his well-cut clothes to attract some attention from people coming in to the restaurant, and more than one woman would have liked to see for whom he was waiting: but he did not notice the taxi-cab that really brought his guests until they came rushing up the steps, the boy walking surprisingly fast with his stick, and both of them flushed and laughing.

"Are we late?" Valentine called out as they reached him. "We nearly got out of the cab and ran, it seemed to drive so slowly!"

"Not a bit." Curton raised his hat and smiled more genially than he felt. "I hope you are not cold, Mrs. Crayshaw? It is a beastly day again."

"It is daring to rain!" said Noel Crayshaw breathlessly. "But we don't mind so long as we have got here."

"It will be a miracle if it doesn't snow!" said Val with a laughing shiver.

They seemed all the same in excellent spirits, and ready to enjoy themselves. People looked at the boy as they came into the warm vestibule, and evidently commented on his good looks, but he did not appear to mind or to notice. Nobody looked twice at his mother. She was quite inoffensively dressed, Curton was relieved to see, in a brown hat and coat, though the coat was more suited to autumn than winter. Her face looked less worn and tired than he had thought it when he first saw her, and her eyes lighted up with interest when they went up to the West Room where he had reserved a table for them.

"I hope this will suit you," he said, as they all seated themselves. "It is not a bad lunch, and we shall have plenty of time to get to the theater."

"I have never been here before," Noel Crayshaw replied. "It is delightful. And what a lot of people!"

"Yes, it is popular." He wondered a little at her frank enthusiasm, and studied her face furtively while she read the menu with Valentine. Her eyes were rather nice, and that wide smile did not spoil her face as he had expected. It was pleasant, even to a disaffected host, to have guests who so thoroughly enjoyed themselves, and he found he was laughing and talking himself into the same mood simply through their obvious pleasure.

"I was sorry the other day that I did not offer Miss York a lift," he said. "I never thought of it until too late, but if she lives in your neighborhood it would have been so easy to have taken her home."

"You would have had to drive her all the way to West Kensington!" Val answered, laughing. "For she lives there. It takes her an hour to reach us by two buses, if she is lucky."

"I am afraid she had a very cold and foggy journey that evening."

"She is so plucky!" Mrs. Crayshaw spoke with a new kindling of her face that caught Curton's attention. It made her seem almost young, and he began to doubt if she were older than her husband after all. "She never fails to come over once or twice a week if we can't go to her. I wish she were not so far off."

"There is no chance of her coming into your neighborhood?"

"She lives at a ladies' Club, which is convenient for her work. She is assistant secretary to Sir Edward Prawn and the Almoners' Society, and has been with him for many years. It would be impossible for her to live farther off."

"It was we who moved," Valentine explained. "We were in rooms at West Kensington too. We have only been at Daisy Hill for the last year."

"I should think you found it healthier."

"It is much colder!" He gave another laughing shiver. "I used to like West Kensington. It was full of such queer people! There was a negro band living opposite, and an old lady who went mad at intervals next door. She came in one night in her nightdress and said she was just going to church and wanted mother to go with her. Society might be a bit mixed, but we were never dull."

"Good heavens!"

Curton's exclamation came from a real revulsion at the idea of living in such a neighborhood. He had always thought that West Kensington was deadly respectable except for the newly married people who were always taking flats and leaving by night to avoid paying the rent. With these delinquencies his work had once or twice brought him in touch, but he had never penetrated far into the North End Road nor did he know the streets of older houses that had been converted into what were called "flats," but were much more like tenements. His dismay was so obvious that Mrs. Crayshaw suddenly and sweetly laughed, her generous mouth opening to let out the sound like a gurgle of water.

"It was not so bad as it sounds," she said consolingly. "The rooms in themselves were much loftier and more airy than you would suppose. But things came to a crisis when my husband saw a pail of dirty water poured over the banisters by a woman who drank and who lived above us. Then we had to move. Val and I were rather sorry."

"There were some quite decent people in the next house —we were unlucky," Val chimed in. "And Lawrence Aylmer, the Cinema star, had just taken a flat there. He's come to the front since. I might have got to know him if we'd stayed."

"Val has regretted it ever since," Mrs. Crayshaw spoke a little mockingly. "He thinks that the pail of water did not equal the advantage of Mr. Aylmer's acquaintance. But unfortunately Horace saw the pail of water and not the charms of Lawrence."

"Your father did not tell me that you took an interest in

the stage," Curton said to the boy. "I thought you went
in for Crossword. He said you were solving all sorts of
those problems."

"Now isn't that like father!" Valentine turned to his
mother with a kind of humorous despair. "All his geese
are enormous swans, Mr. Curton—they hatch out with
angels' wings. I did a trumpery little puzzle in a boys'
paper and it happened to be correct, and I've tried the
better ones once or twice and never had a chance. But to
hear father talk I suppose you thought I was solving
everything I went in for? His mind is a kind of magnifying
glass through which he sees things as he wants them."

"But all his family do the same thing. Horace says it is
because they are Celts." There was nothing to be made out
of Noel Crayshaw's tolerant tone, but Curton glanced at
her a little curiously.

"Is Crayshaw Irish?" he asked. "I have so often
wondered. He has no brogue, and it is not an Irish name,
and yet he has so many characteristics that suggest the
Irishman. His personal charm for one thing."

"He has Irish blood, and Welsh also. One branch of
the family settled in Cornwall and married Cornishwomen.
They are more Cornish than English. It is a large family,
and very clannish, though there is no Scotch strain that I
know of. Horace has numerous relations."

"And mother has only Aunt Anstice," Valentine added,
as if that clinched the matter. Somehow Curton knew that
to the boy as well as to his mother, Miss York outweighed
all the Crayshaws with their various Celtic strains.

They were in such good time that they were able to have
their coffee before even Val's impatience dragged them
away to the theater. It was raining in earnest, but the
theater was within a stone's-throw, and Curton's guests

seemed to take umbrellas and muddy shoes as a matter of course. Their seats were in the third row of the stalls, and Valentine was jubilant at hearing and seeing *Thebos* to the best advantage. His thin face flushed and his beautiful eyes were full of an excitement that seemed to darken and intensify them. People looked at him as they had in the restaurant, and between the acts a lady sitting next to him drew him into conversation, obviously attracted by his good looks and his absorption in the play. It gave Curton a chance to speak of him to his mother unheard.

"He knows a lot about the stage," he said in a guarded tone. "He seems to have grasped the technique of a play and its production. How did he find out?"

"I suppose by talking of it, and asking questions. It seems to you like an obsession, I suppose."

"Well, it is unusual for a boy of his age. Are you satisfied about it? Does it worry you?"

"I don't think it is unusual," she answered thoughtfully. "It has only taken the place of all the other things he cannot do. If he had been like other boys, and at school, I think he would have been just as absorbed in cricket and football. He is not really very artistic or at all abnormal. He has a very vivid brain, and great vitality. It had to find something to feed on, that's all."

"Won't it be a great disappointment when he realizes that he can never act?"

"He has realized it, of course. He hopes to write plays and film scenarios, and to produce them some day. I only hope he may. It would fill his life. And he would be associated with the theater and theatrical people." She had been looking at the safety curtain as she spoke and not at Curton, and her voice sounded curiously subdued. But suddenly she lifted her eyes to his, and her face flushed with a passing excitement and animation that startled him.

"Please don't talk to me of serious things and responsibilities to-day," she said. "Not just while the play is going on, anyhow. I do so want to enjoy it, and to forget who I am and the future and everything. You don't know how I *am* enjoying it. I think it is absorbing! I want to think about *Thebos*—not even about Val."

For a minute he seemed to see her as she must have been when a girl. She looked almost young and pretty. Could a rather spectacular and sensational play do so much for a poor woman, starved of luxury and romance and pleasure in her dull life? He was startled. Horace Crayshaw must have found her attractive, of course, incongruous though his marriage seemed. Perhaps even now, at times——

Curton's eyes, traveling downwards over her face and figure, fell on the hands lying in her lap. She had taken off her gloves, and he saw that they were quite clean, but rough and rather red. The nails were kept short, and there were hard corners to them as if the skin had thickened. They were the hands of a decent working woman, but many domestic servants kept their own better. He had a sudden revulsion of sympathy with Crayshaw. What man could want to touch a woman with such hands! Madame Da Costa's had been perfect. So were Sybil's. Of all things he disliked a woman who was careless about her hands and feet. He felt sure that if he could see Mrs. Crayshaw's ankles her stockings were not properly put on. They would wrinkle, and the seam would be all on one side.

He dropped into silence with apparent acquiescence as the curtain rose, and his companion became so absorbed in the great second act that she seemed to have forgotten him. When the curtain fell again to the applause of the whole house, he turned to her with a smile and asked if she would like some tea? But for a minute she hardly heard him. Her face was all broken out of its control, her chin worked, and there were tears in her dazed eyes.

"Yes, thank you," she said; and then, "I am very silly! I always cry at plays. Val says it is because I have no critical faculty."

But even Val was radiant, chatting to his new friend and turning to include Curton in his comments.

"I've seen Sedley in better parts, but never one that suited him better!" he said. "Doesn't he love it, too! That was his big scene. There will be a long wait now to give him a rest. Tea, Mr. Curton? How topping! Don't give mother anything to eat—she will only choke. She always does, don't you, Mum?"

"Always," said Noel Crayshaw, recovering herself a little. Her eyes shone through her tears, and she began to laugh again at her own emotion.

"You are a delightful audience," said Curton kindly. "No actor could wish for a better. You take it all in earnest."

"I was with Sedley all through that act. How tired he must feel! If he experiences that all again to-night, it is enough to kill him."

"Well, I suppose they get case-hardened. Some of it must be mechanical."

"It did not seem so. It was real."

"I have met Sedley at the Garrick Club," said Curton with a desire to interest her. "He is quite a good fellow, and plays golf and cricket. But I am afraid he is not so picturesque out of that Eastern dress."

But now it was Valentine who was interested, and not his mother. She did not care about Mr. Sedley the golfer, in plus fours. To her he was "Thebos," the man in royal robes who rose above himself in that last magnificent scene, and she took no part in the eager questions and answers between her son and her host. When the curtain finally fell, and they all rose to go, she gave a long reluctant sigh, and looked round the theater as at some well-loved scene that has shrined a happy time.

Curton walked with them to the Tube in Leicester Square, and said good-bye to them there. The rain had ceased, and the air was suddenly mild and fresh as if with the long-delayed spring.

"We can't thank you enough, and so we won't try," said Noel honestly. "But you could see how we enjoyed it."

"Yes, you cried all through the last two acts!" he retorted, rather surprised at himself for teasing Crayshaw's dull, dowdy wife. "I believe even your tea was salt."

"I am not really sentimental, am I, Val?" Noel appealed to the boy remorsefully. "If it had been funny I should have laughed quite as much as I cried. Perhaps that is rather tiresome, though."

"We always yell at comic scenes," Val explained calmly. "Even when we go to the Pictures and other people are bored at the funny man, mother and I roll in our seats. We like to let ourselves go."

"We ought to have warned you!" said Noel seriously. "But you know now."

"I am not easily intimidated." Curton, in his warm, well-cut overcoat and with his massive head, did not look as if he were easily upset in any way. There was a good deal of solid strength in both his mind and body. "If the weather really turns spring-like, I should like to take you for a run in my car. We could lunch at some place on the way, and get back by daylight now. And perhaps Miss York would come too?"

He really did not know why he gave this second invitation. He thought it was Sybil's suggestion again. He should like to please Sybil. And he wanted to see if Mrs. Crayshaw's face could take that odd look of youth and her eyes grow radiant, in spite of her worn appearance and those careless hands and feet. Of course it would be more intriguing still to see her in sharp contrast to her handsome, attractive, well-dressed husband; but as Horace was still abroad that must wait. He was not so curious about seeing them together, either, as he had been. It seemed like ill-nature to compare them, and a cruelty to poor Mrs. Crayshaw. He did not altogether like the boy, who reminded him of Horace so much physically that he fancied the mental resemblance, and it was a subconscious impulse that had made him include Miss York, to square the party. Valentine seemed to pair off naturally with his aunt, and to leave Noel Crayshaw to her host. Yes, it would be an interesting study.

He half expected Valentine to show some signs of discontent that he was not offered another theater party, or at least a cinema, but the boy did not betray it if he felt it. He looked at his mother and laughed.

"You know you nearly cried over the bluebells at Greatoaks!" he said.

"I didn't!"

"Mr. Curton won't be warned. Mother adores the country, Mr. Curton. Do make her go!"

"Are you hesitating, Mrs. Crayshaw?"

"Could you really take us? All of us? It would be so perfect!"

"Then that is settled. What about next Saturday, if fine?" Another golfing day abandoned; but he did not feel that he would miss it when he caught that look on her face again, for a passing minute.

Yes, she was certainly an interesting study.

# CHAPTER X

WHEN Curton arrived at "Lordside," Daisy Hill, the
following Saturday, he found a man with a parcel
at the door, and very naturally took him for a tradesman
delivering goods.

"Have you rung?" he asked, joining him in the little
porch, and speaking with the off-hand civility he used to
a class he considered, without any snobbery, to be his
inferiors.

The man was respectably dressed in a dark suit, with a
soft hat on his head. He was neither tall nor short, thin
nor fat, and his face as he turned it to Curton was the
common type that may be met in the streets a hundred
times a day. Had it not been for a certain keen intelligence
in his eyes, Curton would have taken no further heed
of him, and the eyes themselves, though shrewd, were
nondescript in color and not appealing in any way.

"Yes, I have," said the man shortly, and a minute later
the door was opened by Valentine, already in his cap and
overcoat.

"Oh I say, how awfully good of you to bring it yourself!" he exclaimed as he took the parcel. "Good morning, Mr. Curton. This is Captain Lewison, my boss."

The boy's charming smile made the expression on the
two men's faces the more dour by contrast. They looked
exceedingly like two dogs who have stopped to look at
each other with the hackles rising on their backs.

"Good morning," said Curton, much in the same tone

as he had said, "Have you rung?" "I am afraid I am taking your pupil from you. Mrs. Crayshaw promised to come for a run in the car."

"Saturday is always a half day," Captain Lewison admitted, but there was something grudging in his tone. "Mrs. Crayshaw begged the whole holiday."

"Here's mother," said Val.

She came into the hall in her long brown coat that Curton had thought too thin for the bitter weather last week, and a close brown hat on her head. Her face was very kind as she recognized Captain Lewison, and she smiled that wide smile that was like a silent laugh.

"I'm awfully grateful!" she said to him, even while she shook hands with Curton. "Do you mind coming round this afternoon and putting the other things in the hall? If the tradesmen leave them in the porch they might get stolen."

"Yes, I'll come. Do you want anything done in the house?"

"Well—if you would see to the kitchen fire? I've banked it up, and it will go on for hours. Here's the key."

She gave him the door key, and he nodded. "I'll see that it's all ready for you. Don't you worry. Good-bye, Val. Hope you'll enjoy it."

He raised his hat with a curt nod at Curton to include him in his leave-taking, and stumped off down the row of bungalows. He was not himself exactly lame, but it was evident that he walked with a stiff leg; and on the left hand that looked so natural, Curton suddenly saw that he wore a glove, and guessed that he had lost an arm in the War.

The terms of intimacy which he was on with Mrs. Crayshaw and her son were no doubt almost inevitable from his being tutor or crammer to the boy. But they jarred on Curton none the less, and he wondered how Crayshaw got on with the ex-soldier of the "New Army." For Captain Lewison was not a gentleman either in speech, manner, or appearance. He might be clever; he was certainly not attractive. And yet both Noel and Valentine had treated him with something like affection. It was a pity, Curton thought, that circumstances had forced them into such an intimacy. That door key in Lewison's pocket, his right of entry into the bungalow, his acceptance of domestic duties to help them, were all an offense in some occult fashion.

Miss York appeared in the little hall passage, ready for the excursion like the rest of the party. She was more suitably dressed than her niece in a dark fur coat. It might be seal cony or that mysterious skin called "pony," but it was at least fur, and warmer than Mrs. Crayshaw's.

"Thank you so much for asking me to come too, Mr. Curton," she said, and he recognized that her manner was that of any lady to whom he had given the invitation. However straitened her means, she was a gentlewoman, and quite unassuming on that count.

"I hope it is not too early in the year," he answered, smiling. "Thursday was a lovely day—I wished we could have gone then, but I had no chance even if you could all have come. My senior partner is laid up, and we are very busy."

"I hope it is nothing serious?"

"Poor old chap, I am afraid it is, rather. He has been more or less of an invalid for some years, but this last attack makes us anxious. Are you sure you will not be cold, Mrs. Crayshaw? There is rather a keen wind in spite of the sun. Would you like to bring more wraps?"

"I don't feel the cold." Noel spoke quite quietly, but her worn face flushed a little. She was looking old again to-day, and rather tired. It occurred to him as incredibly possible that she really had no service in the bungalow, and that this outing had meant extra work for her in preparing some meal for their return, and leaving everything in order.

"Why not bring your mackintosh?" suggested Miss York. "You can put it round your shoulders, if you are cold."

"Yes, do. There is nothing so warm as a mac," agreed Curton cordially. "Let Val fetch it for you while I tuck you into the front seat beside me. Here Val, come and help your mother——"

"It is here," said Noel, taking a dark waterproof coat from its peg in the hall. It was obviously well worn and rather shabby, and he realized with a pang that his insistence had brought the blood to her face and made her wince. His manner was the more solicitous as he wrapped the heavy fur rug over her knees and tucked it round her, while he felt his resentment growing against Horace Crayshaw with each revelation of his neglect of his wife.

Val and Miss York in the back seats kept up a running conversation almost from the first. They had a sort of game of guessing the make and name of each car as it passed them, and the elderly woman seemed quite as correct as the boy. Curton heard snaps of "Morris!" "Austin!" "Fiat—no, it isn't—Humber!" "Then that's one to me!—Rolls!" "Daimler!" "Wolseley . . ." as they ran smoothly out of the south of London; but Mrs. Crayshaw was rather silent until the suburbs were left behind and they began to feel the clearer air and see the March sunshine on the fields. It was too early for the hedges to be even in bud, owing to the cold February, but the grass was growing, and the rooks cawing above the leafless trees. One field in especial caught even Curton's eye as he drove.

"That looks like spring," he said. "What a color!"

"It is early trefolium," Mrs. Crayshaw answered as if it were a matter of course. "It ought to be higher, but it is a late year."

"Are you an agriculturist, Mrs. Crayshaw? I should never have suspected you."

"I lived in the country up to the time—until I married. I suppose one soaks it in unconsciously."

"You must miss the sounds and sights—don't you?" He thought, but did not say, "In such a hole as Daisy Hill!"

The patient dullness of her face altered again, but this time to something that aged rather than brought back her youth. It was so like a stab of pain that it was almost a grimace. Then she recovered herself and that lack of any expression that made her seem so unattractive. But all she said was, "They are chain-harrowing that pasture. It should have been done last month."

"Mum," said Valentine over her shoulder. "Isn't that farm-horse a Clyde?"

"Bit of Suffolk Punch in him, I think."

"There! I told you——" from Miss York.

"Don't you get a swelled head, Aunt Anstice. It's quite enough for you to beat me at motor-cars."

Curton laughed, he felt contented and almost happy, for no particular reason unless it were his own good deed in giving up golf to take these unlikely people for a run out of town. The eager landscape before him seemed to get into his blood, and the steady, successful man-of-business mood dropped off his shoulders like a heavy cloak—too heavy for the day.

He ran them down into Kent, and pulled up at a little inn standing in the middle of a straggling village street. "Will this do for lunch?" he said. "I wanted you to see Char. It is one of the few unspoiled villages left. They won't have char-à-banc parties here, and they discourage motor bikes. But they can give us quite good food."

"Topping!" said Valentine.

"But how clever of you to find such a place!" said Miss York.

Curton turned to Mrs. Crayshaw who had not spoken, but then she never did manage to get in her word before her quicker son and aunt. Into her face had come the dawning of the look of youth for which he had been waiting, and to win which he had unconsciously played with fortune. Her features seemed to have sharpened, and there was greed in her eyes—greed of the little irregular street, and the stream beyond with an old-fashioned bridge that would only allow of one-way traffic, and the blacksmith's shop at the end of the village, and the cruel March sunshine lighting it all with sharp edges and patches of white dust; but the eyes themselves were the eyes of a young woman with her life before her and not behind.

Curton came round to her side of the car and opened the door to help her out. She almost stumbled, and he saw that she was not seeing him at all, her dazed vision being all on the picture before her. Miss York and the boy had gone straight into the inn, to explore and exclaim in delight of its quaintness, but Noel stood a moment as if she did not know where she was.

"Would you like to go on to the bridge while I order

lunch?" said Curton gently. He still held her arm, as if he were afraid she would fall.

"May I? I want to look up the stream—river, I suppose they call it. If you don't mind——" She did not wait for his assent but walked away from him to the bridge, where he saw her pause in one of the recesses and look up the flowing current beneath. He had watched her progress to the bridge with real anxiety, for she did not appear to him to look where she was going, or to exercise the ordinary caution of pedestrians, who always seem to hold their lives on sufferance nowadays from the traffic; and Curton was by nature a person with the instinct of self-preservation strongly developed. But Mrs. Crayshaw having reached the bridge in safety, he turned into the inn to see what its resources were in the way of soup and chicken and salad and cream cheese.

Noel remained in the recess of the bridge for some minutes, her body a little swayed backwards and her hands resting on the old stone coping. Her eyes saw the hurry of the water below her quite distinctly, and some low willows along its banks, nothing but reddish bark and branches as yet: but her mind caught the association of another scene that resembled this, and she was eighteen, standing on a similar bridge above the trout stream that ran through her father's property. How painful it was to be young, and to have all of life's experiences ahead! But how wide the world was. . . . There was no Horace Crayshaw in it, nor the burden of matrimony that seemed part of his smiling personality. There was not even Valentine and the tragedy of his lameness. There was just Herself, standing free in the sunshine of the cold, early spring, with wide eyes looking for joy. . . . And the water under the bridge ran away and ran away, faster and faster, carrying the weight of her years with it and leaving her free once more. She wanted to give a great shout and proclaim her own freedom and never, never go back to the woman who had stepped out of Curton's car and who seemed to have gone with him into the inn. This rebel, standing on the bridge, would for the moment have thrown husband and child into the running water and all the long aching years between what she had been and what she was, and seen them hurried away on the current without a regret.

. . . . . . .

"I'm simply starving!" said Valentine, laughing, "Where's mother? I'll go and get her, Mr. Curton." He spoke rather as if she were his hat or coat and were hanging in the hall until wanted.

"She is coming in a minute. No, don't go after her, Val. What shall I order for you to drink? And you, Miss York?"

Anstice York's eyes met his as he spoke with a sudden widening of the lids in comprehension. She looked at him, indeed, as if she recognized a friend, and a queer little flash passed between them over Val's handsome curly head.

"Cider for me, please," she said.

"Oh, and for me!" said the boy.

"You'll go to sleep, Val. You'd better have ginger-ale."

"No, it's too cold. I want alcohol!"

"What about beer?" said Curton, laughing. "Do the thing thoroughly while you are about it."

"Lager isn't bad."

"Really, Val," said Miss York solemnly, "I think you will be sorry. You can get quite heady on lager. I tried it once at the Club and snored all the evening."

"You must have drunk a dozen, aunt!"

Mrs. Crayshaw came in before the drink question was quite settled, and decided in favor of coffee for herself. She would like a large cup with plenty of milk, she said.

"Yes, the wind is too cold—it has made you chilly," Curton agreed quickly.

All the youth had faded from her face which was that of the working drudge again. Yet she looked bright enough to Val, and listened smiling while he pretended to be the landlord and explained the luxuries of the menu to the party with a fine sense of comedy.

"Soup, sir? I hope you'll honor us by trying our soup— made from the mockest of turtles, with real flavoring. And what to follow, madame? Roast chicken—potatoes *à la Char village—choux au naturel*. Alphonse! four roasts——"

"Val, you're absurd," said Miss York. "And you've got an audience."

Another party had come into the dining-room, and were examining the oak paneling and the eight-day clock— three boys a little older than Valentine, and a girl who might have been an elder sister. They sat down at a little distance and discussed the latest flying accident with which they seemed to be horribly familiar. Nothing happened to disturb the serenity of Curton's party until Valentine happened to get up to ring the bell for something the waitress had not brought, and then the other boys looked at him. Later, as they left the dining-room, the eldest of the party said to the girl, "Chap's lame."

Her answer was inaudible, but a younger boy unfortunately made a remark he did not intend to be overheard.

"If I were one-legged and couldn't go in for games I think I'd shoot myself."

Val's face did not alter, to Curton's relief. He thought

the boy had not heard, though he would willingly have thrown the careless speaker into the porch for his indiscretion. A minute later, however, Val began to fidget, and his mother broke her usual acquiescent silence by saying, "I should like to go round to the back of this place, and see if they have got a farm. Anybody ready to come?"

"I'm ready," said Valentine quickly. "Mother's an authority on stock, Mr. Curton. You should hear her price a cow. And she knows a breed of pigs like a farmer."

"I'll smoke a cigarette first, if I may," said Miss York lazily. "Mr. Curton and I will find you in the pigstyes later."

Again some glance of comprehension passed between Curton and the older lady, but he offered her a cigarette without comment until the boy and his mother had left the room. Then he turned to her quickly enough.

"Do you think Val heard what those young brutes were saying?"

"Yes," she answered quietly. "And my niece also. That was the cruel part."

"I wish I had the handling of them!" Curton muttered viciously. "Poor woman!" He smoked in silence for a minute, turning the cigarette in his hard, clean fingers. Then he looked at Miss York with a speculation in his eyes, and found her looking at him gravely, almost sternly. "I think a day off from housekeeping does Mrs. Crayshaw a lot of good," he said. "She looks so much younger, don't you think?"

"How old do you suppose my niece to be?" Miss York asked deliberately, but as if a little surprised.

"I never know a lady's age—but Val is twelve, is he not? Is Mrs. Crayshaw under forty?"

"She is just thirty-two."

For a minute he suspected her of what he thought the usual concealment of the truth with regard to a woman's real age. But the expression on her face startled him into believing her. For it was evident that she regarded her statement as in some sort a tragedy.

"She must have seen a lot of trouble—hardship perhaps?" he ventured.

"She has seen a great deal of trouble—and hardship. She has worked like a laboring man's wife for most of the years since she married—certainly since her child was three years old. She has scrubbed and washed and cooked and nursed, as the working class do, with the disadvantage of not having been brought up to such a life, or having the constitution to stand it. The working-class woman ages very soon, as you may have seen. Noel has aged in the same way. She looks forty or more. And it is not the well-preserved forty of a woman in her prime. You are quite right."

Curton was feeling exceedingly uncomfortable and more than a little shocked. The concentrated bitterness with which Miss York spoke was almost like venom.

"I had no idea that Crayshaw's circumstances were what they are," he said uneasily. "I knew of course that he had no settled occupation or business, but I supposed he had means."

"Naturally. He plays golf, he can afford to go abroad, he dresses well. When he lives at home his expenses are limited because his wife is a general servant to him. He has small private means, and they are spent almost entirely on himself."

"But why does she submit to such a state of things? It is incredible—in these days. No woman would stay with him to be treated like that!"

"Where is she to go, and what is she to do, with a crippled child? If she left Horace Crayshaw and got work she could not take Valentine with her, and even now he needs constant care and attendance. She married against the wishes of her family when she was eighteen—clandestinely, in fact. I think that Mr. Crayshaw supposed she would have money, and that her father would forgive her as she was his only child. He did forgive her, but he had nothing to leave. He died actually in debt, and the sale of the property and everything he possessed hardly satisfied his creditors."

"But surely there must have been somebody to do something for her?"

"We are a singularly poor family," Miss York's face flushed darkly, but she had evidently a purpose in laying bare every cruel truth about her niece's marriage, and she did not hesitate. "There are very few of us left, and those few are rapidly sinking down into the small livelihoods and meager ways of living that just provide a bare subsistence for them until they die. I am fortunate in being able to support myself, and not to be a burden on some charitable institution, but I cannot help Noel—I cannot even give her a home. When my brother died—he was an Admiral—his pension of course died with him. But we did not know, and I think he hardly knew himself, that he had been living on such capital as he had, for years."

The upset of all Curton's former impressions with regard to Mrs. Crayshaw came as a kind of shock to him through Miss York's bitter, modulated speech. He had supposed that she might be of a lower social status than Crayshaw who had the facility of what is called "putting all his wares in the shop window." He had a certain style about him that made him seem better class than he might have done without it, and his familiarity with pursuits that entailed money added to it. It undermined all Curton's point of view to discover that he had been little more than an adventurer, marrying the daughter of Admiral York for the speculation of her inheriting money or property. But it still seemed incredible that he could have reduced her to such servitude as he had.

"Was the child lame from birth?" he asked abruptly.

"No. He was a perfectly healthy boy, and full of life. The lameness was his father's gift to him." Oh, the cruel way she said it, the hatred of this woman for the man who had so injured those she loved! "Horace had been drinking—he was not drunk, you understand, but he was excited and reckless. He was playing with the child, tossing him up in his arms, and he let him fall down a flight of stairs. Noel had called to him to stop, and was running to take the boy, but she was too late. He fractured his hip, and the doctor who set it was not competent—he was only a local practitioner and not a good surgeon. The boy developed hip disease and was handicapped for life. You heard those other boys at lunch just now—they did not mean to be brutal, and after all, it was the truth from their point of view."

Curton was listening with a most unusual amount of expression on his reserved face. The eyebrows frowned above the hard eyes, and his mouth was thin with resentment.

"Crayshaw told me that it cut him up even to look at the boy. He said he felt it more than Mrs. Crayshaw—at least, he insinuated it."

Miss York laughed most unpleasantly. "Yes, the sight of Valentine must be a disagreeable reminder, and he avoids anything unpleasant. Moreover he knows that there are moments when that same sight has made his wife hate him."

They were both silent for a minute. Someone came into the little dining-room and put a glass vase of daffodils on the table and then went away again. The flowers stood in a blot of March sunshine and seemed to have absorbed it into themselves. Miss York was breathing fast and unevenly, and her voice was still full of anger, though she had it under control.

"I have betrayed my niece's private life in telling you this," she said. "But I felt myself justified. Horace Crayshaw always presents himself to people as he wishes to appear, and he succeeds in making them think him a charming man who is very much to be pitied in having a dull wife and a crippled son—ha! ha! He is a charming man, is he not? Well, I told him once that he was nothing but a miserable sinner, and some day he would have to pray for himself on his knees. It will come true. I have never known God fail. Man's justice fails, but not God's." She went on with little alteration of tone, "I hear my niece and Val, coming back to us. May I ask you to respect my confidence?"

"Of course, Miss York." Curton was so shocked as to feel rather stunned. For he had thought of Crayshaw exactly as Miss York described, and it chagrined him a little to have been taken in. But though he allowed for some exaggeration in her bias towards her niece, he did not think that she was either deluded or lying. Her deep eyes, a little sunken in her lined face, were full of grief and indignation, but they were not the eyes of a mad person. She rose up to meet Noel and Valentine, and listened to their account of the live stock behind the little inn, with her usual kind smile for them, and left Curton to recover himself.

He looked at Noel Crayshaw anew, and understood the lines and the vacancy of her face as he had not done before. If she had been more animated she might have been attractive. But she had been a household drudge for so long that her faculties had become dulled. It was only when that strange look of lost youth came back to her eyes that he found her arresting. His quickened interest in her was only the natural pity of a man for something downtrodden and ill-treated, but it made his manner a little different though so subtly that she did not appear to notice it. It was not tender or protective, but it had the shadow of both these feelings in it.

They drove back through Hildenborough, and had tea at the Old Barn—a place which delighted Valentine as something derelict that had been transformed into a commercial success. He was always, subconsciously, building castles in the air wherein he lived with his mother, independent of the domestic Dole with which they gained his father's permission to exist. To make a fortune, and to take his mother away from their present surroundings, was a far more generous purpose in him that Curton would have credited. He wanted to explore each added improvement to the original structure of the tea-house, and they lingered so long over it that the mysterious spring twilight was almost beginning before they left.

"I hope you are not tired?" Curton said to Mrs. Crayshaw gently as he helped her into the car.

"Oh no—but I am a little anxious over the kitchen fire!" she admitted with her frank smile. "If we are late it may have gone out."

"I thought your neighbor, Captain Lewison, was to see to that?"

"So he will. But he can't sit there to stoke it till we come in!"

"We shan't be long in getting back," Curton reassured her, but the simple honesty of her confession was another revelation to him. She was always, more or less, thinking of the kitchen fire, of the meal to be prepared after a long and rather tiring day of pleasure, of the boy to get to bed—and up again to his work in the morning. No wonder that she had little to talk of when this was her daily, hourly life. And when Crayshaw was at home it must be worse. Curton felt his own impotence so much that like Miss York he was angry.

"Are you going away for Easter—I think you said something about Brighton for the boy?" he asked abruptly. It was almost the only remark he made on the way home.

She started, and sat up in her easy seat. Her thoughts must have been far from holidays or Brighton—possibly still on the ashes of the kitchen fire.

"Yes, we are going away for Easter. My husband agreed that it was necessary. I expect it will be to Brighton."

"I am going down to Hove for Easter," said Curton as he switched on his lights to drive into London. "You must give me your address. I will come and look after you and Valentine—if you will let me."

"Mr. Curton," said Val's gay voice from the back seat, "here's a big car coming—don't let's dip till they do—give it to them full blast!"

Noel Crayshaw had not answered Curton's suggestion. She was too surprised.

# CHAPTER XI

"YOU must come down to Southampton and see us off, Hugh. I may want you."

"Oh, of course. A Friday, isn't it? I can take the boat train."

"Yes. We are going down a day or so before, to give John a rest. We shall be at the Sou' Western. I knew you could not afford two or three days just now away from the office, but I must see you to say good-bye before we sail. I shall miss you so!"

"Not so much as I shall you, Sybil. I wish you had not been going by sea. These four days to Madeira seem such a barrier. If it had been the Riviera——"

"The Riviera is no use for John. It is too treacherous a climate. I hear the people die from influenza like flies. Captain Berney told me that they are supposed to bring out the coffins at seven o'clock in the morning by the back doors of the hotels to prevent other visitors knowing! Gruesome nonsense, of course—but it just shows."

"There was no epidemic when I was at Monte Carlo this year. The place had rather a clean bill of health. And Madeira is awfully damp!"

"Damp doesn't seem to hurt John so much as sudden changes of temperature. And I have never seen Funchal. I hear it is charming. Write to him at Reid's Palace, and tell him how things are going on, but don't worry him. I am afraid you will be very tired this summer, Hugh."

"Not more than I have been since John's illness. And I

can leave a great deal to Curtis and to Stephen. They are both regular stickers at work."

"I hope you will get away at Easter. You are looking thin, Hugh, but very fit."

"You think of everyone, Sybil. Don't make yourself responsible for my health as well as John's, or you will wear yourself out."

Mrs. Staine lifted her cool soft face for his kiss with a little smile.

Appreciation was to her what soft stroking is to a cat. It made her purr. She really was thoughtful for the people round her—even her servants acknowledged that—but she was very well pleased with herself for the virtue. She counted Hugh Curton amongst her own possessions, and concerned herself with him as well as with her husband.

"Have you thought about Easter?" she said, returning to the charge.

"Not much. I daresay I shall run down to Brighton."

"Oh, poor dear boy! It will be truly awful. Can't you get a little farther from London?"

"I don't feel that I want to. Every golf course will be crowded, but I know so many men who play at the Dyke that I daresay I shall get a game. I have some business in Hove, too. A property that has been offered as security for a mortgage."

"Don't be too conscientious about the work. Get some golf, but do send your nephew on these inspection duties. What a curious, old-fashioned young man he is! Not a bit like you."

"Stephen has a good head for business, but he lacks experience. I don't myself know the locality, and shall ask a professional friend to inspect with me. Well, good-bye, my dear. You think there is no danger of John's not being able to travel this week?"

"The doctor says not. But I will telephone you on Tuesday before we start."

As Curton walked away from the substantial house he remembered that he had not mentioned Mrs. Crayshaw and the boy being at Brighton for Easter. It did not matter. He should see Sybil again before Tuesday. There was no reason to suppress their being there, but somehow he had hesitated to mention it. Perhaps it was because he was now in the secret of Noel Crayshaw's life, and had promised Miss York to keep it private. If he once began to discuss Crayshaw's wife and crippled son with Sybil, she would ask questions, and he was bound to make reservations which she might detect. He decided that, after all, it was better not to introduce the subject.

The Staines really went to Southampton on the Tuesday, and embarked on the Union Castle liner on the Friday, Curton going down to see them off. His partner looked so frail in the unusual surroundings of the state-room in place of his own familiar bedroom in London, that it came as a renewed shock to Curton. His eyes met Sybil's almost pitifully, and found her looking equally grave.

"Yes," she said afterwards as they stood together at the gang-plank before he left the ship. "You see the change in him more now, don't you? I know that I must face it. He may never come back!"

"My poor Sybil!"

"But it was his one chance. Oh, Hugh, write to me—I shall be so lonely!"

For once Sybil's composure seemed to fail her. She clung to Curton's hand which clasped hers, and choked down a sob.

"If anything happens, I'll come to you," he said hastily. "Nobody will think anything, as I am his partner."

"Yes,"—she still choked a little. "Come to me—I shall want you. You are my anchor, Hugh!"

"Cheer up, little woman. It may not happen. Good-bye, dearest—take care of yourself."

They had kissed in Sybil's cabin, before coming up on deck. It had seemed no treachery to the sick man lying next door, and indeed their private relations to each other had become so settled for a long time that beyond a keeping up of appearances they regarded them as almost legal. Sybil did so, at least. But her experience of men had never allowed her to relax her hold upon Curton, and this journey to Madeira was the first thing that had parted her from him beyond reach of a day's summons. Even when he went to Monte Carlo or Cannes she was complaisant, feeling that her influence was strong enough to bring him back to her at her need. These four days that stretched before her, and being dependent upon the next homeward or outward mail steamer before they could rejoin each other, gave her a sense of impotence that was almost like loss.

"Any more for the shore?"

Sybil still stood beside the gangway, watching Curton's broad straight shoulders going down the gang-plank. He turned at the bottom and raised his hat, then hurried on through the sheds to the train. He had not looked back again. She remembered that he was not a man who looked back.

.        .        .        .        .        .        .

The rooms that Noel Crayshaw had taken for herself and Valentine were in the old part of Brighton, not far from the Old Steyne. They were not facing the sea, nor in one of those narrow streets leading down to it, but in an old-fashioned square tucked away behind the cheaper shops of North Street. The houses in the square were all old-fashioned too—not stately Georgian mansions like those along the King's Road, but structures even older perhaps, built for humbler people before the Regent made the town fashionable. There were two bedrooms at the back of the house, looking out upon somebody's washing and the blank windowless wall of a house whose built-up frames told of the window tax. The sitting room was in the front, facing the square, and was rather stuffy and musty unless the windows were always open. Easter, having fallen early, was subject to attacks of sleet and hail, so that a fire was a necessity and the rooms could only be aired by fits and starts. But despite their undeniable drawbacks, Noel and Valentine got more enjoyment out of the change of scene and the holiday from doing housework than any expensive motor party at the Metropol or Prince's.

There were some boys staying in Brighton for the Easter vacation who knew Valentine and had often carried him off to Sussex Square where their home was. Their parents were friends of General Arthun's, and they were almost the only boys of his own class that Valentine knew with any intimacy. There were three of them, all a little older than Val, but they had a half-patronizing, half-awed admiration for him as a clever youngster who might have made his mark if he could have gone to a decent school. He could get up and stage-manage plays for them to act with amazing energy, and had just completed a boys' drama wherein detectives and criminals and victims chased each other through brief scenes, and which was being hurried through for production during the holidays with dark secrecy and endless betrayal of plot and dialogue through bubbling excitement. The weather was so bad that Valentine suffered less than he might have done through his being barred from most outdoor amusements, for the boys preferred to retire to their own big room in the Sussex Square house, to rehearse and dress the parts and amuse themselves there in preference to facing the elements. Mrs. Crayshaw was only too glad to have them take Val away for the afternoon, and did not always accompany him. She knew the value of independence to a boy of Valentine's age, and it was seldom that she could give it to him with reliance and satisfaction. On her own side there was a secret shrinking from visiting people in the position of Jack's and Ronald's and Otto's parents. They had means, and social position, and were a good deal in request. When she found herself amongst people whose lives seemed to be made up of bridge and golf and motoring and dancing— healthy and normal though it was—she felt her own unresponsiveness as a barrier between them. She was dull, she had no part in all this, no experience to talk of in relation to it. They meant to be kind, but they were too busy with enjoying their own lives to get in touch with hers, even if she had wished it. Sometimes Noel Crayshaw reminded herself of a solitary oyster amongst multitudes of swimming fish, and knew that she closed her shell with the intention of being unnoticed. She was not quite young enough to fling herself into the little circle of personalities in which she found herself in Sussex Square; it was only in excursions taken with Valentine that she could regain the elasticity of her youth to companion him.

So it happened that when Curton called at the unpretentious little rooms in Brighton, to "look up Mrs. Crayshaw and her boy," he found only Mrs. Crayshaw sitting over the fire with a book. She was not reading—she had

lost the habit of reading because she rarely had time—
and her face as he saw it in the spring twilight was star-
tlingly worn and discouraged. It was as if he had chanced
upon her unawares with the mask off. For we all wear a
mask of some sort for decency's sake, and turn a braver
face to the world than we know. For the moment Noel
Crayshaw's face was not even decently resigned. It was as
if she stared at some horrible Head of Medusa in the
coals. The room with its worn furniture and faded cretonne seemed to Curton stuffy and second-rate, and instead of staying to tea as he had half intended he instantly
decided to get her out of it. He really could not sit down
with those antimacassars and oleographs, and Mrs. Crayshaw with that face pouring out flaccid tea.

"All alone?" he said cheerfully as she rose rather guiltily
to greet him. "I came to see if you and Val would come
and have tea at the Metropol. It's a beastly day even to
stay at home—will you brave the weather?"

"Val has gone to some friend of ours—Captain and Mrs.
Mackay and their own boys," she explained. "They are
getting up a little play he has written for them, and they
are all full of it. I am not to see it until the actual performance. May I give you some tea here?"

"No, do come out and have it somewhere with me. I
know the Metropol is full of awful people, but they are
really rather amusing. Or will you come to Prince's?"

"If you don't mind——" she hesitated a little—"I would
rather go somewhere quieter. Must it be a hotel? They are
so noisy and full of smart people."

He felt instantly that she was right. She would be more
shabby and badly dressed at Prince's or the Metropol than
she had been at the Criterion in London. But he ceded

the point as if all she meant was the glare and the jazz music, and not herself.

"If you don't mind a tea-shop I will take you to the China Shop," he said. "It's not so likely to be crowded. But I was afraid you would find it dull."

"Not for myself—I should like it. Val would have liked the Metropol because one sees theatrical people there. He is always wild to go there. And of course you did not know he was out."

Her tone of regret, almost of apology, woke no echo in him. He was rather glad to be rid of the boy with his incessant chatter and vitality, and the old-young shrewdness that Curton deprecated although he quite admitted it was natural in the unnatural circumstances of his upbringing. It would have been a less retired tea-party if Val had been present, even though they had not gone to the Metropol. The boy's unusual beauty, and his eager questions, attracted attention and interest wherever he appeared in public. It was impossible to hide Valentine under a bushel of candles, as one of his father's Irish relatives had once said. Curton feared that as he grew older he must be spoiled, and foresaw him as a young man of the type he detested—vain, posing to attract the notice which would become a kind of stimulant to him, more theatrical than the real stage people, with all his father's vices and less of his charm. He was glad to have Mrs. Crayshaw alone without her son's obtrusive personality. Since her aunt's revelations he looked upon her with a kind of chivalrous pity that almost canonized her.

Noel was vaguely aware that she was being taken care of, and the sensation was a new one from a man of Curton's stamp. As they walked through the windy, inclement streets to reach their goal he took her so carefully by the least exposed route, avoiding the sea front, and inquired so earnestly if she would not like a taxi, and if she were cold, that it gave her an odd little sense of comfort, like warming one's hands at a fire. His tall figure in its thick overcoat seemed to stand between her and the rough blast that met them at corners, and she answered truthfully that she did not feel it, she preferred to walk.

The China Shop was one of those small places that abound in Brighton and Hove, got up in dark wood and willow-pattern cretonne, with gate-legged tables and tea-sets of blue ware that was Japanese rather than Chinese. It was almost as snug as the old inn at Char. There were a few people beside themselves, mostly women, but they found a quiet corner and sat down near the fire without any interruption from music. The place was too small for a band, even for a wireless set.

"Tell me about this wonderful play of Valentine's," said Curton kindly. "Have you read it?"

"Not yet. It is to burst upon us like a revelation. Val has been scribbling at it for weeks in anticipation of the Mackay boys being at home to act it with him. The performance is next Saturday afternoon."

"Do you think that he really has a talent for this sort of thing?"

She hesitated a moment, and her face was graver than he had intended. "I should like to think so," she said. "It would mean a career for him—after all. But I am the worst possible judge, I suppose, because women always think their children are prodigies, don't they?"

"What does Captain—that tutor of his—say?"

"Captain Lewison. He thinks that Val has very good general capacities when he will work. He is idle at times like all boys, I suppose—idler than most, perhaps on account of his health."

"Captain Lewison does not always make allowance for that, you think?"

"How did you guess that? I think he is very much in earnest himself and inclined to cram his pupils if they don't come up to his own standard."

"It was evident that you and Captain Lewison did not always see eye to eye," Curton smiled. "But does he think that Valentine shows any gift for writing?"

"He is rather inclined to discourage it when it gets in the way of maths and languages. He thinks it more a mania than a talent, at present. I had a long talk with him before we came away. He says, quite fairly, that even if Val does become a playwright, he must have an education to help him. He is anxious that my boy should be thoroughly well grounded, and not waste time in trying to train for a profession too early. It is very sensible—but I can't help sympathizing with Val."

Curton's smile had stiffened until it was almost a frown. He had a distinct recollection of Captain Lewison on that occasion when they were all starting for a day's outing in the car, and in his own mind he always referred to him as "that bounder schoolmaster who still calls himself a Captain." He intensely disliked the New Army officer left derelict by the War, though he showed an outward respect for lost limbs and medals. He had himself served in France with a certain amount of distinction; but he certainly never talked about it. Mrs. Crayshaw's intimacy with a man of Lewison's type jarred upon him.

"What a pity that you can't get Valentine into some training school or college where they make a specialty of cases like this," he said. "There are places to meet every kind of handicap nowadays. Of course Captain Lewison may be an excellent coach, but he is not quite the type you want for Val, is he? The Secondary School ideal is all very well for a boy who is going to a working-man's college, but it does not adapt itself to special circumstances like Val's, does it?"

A quick change came into the woman's face as he spoke. Her eyes grew harder and brighter, and for the first time she looked at him with suspicion.

"I should not consent to his going to the kind of institution that you mean," she said with a downright opposition that did not temporize. "I think it is a mistake to herd afflicted people together, if it can possibly be avoided. Of course it is more economical—like mass production. There is certain treatment, and certain reservations, for one and all. But it brings it home to them more than when they are amongst normal people. They become a 'case' and not a free human being. It is bad enough for those who are past boyhood or girlhood. I should hate it for a child."

"You feel that he would miss your care and your personal guardianship," said Curton gently. "But he must grow up and leave you some day, you know. His lameness will not keep him a child!"

"No, but he will have been the child of a mother and not of an institution!" she retorted quickly. "However good the teachers, however excellent the nurses, the advantages cannot equal a home for a boy who is handicapped like mine. If he could have gone to school like other boys, do you think I should have wanted to keep him? I am not such a fool. But he would feel his difference from them more, rather than less, as a cripple amongst cripples!"

Her worn face blazed, and her eyes were dangerous. He

had roused the lioness in her when he only meant to reason and remind her of the inevitable parting of the ways that must come between her and her son. In the background of his mind, also, he had seen it as a release from Horace Crayshaw's yoke, herself a freer agent to act for herself—to work, no doubt, but not for Crayshaw. But the burden of Valentine had been also the one thing that made such a life tolerable, and she was jealous for her rights in him, for the one thing she had to love. Curton was so sorry for her that he laid his hand on her arm gently and kept it there.

"Forgive me—I blundered," he said, and his voice was very kind and more moved than she had yet heard it. "But I should have liked to have helped you."

She sat silent for a minute, her breast heaving and her eyes bright with tears. Her rush of feeling was not all for Valentine. It was a new experience to be thought for and taken care of by a man without having to be on her guard against some secret bias towards herself. Lewison had wanted to help her to independence of her husband more than once, but his reason was his own desire for her; and other men had urged her to leave Crayshaw, but always for themselves in dubious exchange. There was no such thought connected with Curton, in her own mind, or fear of him. They knew each other too slightly, and she recognized her own difference from the women of his world, whose attractions might have made his suggestion more personal. It was only pity for the drab monotony of her life, and her overworked youth; but she valued his pity all the more, and hugged it to her as something she need not refuse so long as it left her Valentine. There were certain things that she had always wanted and never had, and they seemed to make little holes in her life and spoil the pattern, like dropped stitches in knitting. Moreover, like the dropped stitches, the hole might grow larger and spread. Hugh Curton's unlooked-for kindness drew the edges of the gap together.

Somehow the unexpected moment of plain speaking between them seemed to have cleared the air and drawn them nearer to each other. He did not know how it happened, but he began to confide in her in a vaguely general way that a man as destitute of female belongings as himself finds the friendship of a woman all the more precious. He did not speak to her of Sybil Staine, but she was so much in his mind that he unconsciously used her as an example. Mrs. Crayshaw listened quietly, and with another woman's intuition she deduced that Curton had a partner who was married, and that when his ill-health took him abroad the younger man missed the companionship of the wife as much as of the husband. It was a great advantage, said Curton, to be on good terms with your partner, and to get on with him so well. He knew many men in partnership who could work together in business without any private friendship. But in his own case he had always been personally attached to the Staines. Their house had been open to him like a home, and Mr. Staine's health was a grief as well as an anxiety. He would like her to meet them on their return. Mrs. Staine was always interested in and attracted by children—she had a gift for making friends with them.

"Has she none of her own?" said Noel in a non-committal tone.

"No, unfortunately. I sometimes wonder that she does not adopt one."

"It is not the same."

"You say that very finally."

"I know. She has not borne the pangs of it—it is not hers. Do you remember your own mother?"

"Very slightly. She went to India with my father—he was a Judge. They were much away from me, and she died abroad. Perhaps I lost touch with family life. I was trained for the Bar, but after I lost both parents it was more practical to become a solicitor and I joined Mr. Staine. An Indian Judgeship is not what it used to be."

"My mother died when I was three," said Noel almost abruptly. "If she had not——" She turned her head and looked at the modern grandfather's clock in its sticky wooden case. "It is getting so late!" she said. "I must get home. I didn't think it was nearly so late!"

"Never mind—we shall find Valentine awaiting us. I didn't know it was late either. I have enjoyed it—have you?"

"Yes—it's been lovely," she said simply, as a girl of eighteen might have said it, and it struck him that in all social life and ordinary intercourse she had stopped short at eighteen, the time when she was married. It was only in hard experience of life and its sordidness that she talked as a much older woman might have talked. She was like a working woman when she spoke of parting with her child to an Institution education, though she spoke with a wider diction.

"I shall come to-morrow and take you for a walk," he said, as if it were a settled thing. "It is not good for you to sit and brood over the fire. Those small old-fashioned rooms are always stuffy."

"They are comfy little rooms. And it is a rest to be waited on."

She had never admitted so much before, and never complained to him. He felt that she was growing less formal with him, and that in time she might regard him as a real friend. He did not quite know why he wanted to be her friend, for he still thought her an unattractive woman and somewhat dull as judged by his usual standards. But her large, listening eyes had not been dull when he was telling her about his own life, and he felt that she would be a woman one might safely confide in—like Sybil Staine. There was no doubt that he missed Sybil. A man needed a woman's companionship now and then, after the strain of a growing business and its responsibilities.

It was dark as they walked back, and it being the Saturday before Easter Sunday there were many people in the streets on the way to the quieter square where she was staying. Some girls and young men, chaffing and laughing, almost ran into them—would have done so quite but for the solidity of Curton's tall figure and his determined pause.

"Beg pardon, I'm sure!" said one of the girls, half abashed and half impudent. She nudged her companion and added a line from a popular jazz tune:

"Wot's it mattah, so long as it's dark!"

They giggled their way into distance.

"I think you'd better take my arm," said Curton, quite naturally. "Union is strength. If you don't we may both find ourselves down the next area!"

"It is all these char-à-banc people who come down, I think," she replied as she laid her hand on his rough thick sleeve. He did not know that she was glad it was no longer daylight or he might have seen that her gloves were shabby and only "fabric" when new. She felt humiliated afresh because she was ill-dressed and dowdy in contrast with Curton's good clothes and excellent tailor, and at the same time that comfort of being taken care of warmed her through all the bitter wind and her thin coat. The man's feeling was the exact complement of the woman's; he liked the sensation of being on guard over something neglected and too weak to stand alone for all her habit of physical labor. It flattered his chivalry, and made him aware of his strength. When they came to the quiet square and she would have dropped her hand from his arm, he said quietly, "No, don't——" and she left it there.

One other incident remained in his memory of that cold, ugly evening in the Easter holiday. Valentine had got in before them as Curton had prophesied, and had made up the little fire so that the room was full of no other light, and its furnishings were softened to a general harmony. He came rushing to meet his mother as soon as she appeared, his face beautiful with his own excitement, and could hardly wait to greet Curton first.

"Oh, Chris," he exclaimed, "it's a big success! It's going to be topping!"

"Dear old boy, I'm so glad! But do speak to Mr. Curton."

"I beg your pardon—I'm so full of my play," said the boy naïvely. "How are you, Mr. Curton? Won't you sit down?"

"No, thanks, Val—I must be going. I'm glad the play goes well. Good luck to you and your company!"

"I'll come and see you out, and light the gas," said Valentine with a sudden attention to a guest that explained itself a minute or so later when they stood in the passage by themselves. "I say, sir," he said half nervously, and half as if very much in earnest. "Would you mind forgetting what I called mother?"

"What you called your mother?" repeated Curton surprised. "Oh, of course—I only supposed it was your name for her."

"So it is—Noel, Christmas, d'you see? I've always called her Chris between ourselves. But I never do before anyone else—only I was so excited I forgot."

"My dear boy, it doesn't matter!"

"Yes—but—I should be awfully grateful if you wouldn't let it out to my father. He doesn't know, and we don't want him to."

Curton's surprise changed to an unusual intuition. "I will remember, Val—you needn't be afraid."

"Thanks awfully," muttered the boy, evidently a little abashed. "Sounds silly, I know—but he'd use it—make a joke of it—he makes things so cheap!"

Curton turned back from the door, and shook hands with the boy as if he shook hands with a man.

# CHAPTER XII

HORACE CRAYSHAW returned home at the end of April. Himself, his suit-cases, and the general litter of an untidy man unpacking, seemed to fill the bungalow at Daisy Hill and squeeze the other occupants into distant corners. His clothes always appeared too handsome for the furniture and made it the poorer by contrast, and he must himself have been aware of this, for he remarked on it.

"How shabby the place has grown! It was as clean and nice as a new pin when we came here. You have contrived to wear out the chairs and everything else while I've been away!"

"They were not new when we came here, and wicker and bamboo soon get frayed," said Noel in her controlled voice. She was generally severely under restraint in her husband's presence.

"They oughtn't to have gone so quickly, ought they? That's the boy, I suppose. Children never can keep their legs or their boots quiet. Look at that chair—it nearly let me down this morning."

"It nearly let you down in January when you broke it yourself!" said Noel dryly. "I have had it mended once. You had better not sit on it."

"Ah! I'm a heavier fellow than I look!" Crayshaw turned the home-thrust with his ready laugh. "That's the worst of having a fine man for a husband, my dear." Noel received this self-acclamation with unresponsive silence.

She was, perhaps, too busy laying the table for the mid-day meal to respond.

"We want a whole new fit-out, don't we?" Horace suggested agreeably. "But I'm afraid it won't run to it. I had rotten luck at the tables."

"When you won five hundred pounds?"

"Who told you that? I never mentioned it because I knew you would be vexed with me for losing it again—as of course I did next day! I'm a born gambler, I'm afraid—when I have won money I must either give it or throw it away. Something in our blood, I suppose. All Celts are generous."

"It is a pity you were not more generous to me when you had it. You did not give it away or throw it away on your home."

"I hadn't time—I tell you it was gone again in a night. But who told you?"

"Mr. Curton let it out, the first time he came here when you had invited him and then forgot to let him know you were not coming."

"Of course! But I had wired to you."

"I could not know you had invited him. I barely knew of his existence except that you had gone abroad with him, and I certainly did not know his address to prevent his coming. We were as surprised as he was when he turned up."

Crayshaw burst out laughing again. "I should have liked to have seen old Curton's long face when he called and found only you and the boy! What a sell for him. I must get him out of the huffs and play a game of golf with him again."

Noel went on with her preparations for dinner in silence. It was one of her husband's most pathetic complaints against her, in moments of confidence to his own friends, that she never talked and seldom took enough interest in what he said to answer him. It is very difficult to get either agreement or anger from an audience which is strictly silent. He was driven to the direct question as he had been many times.

"Has Curton been here since?"

"Yes."

"How often? What did he come for?"

"I told you. He took Val and myself to the theater. He was very kind in getting tickets for a particular play that Val wanted to see. And he took us for a joy-drive in his car, with Aunt Anstice."

"He must be fonder of me than I ever guessed to stuff himself up with a family party like that! The whole lot of you. Really he needn't have gone out of his way to such an extent—I've never made a special pal of him. Of course I knew he liked me—rather touching, I call it. Taking you all out because I was away!"

Noel lifted her dull eyes and looked at him as if she wondered. After thirteen years of married life with Horace she still got taken aback at times by his point of view though she knew it began and ended in himself.

"I think he was interested in Val," she said at last slowly.

"My dear, you're obsessed with Val. It's really childish. D'you suppose a man like Curton would take the trouble to traipse round with a boy and his mother and his aunt if he didn't wish to do someone else a good turn? I don't suppose he was much struck with Valentine, except as my son. I really must thank him, though—I'll write and ask him to come out on Thursday, unless he'd rather meet me at the Club."

"You had better ask him to the Club and not here, as you think us so shabby."

"Well, you must own that the little shack is hardly the place one wants to ask a man like Curton! I know you do your best, Noel, but coming back to it showed me what a hole Daisy Hill is. It's off the map to start with, and the whole of the bungalows are jerry-built styles!"

He looked round him with dissatisfied eyes, and obvious disgust. He had come straight back to England from the Casa Caralyn where he had been spending his last days, and the wonder of white marble and flowering gardens, the luxury of the life there, was still sharply in his memory. He had hated the narrow confines of the tiny house at Daisy Hill by contrast, and the dilapidated basket chairs and cretonnes that Noel never had the money to renew, though the bungalow had seemed so fresh and pleasant when they moved there from the rooms in West Kensington. He had already decided that when he began his job in Vanstead's office he would get a room somewhere nearer, or live at the Club. He could afford that out of his salary, and keep on the bungalow as well on the allowance he made Noel, and he felt that it was generous in him to do so. Hitherto he had found a home of some sort a convenience to him, and a necessity in his worst times when things were going badly; but now that the tide was turning he resented the disadvantage of a wife and child to provide for when he could do without them. It was like a millstone round a man's neck. He did not even see how it could be done more cheaply than as things were, and supposed that the home at Daisy Hill must remain as a disagreeable background to his life even if he got more and more free from it.

Valentine came home to the midday dinner from Captain Lewison's morning tuition. It was an uncomfortable meal, because Horace was in one of his Celtic moods, and felt himself misunderstood and suffering from a vague grievance. Valentine was in pain from his injured limb and irritable with his father's presence, though he did his best to hide it for his mother's sake. Noel was sufficiently occupied with feeding and waiting on her menfolk to have little time for conversation even if she had wished it.

"You can do something for me when you've had your grub, Val," Crayshaw said as he ate his meat. "I want my boots cleaned—give them an extra shine, and remember it's for your old father who works for you!"

There was a faint flush on the boy's thin, handsome face as he glanced at his mother. He cleaned her shoes and his own with a good will, but he had many times resented being set to like tasks for his father.

"I want Val to rest for an hour before he goes back to his work," said Noel quietly, but with instant decision. "You must look after yourself to-day, Horace. We can get your things in order to-morrow."

"If he can go back to work he can do what I ask first. What's the matter with him? He was all right this morning."

"I want him to lie down," said Noel, looking straight at her husband. "His leg is painful. I don't think he will go back to Captain Lewison to-day."

"I'd rather go——" began Val eagerly, and his father turned on him instantly.

"You do as your mother tells you—if you are as bad as you say," he said almost fiercely. But his eyes had fallen before his wife's and he looked furtive. "It will do you no harm to stop away from that second-rate prig, Captain Lewison!—New Army ranker, and Elementary schoolmaster! I wonder you can stick him as you do, Noel.

The boy's getting just the same common accent from learning from him."

"He's got a decent War record, and he's been a good pal to mother and me whenever we wanted one!" Val burst out in defiance of his mother's warning glance. "I can't help it, mother—I won't sit here and hear Lewy run down just because he's made himself off his own bat!"

"We don't want to discuss Captain Lewison, Horace," said Noel firmly. "He has been a good friend to us, as Val says, and you agreed to his coaching him."

"Oh, you two are always ready to back each other up, and in league against anything *I* say! Well, make a friend of the little bounder if you like, only don't ask me to meet him. I'm going off to see Vanstead."

"You had better eat your pudding first," said Noel sensibly. "You will only be hungry before you get to the City."

He ate in silence. It was plain food, well cooked and perfectly wholesome. Chosen for the boy, of course! He had grown used to French cooking, and his palate resented the absence of sauces and flavoring. He thought that Noel was no good at cooking—hadn't the same *flair* for it as a Frenchwoman—and pitied himself for being obliged to eat food prepared by an amateur. It was not every man who would have sat down to a midday dinner with his wife and child! No, the majority would have gone to the Club. He nursed his grievance, which had now grown definite, until it justified him in having another and better meal to-night with Vanstead. Then he got up, threw his napkin on the table, and by way of grace said he shouldn't be in till late, and should grub somewhere else.

"Then don't forget your latchkey, and do come in

quietly. I will leave everything you want in the kitchen," his wife agreed indifferently.

The little room felt healthier when he was out of it. It had held too much anger for its size. By and by they heard him go out—Noel was in the kitchen again by then, washing up, and Valentine was drying the plates and dishes for her—and he passed into the road to wait for the omnibus, looking as if he ought to ride in a Rolls Royce. It was a characteristic of Horace Crayshaw that he always looked expensive even when economizing. He had really been so disagreeable all the morning that Noel felt the relief of a person suddenly recovered from a painful attack of indigestion, and she drew a deep breath as of thankfulness for a happy release.

Valentine was glad to lie down in the sitting room on the spinal couch and to fall asleep. If it had not been for the blister of his father's presence he would not have suggested going back to his work that afternoon; but his mother put on her hat as soon as he was comfortably settled, and walked along the row of bungalows to Captain Lewison's to tell him not to expect his pupil.

Though it was the 1st of May, it was still a chilly spring, and the wind was sweeping through the little garden suburb and buffeting the young green of the slender trees. Mrs. Crayshaw liked it. It seemed to blow away the atmosphere of her own house and Horace and his moods. She threw up her head and sniffed the air which seemed to her faintly sweet with budding lilac and wallflowers. Some of the gardens to the bungalows were gallant attempts to grow bulbs and perennials, and one or two had striplings of lilac and laburnum. Captain Lewison's front plot was bright with forget-me-nots and double white candytuft, and it was wonderful how much he contrived to do in his small borders with his one hand and arm. She almost trampled on his crouching figure as she came through his gate, where he was lovingly weeding and hunting for "garden pests."

"I'm sorry, Paul—I didn't see you," she gasped breathlessly. "Don't get up—I only came to say that I'm keeping Val at home this afternoon. His leg is bad."

Captain Lewison remained kneeling, literally at her feet, but he threw his head and shoulders back to look up at her.

"I know," he said. "I nearly sent him home this morning—only he begged to stay. Did you want him home?"

"No. His father takes up rather a lot of room, and Val wants to be quiet. My husband happens to be out this afternoon."

"But you——"

"I can manage."

His face altered suddenly to an ugly red flush and frowning brows. She foresaw an outburst, and put out her hand as if to stop it. What was the use? She knew of that devotion of which Miss York had spoken, and that Horace Crayshaw's proximity sometimes maddened Lewison into unwise speech. It had all been talked out between them months ago. It was impossible to disguise her relations with her husband, to Lewison, who had become intimate and in some sort necessary to her. But she had never accepted him as anything but a friend, or confided more in him than had been imperative for Valentine's sake. The love was all on his side. Yet she had not disguised the fact that had his circumstances been different she might have left Horace for him—and made the best of it. He was too poor to make the exchange possible. His sister and himself found his pension and what little she could earn at home (she was a skilled and clever knitter) almost too small for the common needs of life as it was. And Edith Lewison could do everything for him that Noel would have done in the house. She and the boy would have been a heavier burden than they were to Horace Crayshaw. It had been nothing but the desire to escape that had made her think of Lewison as the lesser of two evils, and now she wondered suddenly if it would not be out of the frying-pan into the fire? For this man kneeling at her feet would have made demands upon her that she was able to evade from her husband whose infidelities were becoming an ironic comfort to her. She need not at least pretend to love Horace. She would have to pretend it for Paul Lewison unless they were to be utterly miserable.

"Don't say anything, Paul!" she pleaded, laying her hand on his shoulder.

"I can't bear it—when he is with you!" he muttered, trying to regain his control.

"It is no worse than usual. He happens to be in a bad temper, that is all. He has gone out for the rest of the day."

"He will try to get round you—after he has done quarreling. Don't forgive him!"

She knew what he hinted at, and steadily ignored it. "Oh, Horace is sure to be extra amusing and entertaining after a fit of temper," she said. "He cannot bear being unattractive! But we have learned to put up with that in due course, Val and I. Don't worry, Paul!"

"How can I help it? I'm always thinking of you. You know that, Noel!"

"You don't think in the right way," she said simply. "I'm very strong, really, and the work won't break me down. And I get a lot out of life. When I do get a holiday—like that fortnight at Brighton—I enjoy it ten times as much as people who can go away every week-end."

She had hoped to divert him, but instead she turned his thoughts into another dangerous channel. "Because that man was with you, and could take you about. That's why you enjoyed it. And a poor devil like myself can't do anything for you. Have you seen him lately?"

"No." Somehow she was relieved to be able to say no. "He is only a chance acquaintance, and you are our friend. He was really awfully good to us. But I don't expect to see him now Horace has come back—they will meet at the Club."

She was aware that his deeply set eyes were searching her face, and had a panic fear that she might flush—for no reason save that he was expecting it. She laughed instead, thankful that she had learned to laugh for Val's sake when her mind was most serious, and without entering the house said good-bye to Lewison and left him to his flowers.

As she walked back it struck her that his voice was rather nasal, and that he spoke too carefully for good breeding. He had been taught to speak, but had never acquired the right accent. And his face was common despite its look of hard intelligence. She wondered why she saw these things more plainly to-day. Was it by contrast to Hugh Curton, and his well-groomed surface? She had not found him attractive at first, and did not now regard him as a friend, as she did Lewison. But his recent air of protection supplied a want in her existence that altered her whole attitude towards him. It was too subtle a feeling to analyze, and too vague to call a sentiment. He merely gave her something that she did not ask for but which seemed to belong to her.

She wondered when she would see Curton again, and if he would now drop out of her life as he had dropped into it—by Horace's selfishness. She never met his friends when he was at home, except such women as he had tried to bring into the house to suit himself, and against whom she had protested once and for all. It seemed to her unlikely that Curton would come again, and she did not know that she wished it with Horace present. He would so predominate the foreground that she and Val would be pushed on one side, and he would somehow present his own point of view of himself as a good fellow unluckily handicapped by a dull wife and a lame boy. Horace was always apologizing for her by his own charm. He did not say it, but it breathed from him like an essence.

The word occurred to her mind, and reminded her of something she found puzzling in Horace's protracted stay in Monte Carlo. On most occasions of his return home after a long absence he brought her a great deal of mending to do amongst his clothes. But this time everything was in such perfect repair that as she looked through socks and shirts she marveled. Either the *femme de chambre* in the hotel had been a pretty woman and Horace a favorite, or else he had not spent all his time in a hotel. He had told her that his stay had been lengthened on account of influential friends he had made who might help him to considerable business. More particularly he had mentioned one man whom it was unwise to disappoint. He had been to Cannes with his new friend, and returned with him to Monte Carlo, and they had traveled as far as Paris together. It was unfortunate for Noel that when her husband was expansive she had learned to mistrust his statements. He always embroidered, if he were not lying for sheer love of it. She did not believe in the man friend, unless he had a wife (Horace had said he was a bachelor, which made her think he might be married), in which case they might have been spending the winter abroad in a villa, and have asked Horace to stay. It must be a well-run house in which the guests' clothes were so carefully looked after! She shrugged her shoulders, mentally. Bachelor friends did not look after these domestic details. Perhaps the sad thing was that she cared so little now that she only suspected Horace through habit, and hoped the lady in the question was safely left behind in Paris.

Curton did come to call at Daisy Hill, despite Crayshaw's invitations to his Club. He appeared on an unfortunate occasion when one of Horace's numerous relations had come to lunch without an invitation and lingered on to tea. She came of the Welsh branch of the family who called themselves Crayshaw-Morgan, and had married a cousin. Horace was always delightful to his connections and invited them to meals at any time, explaining with his hearty laugh that there was nothing but bread and cheese in the house unless Noel could knock up some soup! (He had a rooted idea that soup can be made in five minutes, which his exasperated wife could not dispel.) Mrs. Morgan had accepted the "pot luck" without reference to her hostess, and rushed into staccato praise of Horace's looks before she was in the sitting room.

"As handsome as ever, Horry!—are you not proud of having such a man, Noel? Ah, it is the real Welsh color in you that puts every other nation to shame. I have said over and over again that it takes a Welshman to get violet eyes and black hair and a warm heart!"

"But I'm not Welsh, Cousin Gwenyth. I'm Cornish just as much, and a dhrop of Irish blood in me I'm thinking!"

"Don't forswear your lineage, man—it's your heritage. Your Cornish strain would have made you little and dark, and your Irish wouldn't have given you a feature."

"My mother was a Blake and the most beautiful woman in County Cork!"

"I saw her before ever you were born—we were near the same age. A poor slip of a thing with gray eyes and no bosom!"

Mrs. Morgan was, herself, a small woman, with dark hair and chocolate eyes. Her color rose easily as she spoke, and in a minute there was an argument between the two Celts, neither waiting for the other and each raising their voices in contradiction.

"I tell you——"

"I won't listen to it——"

"You are wrong then——"

"Don't you think that you are wrong to say so?"

Noel went away to make the soup with such means as were at her command, leaving them to quarrel. They would do so several times, she knew, before Mrs. Morgan left, and afterwards Horace would reproduce her, manner and speech, with a mimicry that was not entirely kind but certainly very funny. She and Val had laughed at it many times.

On this occasion, however, Cousin Gwenyth had a surprise in store for them. During the impromptu lunch (Horace had been going out to lunch, so that there was really little to eat in the house) she became serious, and told them with some melancholy that since last she had seen them she had become religious and knew herself saved. Horace of course made a joke of it, whereat they quarreled again, to Valentine's obvious enjoyment. But they were none of them prepared for her sudden desire for their conversion, particularly Horace's, and when they were all in the sitting room after the meal was over, she startled them by going down on her knees and praying out loud for their souls with a fervor that caused her to rock her body to and fro. The cigarette dropped from Crayshaw's lips in his amazement, and for the moment he was nonplused. Noel rose swiftly and put her hand over Valentine's mouth, checking the giggle. Mrs. Morgan prayed on. Valentine, struggling with his mother's hand, pointed to the window, and there, outside the little gate, was Curton's big car and Curton getting out of it.

"Amen!" said Noel loudly, cutting short a request for pardon for her own shortcomings. "Horace, there is Mr. Curton."

Crayshaw's expletive is better unprinted, and making a dive for Mrs. Morgan he dragged her up from her knees and sat her down in a chair as if she were a doll.

"Another time, Cousin Gwenyth," he said flurriedly. "Here's a man to see me on business——"

"Then let him hear me too!" said the convert, still beating her breast in her excitement. She had worked herself up to a kind of frenzy and looked as if she were in a trance, and Noel saw that Valentine had in a sense caught the reflection of her mood. He was nearly as excited and almost hysterical with laughter or fear.

"Go and meet Mr. Curton at the gate, Horace," she said quickly. "And you come along with me, Val—Cousin Gwenyth would like to be alone for a little."

She swept her menkind out into the hall-passage like a

whirlwind, and turned the key in the sitting room door, locking Mrs. Morgan in.

"Why the deuce didn't you stop her? Throw some cold water over her or something?" stormed Crayshaw. "She's mad. I've never seen her like this!"

"She is only over-excited, and it makes her seem delirious. She will come round if you let her alone, and we can all have tea. Take Mr. Curton into the dining room while Val and I get it."

"But suppose she breaks out again before Curton! I say, Noel, is she drunk?"

"You know she isn't. She has only had lemonade to drink at lunch."

"She might have something in that bag—elderly women take nips about with them."

Val began to giggle again, and Crayshaw, who liked applause, made a funny face at his son as if they two were in collusion about Cousin Gwenyth.

"Mr. Curton is waiting, Horace."

Crayshaw turned to the hall door just as Curton pulled the bell, and Noel and Valentine heard his hearty voice in surprised welcome as they scurried back into the kitchen to get the tea. "But what will you do about old Gwenyth, Mum?" said the boy eagerly.

"Don't call her that, Val. You might get into the way of it, and it's rude."

"Well, father does it—but then he's often rude."

"Never mind. He's a man. You can decide whether you are going to be rude or not when you are one."

"I hope I'm not going to be like *him!*" said Val, rather offended. "I shall at least be a gentleman."

"It is rather difficult to be a gentleman."

"You're thinking of Lewy," said Val quickly, with the

uncanny habit he had of following his mother's mind. "But that's only his voice and his manner. He's a *pukka Sahib* inside all through!"

She smiled at his loyalty, but went on busily cutting thin bread and butter. "Make the toast, Val," she said.

"All right. I say, do you think Curton is?"

"Mr. Curton. Think he is what?"

"A *pukka Sahib.*"

"My father used to say that people who couldn't express themselves in English didn't know what they meant!"

"Well—a gentleman?"

"He acts like one, anyway."

"He doesn't like me," said Val shrewdly. "He never did, from the first. Chris, you don't like him *really,* do you? Better than Lewy? Better than the General?"

His mother's breathless pause had hardly been long enough for her to question herself or to realize that she had been taken by surprise. She let the first part of the indictment go, and found that she could answer the last.

"No, of course not. No one is like General Arthun!"

"He is a dear old boy, isn't he? And he is fond of us both. He seems to belong to us—but father's not in it!"

"There—I've made the tea. Be quick and take the toast in, and open the dining room door for me and the tray."

Val rushed on in front to his mother's relief, but he was not the one to open the door for her and the tea-things— Curton did that, standing tall and immaculate at her service, and trying to take the tray from her hands. She greeted him with her usual manner, apparently pleased to see him and as friendly as she would have been to the rector or the doctor or Captain Lewison—the few men who came into her life. Then she went away to bring Mrs. Morgan in, and returned with her after a few minutes, as

if nothing had ever occurred to enforce her being impris-
oned in the sitting room. Cousin Gwenyth hardly seemed
aware of it either. She was introduced to Curton and began
to talk to him volubly so that she and Crayshaw practically monopolized the conversation. Noel Crayshaw was
rather silent, but then she often was when there were
greater talkers present. Curton missed nothing in her quiet,
for he was a little *distrait* himself. But perhaps if Valentine had not asked those questions respecting him, Noel
might not have retired into the patient hostess, seeing to
everybody's wants and too busy to be spoken to.

Curton's slight stiffness of manner was not due to Mrs.
Morgan's unexpected presence or her Welsh accent, to
which of course Crayshaw attributed it. "Curton was
always a bit of a snob," he decided. "Old Gwenyth is
too tough for him to swallow." As a matter of fact Hugh
Curton hardly realized that the surprising lady with the
dark coloring and emphatic manner was present, or for
that matter, Horace Crayshaw and Valentine. Suddenly
and in a moment, it seemed, he found out what was
happening to him, and had been happening for some
weeks with regard to Noel Crayshaw. He had fallen in love
with her. The thing was so incredible that it seemed
slightly ridiculous; but he found his heart quickening and
his mouth dry whenever she chanced to speak or look his
way. He had fallen in love before, of course, but with a
deliberation that had never allowed him to be taken by
surprise. It had always begun by his approving of a
woman and then admiring her. Later, if circumstances
permitted, and the lady reciprocated, he either became her
lover, or—prudently went away. Most of these affairs had
been with married women. He did not intend to marry at
present, and seldom or never made love to girls or young

women without a husband. In particular he avoided widows. At the present moment, if asked by his conscience, he would have admitted being in love with Sybil Staine, and if anything should happen to poor old Staine that he would eventually marry her. It seemed the inevitable and decent thing to do, and he thought he wished to do it. That is, until the middle of a commonplace tea-party at the little bungalow in Daisy Hill. Then he found that he was no longer his own master, that he loved Noel Crayshaw to the exclusion of all his principles, and that he could not marry Sybil or any other woman so long as Noel was alive. It was so much more real than any feeling he had ever had before that it frightened him.

Horace was speaking, and laughing, and looking as handsome and happy as if he were really the model husband he only acted, and as if that woman in Monte Carlo had never kept him away from his wife. Curton was convinced in his own mind that she had done so. He knew rather more of Caralyn Da Costa and her reputation than he had told Crayshaw. He began to hate Crayshaw as suddenly as he had begun to love Noel, and that also was the most genuine of all the aversions in his life. But Crayshaw was talking to him, running on in that light, easy way that made him such a social favorite.

"I was a perfect 'deader' for a week after you left, Curton—not a soul to speak to or play a decent game of golf. 'Pon my soul I moped so, people in the hotel thought I'd been turned down by a woman! How's that for a man's companionship, Noel? A woman who's lost her pal goes out and has her hair waved and is consoled. A man who's got used to another misses him like hell! Is that old partner of yours better, Curton? He did all the mischief by crocking up. Still abroad?"

"They went to Madeira." Curton took hold of himself and forced himself to talk in his turn. "And came in for that revolution in April. It was most unlucky."

"Funny thing—we were expecting a revolution in Monaco that didn't come, but it broke out in Funchal! Just like some volcano affecting another range of mountains miles away. What become of your partner—Mr. Staine, was it? Did the old boy stick it out?"

"No, they were obliged to leave by the first chance they had, and that happened to be a mailboat to the Cape. Mrs. Staine was very upset by it all, but I had a letter from her before she left Madeira, and she could only hope the voyage might do her husband good."

"Did she tell you anything about the revolution? This grows interesting, Val! We ought to have been there."

"Very little. They got away before the thing really became serious. But she told me a piece of news that affected me much more personally, in as far as it related to myself. It was rather a curious coincidence. Mrs. Staine met some globe-trotting Americans in Funchal, who had been in Monte Carlo and Cannes. They asserted to her that they had met me in Monte Carlo, at a most sumptuous villa where I was staying, and that I was seen driving about with a lady, long after I had come back to England! I can't quite make it all out, unless I have a double in Monte Carlo. They were told that the man was Hugh Curton, anyway."

Crayshaw began to laugh, as if the "Comedy of Errors" struck his sense of humor.

"I say, old Sport, that's a nasty one for a respectable Englishman!" he said, grinning. "Did you hear who the lady was?"

"No, Mrs. Staine did not say."

"A double!" said Crayshaw more thoughtfully, as if searching his memory. "That's the worst of being typically British. I do remember seeing a man at the tables who struck me as like you, but he was not a twin brother. I could see the difference—but then I know you so well. The Seatons—you remember the Seatons? Little man and large woman—said they thought it was you and spoke to him!"

"Did you hear who he was?" asked Curton quickly.

"No—never thought any more about it, except to rag the Seatons. I believe there *was* a lady with him. I told them they ought to have known you better, old Thing!" Again that hearty, boyish laugh—but Noel looked at him with those undeceived eyes and wondered why he was lying so fluently; was it to reassure Curton, or to help him to an explanation with his partner and his wife? Horace could be good-natured sometimes, and a fellow-feeling might make him kind. She did not believe a word of his story, or think that he had seen any man resembling Curton after the latter had left Monte Carlo, until it was put into his head by the coincidence. She was puzzled, but as usual she kept silence.

"I suppose that was the beginning of the mistake?" said Curton half indifferently again. His momentary spurt of interest seemed to have died down, and he soon after took his leave. Mrs. Morgan took hers at the same moment, so obviously in the hope of a lift in the big car at the gate that even Crayshaw's easy temper was ruffled.

"Old Gwenyth is the limit!" he said when he had seen both guests off with jovial hospitality. "I'm damned glad that Curton turned his back on her and left her to catch a bus. She might have broken out again, and prayed for his salvation! She reminded me of Anstice York, this afternoon—d'you remember your aunt's loving way of calling me the Miserable Sinner? Old Gwenyth was just the same."

"I don't think so, Horace. I think she was praying for me rather than for you, that I might see my wifely duties!"

"She's off her nut, anyhow. She always was a bit nicked. We all are at times—we're Celts."

Noel smiled absently. She was really not listening. Her mind was hanging on those last few moments when Curton was saying good-bye and her hand lay in his. It had lain there for quite an unusual time because she could not draw it away without a wrench, he held it so closely and warmly. He had never done this before, and she wondered if that were his silent way of telling her that he sympathized and understood at last. She had never discussed her married life with him, and had taken it for granted that he liked and admired Horace as all his other friends did, and regarded her as rather a drawback to such a good fellow. At least, that had been her feeling up to a certain point. Lately, it is true, and particularly at Brighton, she had begun to think that he did not regard her as a drawback to Horace—or to any man. But still she had not confided in him. She was not the type that pours out her soul to any one who will listen to her own point of view, and her pride stood in the way. But when he held her hand so closely just now, and looked down at her from his goodly height, there was something in his eyes that seemed to protect her and to promise mutely that he was ready to do her service. It was not the look of passion and worship that she had been obliged to acknowledge in Lewison's eyes—it was a stranger look that seemed to search her and to claim her at the same time. It was all the stranger coming from Curton. She wondered if he also were conscious of some new bond between them, some advance in their relations to each other?

Curton, driving home with mechanical care and skill, was quite as upset and far more stirred than she. Her hand still seemed to lie in his—the work-worn hand that he had fastidiously said no man would care to hold!—and to send a thrill over his substantial body. He was not a sentimental man, and it seemed to him incredible that he should be in love with a woman like Noel Crayshaw to the extent of tingling all over at the mere touch of her. She had no dear little vanities like most women. She was like a clean, bare room, swept out even of the litter of living by a ruthless sweeper. The sort of room that hardly looks as if it were lived in, he thought, with unusual imagination. Probably she had not noticed anything of his excitement. And yet his heart had pounded so for the few minutes that they stood together, and he had felt so strange, he wondered no one had seemed to notice them. But Horace Crayshaw was busy bustling his old relative out of the house, and had sent Val on ahead to stop a bus if it passed, and Noel's clear eyes had only looked at him once, and then seemed quite unembarrassed. The truth was that he had been too taken up with his own emotions to notice hers. And for the first time, perhaps, Hugh Curton was uncertain of himself, and of the effect he produced on a woman.

If it had not been for Val's question he might have been right, and beyond a passing wonder Noel really might not have realized his meaning. He could not know that even as he drove away she was repeating the boy's question with a new application to herself.

"Chris, you don't *really* like him, do you?"

# CHAPTER XIII

A NSTICE YORK was unable to take her holiday at the usual time that year, owing to a reorganization of the office in which she was still fortunate enough to have work. She knew—no one better—how slender a hold she had on employment of any kind, and how few women of sixty were still earning a salary as she was doing. Sometimes she woke in the night and wondered whether she would be lucky to the end—which meant that she would go on until, suddenly, brain and body gave out, and after a short merciful illness she died.

Until her brother's death, she had had a refuge in his home if she desired it: and it was for personal and very feminine reasons that she had sought out work for herself and established herself independently in London. She was at this time forty years old, and as she had not married, it seemed problematical whether she ever would. Her desire for independence was attributed to the restlessness of women who have reached middle age and are still single; but when Admiral York died with his affairs in confusion, Anstice's friends said how merciful it was that she had already earned her own living, and congratulated her as if it had been a provision made for her and not her own effort in the face of some dissuasion. She had not known, any more than anybody else, that her brother was actually living on his capital, and the loss of his kindly hospitality, and some one to depend on should her health fail, was as much of a shock to her as to his daughter.

It was the tragedy of her later life that she had been unable to make a home for her niece and grand-nephew instead of leaving them to the tender mercies of Horace Crayshaw—but at least she had been, herself, a burden upon nobody. She had, besides her meager salary, an annuity of forty pounds a year. Even if she had the Old Age Pension when she could no longer work, she could hardly keep herself, and the dread of some painful illness, and crawling through the remaining years of her life, sometimes broke out in a cold sweat upon her. But she was generally so far tired that she slept. And after all she had become used to the outlook before her, as thousands of other women do.

Anstice had been in her present employment for twenty years, and had seen many alterations in the staff. But so long as Sir Edward Prawn was the Secretary of the Almoners' Society, Miss York was likely to be his Assistant. He was not an easy man to get on with, and he was surprisingly fastidious as to his associates. Miss York suited him for two reasons; she was a gentlewoman, and she wrote an unusually beautiful hand. In the outer office the clerks wore their hair short and used typewriters. He hated both these things, though he admitted their practical use. But in the little inner room where Miss York usually worked alone (for he was only there once or twice a week) he shuddered to think of a smart, business-like young stenographer and the click of her machine. Those neat, beautiful copies of his vague notes in pencil, and the filling in of certain forms which could not be typed, assured Anstice York her livelihood. She was very thankful for her good fortune.

Nevertheless she would have liked to go away in August as usual. It is generally the rainiest and worst month

of the summer, but General Arthun had a conservative
idea that people who lived in London must always be asked
out of it in August, to give them the full compliment of a
country house visit. Miss York was always asked to Greatoaks when Noel and Valentine went, and had generally
been able to go, at least for part of the time that they
were there. This year she had been obliged to lose that
brief glimpse of a life and surroundings that had once
been familiar to her.

General Arthun had been her brother's friend since they
had been at a preparatory school together as small boys;
but she had not known him until she was a girl of twenty,
and he thirty, and Senior Subaltern in his regiment. He
had liked her, been a little sentimental over her, got over
it, and finally became a staunch and valued friend. But
while these processes were going on she had quietly fallen
in love with him and never been able to outgrow it.
Gerald Arthun had, without blame on his part, prevented
her marrying while she still had the chance, and been the
motive power that drove her to an independent life in the
vain hope of forgetting him. She had gone on loving him
instead, and suffered all that a woman may in jealousy of
other women—fear that he would marry—hope that even
at last he might want her in his life, though they were
elderly people. He never had married, but she could not
say that she knew of any disappointment in his life or
any definite love-affair. While he was on Foreign Service
it might have happened without her knowing, but he did
not seem an embittered man. At seventy he was handsome
and upright and able to shoot and ride still in moderation.
Like most men who have held a good official position and
retired to live on a pension and private means, he was not
so well off as he expected to be. Increase of taxation, loss

on investments, cost of living, had all helped to straiten his means. But he still lived at Greatoaks House, curtailing his expenses as far as possible in a bachelor establishment. It was not a large country house, and he had not more land than he wanted. But year by year he was driven to selling, until even the rough shooting which was his principal enjoyment shrank to inconsiderable dimensions.

If he had only loved her, or cared for her enough to marry her and let her love him, Anstice York felt bitterly that she could at least have made him comfortable, and economized as only a woman knows how, leaving him a larger margin for his sport. They could have had Noel and Valentine to live with them without letting him feel the extra burden, and though they might have lost the hope of children of their own, Noel would have been a daughter to them, Valentine a grandchild. General Arthun was very fond of his old friend's daughter and was, in fact, her godfather. He had held her in his arms at the font in the old Devonshire church, and regretted her marriage to Horace Crayshaw only less than Anstice did. "If only he had loved me!"—thought the woman of sixty, still yearning secretly to the gray-haired man who never seemed to have loved any woman enough to marry her.

The explanation was a very ordinary one, though it had not occurred to Miss York as possible. Gerald Arthun had formed an illicit connection with a woman when he was fifty-eight, and she considerably younger. With the surprising faithfulness of elderly men to their mistresses he had had no other affair after meeting her, and might even have married her had she wished it. Not being a "professional," or an adventuress, she did not, and their intimacy was continued under the same terms until she— quite unexpectedly—died when the General was sixty-eight. It had been a great shock to him, and he had not attempted to fill her place in his life. He had grown used to Isobel, though she was exactly what Miss York would have expected him to dislike. She had a flat in Chelsea, and a large and very Bohemian acquaintance. When the General visited her she cleared the flat as if by magic, and shared it quietly with him, and only once had she been to Greatoaks for a few days when one of her own friends accompanied her for the sake of outward decency. She had been, privately, horrified at the place—its size, its loneliness, its suggestion of monotony once one had to live there most of the year. Being a wise woman she foresaw that if she were to keep the General happy, and be happy herself, their present relations had better not be disturbed. He was too obstinately attached to his home to leave it and live in London, and the effect of a country life upon Isobel would have been to age her quickly. So they remained very tenderly attached, and bound to each other by what is often a much more lasting tie than matrimony.

The effect of a *liaison* upon the character of such a man as Gerald Arthun was to make him rather more rigid than less as to the proprieties with other women. Some uneasy sense of his private lapse may have driven him into an old-fashioned strictness with regard to morals before the world. When Noel went to Greatoaks he always asked Miss York to countenance it (though she frequently outstayed her chaperon. However, Anstice was always there to begin with), and on the few occasions when her aunt could not go, one of the General's own family was called in to silence gossip. Anstice knew that, on the present occasion, her place would be taken by the widow of a clergyman, a distant cousin of the General's, and that Noel and Valen-

tine both thought it a great bore. She went to see them at
the end of July to say good-bye and condole with them,
and found that Noel had already got the rooms into that
packed-up appearance which suggests that the house is
going away far more than the occupants.

"Has Horace left London already?" she asked, looking
round suspiciously for signs of the Sinner who was so
seldom Miserable. She always timed her visits to find him
away if possible.

"He is going to stay for a time with this Mr. Vanstead
who is giving him commissions," Noel explained. "They
are dining together to-night. He really goes to-morrow."

"He left mother about ten suit-cases to pack," said
Valentine dryly. "And then wouldn't take a single one
with him, though he was going to Mr. Vanstead's flat!
We are nearly crowded out with his truck."

"Val, I wish you'd go along to Captain Lewison for tea.
I can't get it yet, but you need not wait," said his mother
as she hastily cleared a chair of a pile of things, for her
aunt.

The boy lingered wistfully. "Can't I help you, mum?
You look so awfully tired!"

She did. Her face was as careworn as it had been that
pinching time in the winter when Horace failed to send
home the weekly allowance; and her eyes were unusually
clouded. But she laughed at Val, and her face seemed
to brighten as by magic.

"I'm all right. If I can once get everything finished I
shall go to bed at nine and sleep it off. Aunt Anstice will
help me. Get along!"

"I hope Father won't wake you," Val grumbled as he
took his cap. "He never comes in till one o'clock when
he dines with the Vanstead man."

"He isn't coming back to-night—Vanstead is putting him up," said Noel, with a relief in her own face that she hardly realized.

Miss York had quietly found a place for her own coat and hat, despite the mêlée in the small rooms, and was busily folding the boy's things by the time he had shut the hall door and limped off down the road.

"Do you know anything about the Vanstead man, as Val calls him?" she asked as she worked.

"Nothing—except what Horace doesn't tell me. I think he is an influential man, and that he really does all the paying, because Horace complains that it involves him in a lot of expense knowing Vanstead, and that what commission he gets hardly makes it worth his while. When he says that, it generally means that he is getting a good deal out of his friends."

"Percy Vanstead," said Miss York thoughtfully. "I have seen the name on some prospectus for an investment—something to do with a new Company that was being started with a huge capital, I think."

"Very likely. It may be quite a good thing for Horace to know him, but it has not made him more generous to us!"

"You have not met the man, yourself?"

"No. Horace never introduces us to his friends."

"You forget Curton."

"That was a mistake. Horace never meant him to come here unless he was here himself to keep us in the background. I do not think he was really pleased that Mr. Curton should take Val to the theater, and then for that motor drive. Horace is very greedy about pleasure, and he felt as if something had been stolen that ought to have come to him. He expected that Mr. Curton would always drive him down to Byfleet or Roehampton when they played golf, but I gathered that Mr. Curton did not offer, and somehow Horace puts that down to us."

Miss York shook Valentine's jacket almost viciously, and made a noise in her throat. "You saw quite a lot of him at Brighton," she remarked irrelevantly.

"Yes."

"Does Horace know that?"

"I did not count Mr. Curton's visits."

"Have you seen him since Horace came home?"

"Once—no, twice. He came that day that Cousin Gwenyth was here and had just gone demented with religion. I told you."

"Quite enough to drive any man away! But he has been since?"

"Yes. He came last week. We had not seen him for nearly two months. I think he has found Horace out, and as he can do nothing he simply stays away."

There was a pause while both women busily filled and strapped suit-cases, and cleared the sitting-room somewhat of the confusion.

"I don't know how Mr. Curton found out the way that Horace treats us," Noel said at last. "It is obvious that we have no servant, of course, and that we live like working people while he goes out and enjoys himself. But I have never quarreled with that, and I never confided in Mr. Curton."

"I did." The words burst from Anstice York as if against her will. "I told him. That day at Char village."

A distressed flush came into Noel's tired face, and when it faded she looked almost haggard. "I wish you had not done that," she said. "It would have been better to let him go on pitying Horace for his sordid home life!"

"I wanted him to know. Why should Horace always come off free from blame and be thought delightful?—the Miserable Sinner! Why should you drudge for him for the sake of the bare living he gives you and the boy? It is monstrous!"

"It does no good to make a show of the skeleton in the cupboard. If it did, *I* would not keep it locked up. But I don't want to be pitied. I have chosen to stay with Horace."

"Yes, for Val. I wanted Curton to know that—I wanted him to see Horace stripped of his false manners, and his false charm, and his false representation of his own sentiments!" As when she had spoken to Curton, this woman's passion was terrible to witness in her hatred of Crayshaw. "Sometimes I feel I cannot bear it, Noel."

"I have come near that—lately," said Mrs. Crayshaw slowly. "I have even wondered if I would take refuge with—Lewison."

"You poor child! you poor child! It would be a desperate exchange. Has Horace molested you lately then?"

"Oh no. I think he has a new mistress. All his clothes have a faint scent about them—a very subtle scent that must have cost money. I expect he has been staying with some one who has a wife." She laughed a little, with an irony that made Miss York wince. "It is only that I am tired," she said. "So tired that I feel I can't go on any longer. Come into the kitchen for tea, Aunt Anstice. I don't want to bring it in here."

"I will make it for you, while you sit still."

"I can't sit still. I have lost the power. I believe if I came into money and could do as I liked, I should never be without some sort of occupation for my hands. It has grown such a habit that I have to *make* myself sit down to rest."

"You will rest at Greatoaks. You will feel different when you come back. Look after Gerald for me, and don't let him do too much. He does not like to think that he is no longer forty!"

"I wish you could come and look after us all, yourself. I shall be glad to get away. I wish I need not come back."

"Noel, I never saw you so despondent. Has something happened?"

"Not yet."

"You don't mean Hugh Curton?"

"You will think I am blind with vanity, Aunt Anstice. I have nothing really to go on—but I don't want to be alone with him."

"You don't want him to make love to you? It might end in—rescue."

"No!" said Noel in a hard voice. She spoke as if denying herself. "He would try to part me from Val."

Miss York put her arms round the heaving shoulders, and drew the roughened brown head to her own. "You are worn out, dearest," she said. "That is all. Just worn out. Don't be frightened. You are going away to-morrow—nothing can happen now before you go, and you will have time to get a grip on yourself."

She left soon afterwards when they had had their tea, and nothing more was said of Curton. At the door Anstice York turned back to say "Give my love to Gerald"—that was nothing, she had always called the General "Gerald," and he called her "Anstice." But as she went home to her bleak Club and its mockery of home life, she felt how easily elderly people's faded interests are crowded out by the more instant affairs of the young. She would have

liked to talk a little about the General, and to ask Noel
to do various things for him that she had always done
when at Greatoaks—things he hardly suspected, but might
miss. She would have liked, in fact, to mother this man of
seventy from a distance, through her niece. But Noel had
her own trouble to think of, and it swamped the long
dragging pain that the older woman had borne for forty
years. It was very natural, and even Miss York thought
more about her niece and Hugh Curton on the way home
than of herself and General Arthun. They did not matter
—they were old and had outlived their future. But Noel
was a young woman with the temptation of a man's new
passion to fight. It was very natural. . . .

Noel managed to finish the packing, both for herself and
Valentine, and for the house, at any rate, and got the boy
and herself to bed by ten o'clock—an hour later than she
intended, but still early enough for a long night. She had
the advantage of using her own bedroom too, Horace being
absent, and lay down with a sigh of relief to fall into a deep
sleep.

How long she had slept she did not know, when she
was awakened by a light in her eyes and somebody moving
about the room. She had not heard the front door open,
but she had forgotten to put up the chain on the door and
her first thought was that a burglar had got in and was
coolly ransacking the house. She sat up, checking the
cry in her throat, and saw her husband standing by the
bedside.

He was in evening-dress, and his face was slightly
flushed, his eyes dangerous between the half-closed lids and
the fringe of lashes. She knew at once that he had been
drinking, though he was not drunk, and her pulses
throbbed an alarm. She instinctively drew the bedclothes

up to her breast as if to shield herself from those horrible eyes, and spoke involuntarily.

"Horace!—how did you get in?"

"With my latch-key, my dear, as the master of the house should," he responded with a low laugh. There was something quiet and almost stealthy about his movements and his voice, as if he did not want to be overheard, even by Valentine who was asleep in the next room.

"I forgot to put up the chain," said Noel blankly. She did not quite know why; but she wished she had put up the chain and forced him to announce his return. She would not then have found him in her room—here—close to her, without warning.

"Well, you don't want to bar your husband out, do you?" He sat down on the side of the bed and looked at her with the expression she knew was familiar to many other women, but—thank God!—not to her for many years. His long, shapely hand fell on the outline of her foot under the bedclothes and clasped it. She felt his fingers close and unclose as if he caressed it, and tried to draw it away. "Do you want to shut me out, Noel?" he persisted.

"You know I never use this room when you are home," she said rigidly. "You told me you should be out to-night. I will get up and make a shakedown in the sitting-room. One of us must go there."

"Why?" His smiling, translucent eyes darkened to resentment. "We can finish the night together at least. Don't be a fool, Noel—I've a right here. And when a man wants her, a woman shouldn't turn him down. Youth won't last forever, you know."

She shuddered all through her tired, strong limbs, but she did not reply except to scramble out of bed and catch her dressing-gown from the chair where she had left it. Folding it round her she made a rush through the door and into the sitting-room, careful even in her haste not to make more noise than she could help. She felt how little dignity there was in her retreat, but at least she had escaped and proved her intention of making up some sort of bed in another room.

After a minute she heard the door of her room open and Horace following her. He stood in the doorway, watching her pile the cushions and a traveling-rug into some sort of bed on Valentine's spinal couch, and he seemed uncertain how to proceed with her.

"Of course if you won't stay in our room I can come in here and leave you the bed," he said at last sulkily.

"You had better sleep in the other room. I shall be all right here." She spoke shortly. "I am very tired. Please don't keep me up. Go away now and get into bed. I am sorry I have not time to remake it."

He drew himself up suddenly with a solemnity that made him seem far more drunk than when merely amorous.

"You realize that you are refusing me, Noel? You have complained in the past of—other women, but you are driving me away! Even if you don't love me—which I can't believe—you ought to think of your duty as a wife!"

She was less frightened now that he was plainly not sober. It was wonderful that his speech was clear, but his eyes began to look dazed.

"Go to bed, Horace, and don't talk nonsense," she said sharply. "And don't wake the boy."

He came across the room to her, swaying a little. "Say good-night to me, at least, my wife!" he said in a broken voice. She saw that his eyes had filled with easy tears which hung on the black lashes. "I'm so lonely, Noel!"

His arms tried to embrace her, and she feared a struggle. He was a big man, and strong. Once his passion was roused again she could not throw him off without a noise that might bring Val on the revolting scene. With instant decision she seized him and pushed him backwards down on the couch, rushed across the room, blowing out the candle as she reached the door, and slipping out into the passage locked him in. It reminded her of the day they had locked in Mrs. Morgan with her prayers, and she laughed. Celtic natures seemed to call for drastic imprisonment in their uncontrolled moments.

When she got back into the bedroom she listened for a moment, wondering if he would blunder to the door and shout. But there was no sound, and before she could fall asleep again herself she heard his heavy breathing, regular, almost stertorous, and realized that his intemperance had at least done her that much good. He would not waken till morning.

.    .    .    .    .    .    .

"I say, Chris, what made him come home?" said Valentine as they got the breakfast together.

"Some of those suit-cases. He was afraid the carrier might not call."

"But he had his key—he could have got them after we'd gone, any time."

"It was more convenient while we were here. I shall have to do down to the garage and order a cab for him—hurry, Val!"

"I heard him come in," said the boy suddenly, as he laid a tray in the little kitchen.

"I'm sorry you woke——"

"You went into the sitting-room——"

"Yes, to make him up a shakedown on your couch."

Valentine put another penny in the slot of the gas-stove, and began to make his father some dry toast without asking advice.

"I heard you lock him in!" he said quietly.

## CHAPTER XIV

WAS there ever such a wife! Crayshaw felt himself so much in the right, so much the injured party, that he was almost consoled for his discomfort. To sleep on a couch in his dress clothes, ignominiously locked in because he claimed his rights as a husband, made Noel appear a virago when the scene was retailed to himself. He had paid her a great compliment in coming home to her on her last night, knowing that he might not see her for a month, and she had turned him down! It really was a great compliment from his point of view, for she was looking very dragged and old and had no right to expect him to love her. And when he attempted to touch her she had been quite violent and behaved like a cave-woman!

He had slept deeply, and woke with no headache (Vanstead's wine was always the best), but hot and uncomfortable in his tumbled clothes. The door of the sitting-room had been unlocked, and when he went across the passage he saw Noel bending over the gas-stove and Valentine helping her. The boy said, "Good morning, father," in a perfectly drilled tone that might yet have had a hint of mockery in it, and Noel added, "Be quick if you want some breakfast, Horace. It is all but ready, and we have to get off to catch our train." Neither of them took any more notice of his tousled head and rumpled clothes.

Crayshaw did not answer. The kitchen fire was not lit, which meant that the bath-water would not be hot, and he hated cold baths in England. He stalked into the bedroom

where his suit-cases were already packed and standing in a
row, and locking the door proceeded to open and shut
drawers, throwing his clothes about and leaving his dress-
suit in a heap on the bed which was made and covered
with the counterpane. By the time he had shaved and
washed his face, which he did deliberately, and came into
the kitchen in his morning-suit, Noel and the boy had
breakfasted and had their outdoor clothes on.

"There is your breakfast," said Noel, pointing to the
covered plate on the stove. "And the kettle is boiling—
you can make fresh tea. Don't forget to turn the gas off
at the main, and to lock up before you go——"

"But you don't expect me to shut up the house!" said
Crayshaw, aghast.

"You must, or we shall miss our train, and the General
is meeting it. There is nothing to do but to turn off the
gas and draw down the blinds. Every other room but this
is closed. Go out by the front door—you have your key if
you have to come back for anything."

"What about my baggage?"

"I was going to send it all off early when we sent ours,
but as you came home I thought you had better take it
with you. You might want something out of the suit-
cases."

"Thanks," said Crayshaw sarcastically. "And how am
I to get a taxi in such a neighborhood as this?"

"There is the public telephone at the corner of the road—
you know we always call up a cab from there." For the
first time Noel spoke with impatience. "Don't be a baby,
Horace. We have no time to go for you to-day. Come
along, Val—we shall lose the bus."

She put her hand on Valentine's shoulder and gently

pushed him out of the door. Then she turned and looked oddly at her husband.

"You swine!" she said, and she said it as the working woman does to a man she has learned to despise and not to hide it. It is difficult to live as the laboring classes live and not to catch some of the bitterness of their spirits and the bluntness of their speech. Noel Crayshaw was nothing but a working-class woman at the moment. "Go to the filthy harlots who will take you anyhow, drunk or not, and sleep with them. But don't you dare to touch me or I'll drive my fist into your lying mouth."

She walked out of the bungalow without haste and shut the door behind her. Her anger was still cold at her heart, but it beat a little irregularly as if some undercurrent of consciousness disturbed her. Would she have found Horace quite so insufferable if it had not been for that new fear of being alone with Hugh Curton? Horace had come home before with after-dinner emotions that had sometimes roused his desire for her and sometimes made him merely sentimental about himself. She had nipped his advances in the bud, it is true, since she had no liking for alcoholic love; but she had never felt so nauseated as last night. It troubled her spirit even as she ran after the bus to catch it with Val. She dared not quite ask herself if Curton were making Horace still more detestable by contrast with something that might have been, that waited on her pleasure if she willed it. She turned with a sense of relief to the month immediately ahead of her, that would be safe alike from Horace and from Curton. General Arthun belonged to another, safer period of her life, the time when she was free of men, a girl living at home in her father's country house. There was a kind of aloofness in her feeling about General Arthun, as if the ordinary sins and temptations of daily life could not reach his atmosphere. She had no undercurrents, no painful associations with him, at least.

The less said of Horace Crayshaw's shutting up the bungalow and repacking his own baggage, perhaps the better. What he did not slam he left as it was, and when Captain Lewison came in the same evening to see that everything was safe (Noel had not told, though she had given him the back door key) he found an untidy kitchen and remnants of food that cried for the dustbin. He looked actually ugly (he was always a plain man) as he tidied up and washed Crayshaw's breakfast plates and dishes.

"That's his cursed Irish blood, I suppose," he said savagely. Like most Anglo-Saxons he failed to differentiate between breeds of Celtic origin. "He'd leave his dirt and mess for a month to rot and breed fever, until she comes home to it—curse him!"

He went into the bedroom with an odd hanging-back movement. It seemed almost like an intrusion, since Noel used the room when Crayshaw was away. She did not keep her clothes in the wardrobe or chest, however, because Horace had so many that he would never have respected any drawer or peg as hers. What she had she kept in the attic room under the roof where she sometimes refuged for sleep. But the larger bedroom was almost as disordered as the kitchen, with a soiled dress shirt and collar lying in one corner on the floor, and a pair of old slippers (in which Crayshaw had done his own service) lying on the pillow. There was the end of a shaving stick and a blunt razor on the dressing-table and none of the drawers in the chest, nor the wardrobe, were shut. The room seemed to Lewison to smell of Crayshaw, his stale pipe and his toilet soap. He had learned hygiene and neatness adversely,

in the contrasting horrors of the War, and he longed to
have Crayshaw for one month in his platoon. I think he
would almost have gone back to those years of horror for
the devilish satisfaction.

He made a clean sweep of the mess, of course, and
lingered, smoothing the washed-out counterpane and setting everything in the order in which his pathetic fancy
saw Noel in her daily life. One of the profound mistakes
which Lewison made in his love for her, was to think that
she had a mind like his own, though in his worship he
assigned her a much higher nature. He had, of the two,
by far the more poetic temperament, and he idealized as
she had never done since the initial error of her marriage.
Lewison always imagined Noel as a starved intellect, unable
to reach out to the things which really attracted himself,
through her narrow circumstances. It was her body that
was starved more than her soul, her capacity for enjoyment
rather than her mentality. But this he did not see. He laid
his hand upon the pillow (it was more often Horace's
black wavy head that lay there than Noel's brown one)
and said:

"Where she has rested
Her sleep makes all things white!"

Noel would simply have wondered where the quotation
came from.

Then he bent his head and kissed the folded sheet that
might touch her face, and drew back suspiciously, glaring
round him. But there was no one by to laugh. . . .

Horace had by that time recovered his good temper
and was driving to Victoria. On his way through Daisy
Hill he had stopped at a post office and asked for letters in

the name of Hugh Curton, and was handed one. The post office was one reason why he had come back last night, after really intending to stay in the Mansions where Percy Vanstead had a suite, and where he himself could engage a bachelor room when he wanted it. But it had occurred to him that Cara might have written to him again in answer to his last letter, and he did not wish to leave the letter unclaimed while he was abroad.

For he was not going with Percy Vanstead to shoot in Yorkshire as he had led Noel to believe (only she never did believe him, and merely wondered if he were staying in London and for what—feminine—purpose) but was going back to the Riviera for a flying visit. Vanstead really was in the north, but he had not asked Crayshaw to join him until later, though he advised his new secretary to take a holiday while he could.

"There is nothing doing, for you, in August," he said. "Everybody is out of town except the politicians, and they are not investors in our stuff. No one will come to the office who can't be dealt with by Morton. Go away, dear boy, and join me a little later."

The release had fitted in well with Crayshaw's other claimant on his time and services. Cara Da Costa had written to him to return to her as soon as possible, and he had found it rather difficult to represent himself as of sufficient importance to his business (Curton's, of course) to detain him in England. He had so far made out that he was of very little use to Staine & Curton, but was given a clerkship on account of his relationship. He was obliged, you see, to account for his long holiday in the early spring, and yet to make it possible for him to be kept in England.

"I have had such long leave already in those blessed three months I spent in Monte, that I feel I ought not to ask

again. I'm a conscienceless fellow, but even I have hardly
the face to go to old Staine and tell him I want a holiday,"
etc. Whether Cara believed him or not, she did not say. She
wanted him, and told him that he must come back to her,
somehow. She had been to Paris in June and had caught
cold. She was bored with taking care and with doctors. She
wrote like a hungry child crying for sweets, and Crayshaw
felt that it would be wise to satisfy her.

He had already booked his place on the Blue train when
he went home to Noel. He could afford to travel by the
Blue now, though he did not find that his salary went
as far as it might have done if he had not been Vanstead's
confidential secretary and in constant companionship with
him. Vanstead lived like a rich man, as he no doubt was,
and Crayshaw could not avoid the shadow of his opulence
falling upon him even though Vanstead seemed always
willing to pay for his society. It was part of Crayshaw's
"job" to mix with the better-class people who came to Vanstead for advice, and to meet them on equal terms. He was
paid for his personality. Vanstead had made no secret of it,
and the people who had to be kept off when Vanstead was
busy, found Crayshaw's personality so charming that the
business acquaintance frequently resulted in his being asked
to houses where he could not afford to be on anything
but a well-dressed equality at least. He had not been able to
make Noel a larger allowance for the little bungalow at
Daisy Hill, though he told himself that he had fully intended to do so, and told himself so often that he really
believed it. Life was too expensive just at present even
though his own private means had increased through Vanstead's advice in investments. Crayshaw had sold out his
small capital, mostly in industrials whose dividends fluctu-
ated, and had reinvested on the broader basis of Vanstead's

knowledge of markets. This also he had not told Noel, whose knowledge of his business affairs had never been really complete.

London looked as played out as her population on the day when Crayshaw left Victoria. It was like a very dirty vapor bath. Hardly any one was going south at this time of year, and the porters paid the well-dressed, large-limbed man a flattering attention. It felt like an unclean oven on the platform, but he had only to shut his eyes, and there was Monte Carlo—a red-tiled town with palms growing out of it, and colored balconies, blue and green, clinging to the houses.

The passage from Dover to Calais was as smooth as a pleasure trip up the river. He sat in a chair on deck and smoked and looked at the white cliffs fading away with the feeling of a schoolboy off on a holiday rather than a lover going to his mistress. And indeed it was partly the change of scene that made him happy and the memory of the Casa Caralyn as well as Cara herself. It would be hot, at this time of the year, but he did not mind heat, and he had loved the lazy, luxurious life whose beauty even of scenery appealed to his senses.

He had never taken any interest in the country as far as Paris or for some way after, but because the whole journey was taking him back to love, and laughter, and the sun, he looked out of the window of his sleeper and felt an affection for the whole route. The quiet cultivated fields that stretched everywhere and had no boundaries, seemed a kindlier country than England. Association is stronger than beauty. He watched the peasant farmers working until the light failed, and thought how different they were to the British. He, who had never willingly done a day's work in his life, applauded their labors.

It grew dark. He sat and smoked and read the English papers he had brought with him, and fancied that each mile brought him nearer to a glorious to-morrow. . . .

The train was an hour late at Paris. The city flashed out with her lights as they went round the environs, and the night was misty. . . .

He dined, with pleasure, his face so infectious in its satisfaction that the people sitting opposite to him smiled at him and got into conversation despite their English habit of suspicion.

"He looked so happy and handsome," a woman said to her husband, "it made even that bad dinner bearable." For it is the fashion, even on the Blue, to abuse the food. One secret of Crayshaw's charm was that if he enjoyed a thing, even food on a train, he showed it frankly. He was not tired, but he went to bed early for the pleasure of lying down and thinking of his own enjoyment. Then he slept, to make up for that beastly night on Valentine's couch. . . .

The cold of the dawn and then the chill sunlight woke him early. He got up to look out for the first vineyards. The South was coming—coming—and Cara. By the time he had dressed they were nearing the country about Marseilles, and her bare, rocky heights. He had no memories connected with the great seaport, and went to have breakfast; but afterwards he could not leave the window.

The coast flashed out at him with its artificial blue sea and white villas and green patches. The first palms rattled in the sun and wind, and the houses all had green venetian blinds. He felt that he was shut of England, of Daisy Hill, of Noel and Valentine, of discomfort and reproach, with those blinds. Curious that such a little thing should appeal to him so.

Toulon. It was a bright glare, with the tenderness of summer blazoned to hard colors. . . .

To a disillusioned mind it had the cruel crudity of an oleograph, a country too dry to be restful, with hard shadows in its white slopes. Even the vegetation was bright and hard. But to him, it was like coming home to a bad Paradise.

Cannes—a sophisticated Tropics. . . .

Between Cannes and Nice the country was a glorified Bournemouth, but he did not know that. And even if he had, he liked Bournemouth. There were the pines, the bays like chines, the broad expanse of blue sea that was no bluer than an English summer sea. But there had been no summer in England.

Gradually he grew more eager for Cara as he drew nearer to her. The background was less to him, and the woman more. He was naturally happy because he had no conscience, his equivalent for one being merely a dislike of people's disapproval. In England he had always the one pinprick of the little home at Daisy Hill where his wife and son led narrow lives of which he need not think so long as he was comfortable. Of late, thanks to his association with Vanstead, he had been very comfortable; but still the bungalow was there, and the faces of its inmates. Noel's was jaded when he saw her last, the boy looked thin and invalidish. Both, no doubt, wanted the holiday that General Arthun was giving them. The responsibility was taken off Crayshaw's shoulders, but he could never be quite comfortable when he allowed himself to think of them. They did not exactly reproach him, but they had shut him out of their lives. And a still more rankling thorn was Miss York when he chanced to encounter her. She hated him, as he knew, and he never could get over the surprise of it. Probably she was the only woman he had ever met who did hate him. He sometimes fancied that it was her influence that had made Noel more and more silently hostile to him of late, so that he had almost grown afraid of her. And yet, as regarded their marital relations at least, he felt himself the injured party. She had denied him his rights, she had thrust him into another woman's open arms, and—well, here was Monte Carlo!

Madame Da Costa's car met him at the station, but she had not come herself. He felt a fresh impatience to see her, to clasp her again, as they drove out through the hot streets of the familiar town to the cooler road leading along the coast. A fresh wind came up from the sea as they turned in at the big gates and past the white lodge. He put his hand impatiently on the door, almost leaped out of the car before the silent butler had got the doors of the Casa open, and looked into the vast marble spaces of the hall with eager eyes. She was not there. He followed the servant with impatient steps, the palms of his hands moist and his heart beating violently. The thwarted sex in him was making him as hysterical as a woman. The sun-blinds outside the salon made it all a golden gloom, and a scent, insistent, permeating the air, came in from the garden and from the vases of carnations that were in the room. He seemed to draw in the richness of the scent with his very breath, to be steeped in summer, and there on the couch was a white-gowned figure, golden also in the shaded light, with a face whose beauty he had surely forgotten since it made him gasp anew.

"You are my dream come true!"

The words of Signora Gazzi's song came back to mind with lovely meaning as he knelt beside the couch to take her in his arms, and she clasped her hands behind his dark head and drew his lips to hers.

"My lover!"

"My beauty!"

The tears filled his shallow gray eyes and made them iridescent with light and color, but hers were dry and dark with passion. Through the loose folds of silk he felt her shudder as if her yearning were too much for pleasure, and laid his lips against her breast to kiss away the pain. She was milk-white and soft as her silk to touch. . . .

The carnations breathed their hearts out in the quick silence.

# CHAPTER XV

THE week passed like one long burning day of summer. Crayshaw had been strong-willed in limiting his visit to a week, and would not overstay it. Cara raved and stormed, and cried like a stormy child, but she could not move him. He had never been a weak man in what concerned his own advantage, and he knew that unbridled passion saps body and energies alike. He did not wish to quarrel with Cara this time, or to let her turn upon him in a reaction of her senses. It was a lucky thing that they could not marry, but then he was nearly always lucky! Her husband's stipulation in leaving her his fortune provided the necessary drag on the wheel, and left her acquiescent to separation if not reconciled. He admitted to himself that he could not have lived with Cara for the years that he had lived with Noel, even with the aid of money to grease the wheels. Cara lived on the crest of the wave of her emotions, and when the wave subsided she went down to an equal depth. Even in the delirium of his passion for her he knew that it must be periodic and not continuous, that it could not go on at the height and heat of their mutual feeling. But he meant the period to recur at just such intervals as should whet the appetite again.

She did not come into Monte Carlo to see him off, any more than she had come to meet him. She had really been laid up in Paris, and the effect of her illness had been to refine and spiritualize her face so that she was more lovely than she had been in perfect health. His visit, exhausting though it was, seemed to have done her good and acted on her like a tonic. She had shown no flagging vitality while he was with her.

"I shall go to Italy again after you are gone," she said half pettishly. "I cannot bear this place without you now. The Gazzis are at Analdi, doing a cure. I shall join them, and not come back until October."

"And in October I shall be coming back too!" he said gayly.

"Will you, Hugh? Will you? I want you more and more as time goes on. I would almost marry you, if there were enough money left to live upon. But José was so mean. I hate his memory. I would like to follow him down to hell and spit at him still!"

"Never mind—he cannot harm us now. And we are happy without him."

"Why cannot you have some place in my household—secretary, manager, adviser? I could pay you more than you earn in that damned lawyer's office."

This was one of the perils of his position, for had it not been for the uncertainty of Cara's temper, and his own encumbrances of Noel and Valentine, he might long since have done as she suggested. He always fell back on his pride, which, in reality, did not exist.

"You know I can't live on you, Cara."

"You fool! I'd give you the whole of José's fortune as soon as not. Only then you might throw me over."

Crayshaw suddenly lifted her into his arms and carried her over to a great mirror. It reflected them like some dissolute picture, his own striking face and big frame, and the woman's figure lying across his arms, her warm head thrown backwards and her throat and bosom as white as pearl. He held her yielding limbs towards the glass.

"Look!—do you think a man would ever tire of that?" he said softly.

She stretched her hand to a great jar of carnations that stood on the floor of her bedroom, and pulling out one of the yellow tipped with red she laid it between her breasts, turning to stare at herself. The delicate, rich-colored thing made her flesh more delicate by contrast, and the perfume seemed her own. It caused his nerves to twitch in some odd way to see and smell the flower from her bosom, and he seized her hand and crushed it, flower and all, in a cruel way that bruised both flesh and petals and left a stain as of juice on her skin.

"You make me feel that I want to crush you like the flower," he said thickly.

The carnation dropped from her breast, between her knees, on to the floor. It had lost its beauty and its scent and its life all together.

Noel and Valentine were still way, and the bungalow was shut up when Horace returned to London. He went to a hotel, his Club being in the hands of painters and white-washers, but when he called there for letters there were none of Vanstead's, though he had expected to hear from him, and the date when they were to shoot together in Yorkshire. It did not much matter, and he was glad to have a day or so to recover from the excitement of the Casa Caralyn. He spent two or three days, as it happened, seeing his tailor and lunching or dining with a few people who were still in London waiting on the Government. For the rumors about the financial situation were beginning to stir a certain section of the public, though its full gravity was not yet realized. Crayshaw did not let it worry him—he felt too safe personally: but it occurred to him that Vanstead might have written to the office as the surest and most permanent place to find him. He had not troubled to follow the markets while in Monte Carlo, and would gain more authentic news from the managing clerk than from the financial page of the daily papers.

As he drove to the City he thought idly how great a contrast it was to the scene he had lately left—there surely could not be a greater than Vanstead's offices in the dull rain that was falling in London and the Casa Caralyn in brilliant sunshine. Yet the one was in some sort the complement of the other—a place where men made money and a place where they spent it!

He went up to Vanstead's offices by the lift though they were only on the first floor. What first struck him was that the landing and passages should be so full of people, for Vanstead had most of the space on this floor, and they could not be going elsewhere. It looked as if the offices had suddenly become a center of news or of crisis. Where had all these people come from? What were they doing? He pushed his way through a loose crowd to the familiar glass doors, and found them closed.

Even then it meant nothing to him, except an odd thought that it must be Sunday or a City holiday. But the people on the landing were all either trying to get in at the closed doors of the office, or talking about it amongst themselves. There was a sense of anxiety, or something wrong already that communicated itself to Crayshaw so that he drew nearer to a man with a notebook who was talking to the lift man, to gather what they were saying.

"I don't know," said the lift man shortly. "We've had no notice. All we know is that the office was closed this morning, and the staff gone away."

The man with the notebook asked a rapid question.

"Haven't heard. He's not been here for a week or so. The police may have more information than we have."

It was then that disaster seemed suddenly imminent to Crayshaw's mind, as if it came in a blaze of light. He saw the reporter move away, and turned quickly to the lift man, who of course recognized him.

"Can you tell me where to find Mr. Morton?" Morton was the managing clerk who was acting for Vanstead during his absence.

"I think he's gone to the bank, Mr. Crayshaw—he knew no more than any of us. It's come like an almighty smash. If I were you, sir, I wouldn't stay here in case any of these people recognize you as his secretary. The Lord knows how they've found him out, but they have. They're getting frightened, and they'll be angry next."

The same thing had occurred to Crayshaw, and with it the instinct of flight. He had not seen any one in the excited crowd on the landing who was of sufficient importance for him to know, for it had been the big men, the larger investors, whom he had been told off to deal with. But it was quite possible that some one might recognize him as Vanstead's confidential secretary, more deeply implicated than the usual staff if anything were greatly wrong. He did not wait for the lift, but ran straight down the stone stairs and dashed into the street.

The next few hours were so confused in his mind that he did not remember where he went or exactly what he did. He chased Morton to the bank, only to find him gone, and then by merest chance saw him getting into a taxicab a few yards down the street.

"Morton!" he said breathlessly, though he did not know that he had been running. "Let me come with you—tell me what this dreadful thing means."

"I don't know, Mr. Crayshaw. I thought you might have told us, being in Mr. Vanstead's confidence."

"Good God, man, I know nothing! I left him nearly three weeks ago, with the understanding that I was to join him in Yorkshire when he wrote. Where *is* Mr. Vanstead?"

"In Paris, I'm afraid, unless he got clear off with a hundred and fifty thousand!"

They were sitting side by side in the cab, going slowly along the crowded streets—for the City has no real dead season—and Crayshaw leaned back, shaking all over.

"Is it a smash, Morton?"

"Almost as bad as Hatry's. I knew there was something rocky about those shares we've been putting on the market of late, but I thought it was a gamble. We are all into it, Mr. Crayshaw."

Crayshaw did not answer because he could not. The solvency of Percy Vanstead had been such a bed-rock that to have it slip beneath him seemed to bring all finance tumbling about his ears. He did not even remember for a minute that his private means had gone too; he could only remember Percy Vanstead's compact, cool face with the flaxen hair and shrewd eyes, and his friendly manner of advising him about secure and insecure investments while he was really worse in every respect than Hatry. For Hatry laid his cards on the table and faced his public; but Vanstead had played a lone hand and then slipped away. . . .

He had known incredibly little of Vanstead's business methods, despite their daily association. His position as confidential secretary was the ironic one of never having had his employer's confidence. Some of the companies that the financier had floated had been a success up to date, and some were less so. Crayshaw was not scrupulous about such things so long as his own investments were amongst the safe ones, and he put his trust in "The Boss" to keep him off a loan that had no sound basis. He had a fair capacity for business, and he did not ask questions. Vanstead contrived to give him enough to do without letting him into his secrets any more than the clerks in the outer office. He had chosen Horace Crayshaw for his secretary in place of men who might have become suspicious and gone into accounts too closely. He knew his man. It was Crayshaw, with his easy morals, who had been the dupe.

By midday extras were being sold in the City with the grim truth about Percy Vanstead and his escape out of England. He had a week or so's start of the hue and cry, and might have got off with his booty so that it would be difficult to bring him to trial. The police wanted evidence from the whole staff, but neither Morton nor Crayshaw was detained. Morton went home, quietly, to his house in Hampstead where he was within call on the telephone. Crayshaw gave the name of his hotel, but did not immediately return there. His brain was beginning to work again, too fast as it had been too slow. He dared not face his wife and tell her that he was ruined and had not even the means left to provide for her and the boy on the narrow terms in which they lived. He was absolutely cowed to think of her eyes. Besides, he must tell her about his position in Vanstead's office, since it would all come out in the papers. She would know that he had had a good salary, larger dividends, for a while at least, and had done nothing to improve her life or Valentine's. He felt afraid of her, of her last angry outburst before they parted.

There was no letter for him at the post office near Daisy

Hill, at which he called for them, though Cara had had time to write. He had turned to the thought of Cara at once when he realized his own disaster arising out of Percy Vanstead's flight. Cara was a rich woman—she would help him. She had offered him half her fortune in the intoxication of her passion, and he felt the ground once more stable under his feet. In the confusion of the moment he had not had time to think it out, but if it seemed necessary he must leave Noel and go and live at the Casa Caralyn in some capacity as Cara had suggested. He could get it arranged on some business basis whereby he need not be dependent on Cara's whims and caprice, and he trusted to his power over her, over any woman, to make life tolerable. Noel would no doubt divorce him, and General Arthun must give her and the boy a refuge. Now that he found himself obliged to come to such a decision it seemed a better plan than when he was independent. Cara, with her temper, her exactions, her greed of pleasure, might be difficult to live with, but he did not doubt the lever power of his own colossal selfishness. It had stood him in good stead throughout his life.

He wondered if it were a good or bad omen that Cara had not written, for his nerves were so far jumpy with the recent shock that even a slight set-back made him superstitious. He thought of wiring to her—then decided to wait at least until to-morrow when he must pass the post office again on his way to Daisy Hill. A nuisance—but at least he need not go to the damned bungalow until he made a final sweep of all his belongings and quietly absconded, leaving it on Noel's hands.

Supposing he were detained by the police! His evidence would certainly be wanted. But so far he had escaped questioning, and he might get back to Monte Carlo before an "official inquiry" and proceedings against Vanstead could take place. If Vanstead were never caught, there would be no case, and he was free. . . .

What he could not get over was the implacable, merciless attitude of Vanstead towards himself and his own small capital which had gone into the melting-pot with the rest. One hint—but there had been none. That safe-deposit face of Vanstead had never been more pleasant or undisturbed than in persuading him to sell out and reinvest under his advice. If Vanstead had really liked him he must have felt some reluctance, some twinge of conscience—and he had shown none. It touched the vanity of the victim even in his greater disaster.

He lunched on his way back to his hotel, at a small restaurant that was not for that reason cheap. But he had grown so used to spending money that it was difficult to pull up. He still had a balance at the bank and could leave England again when he pleased, but he wanted to know more about Vanstead first, and the inexplicable collapse of everything that had seemed so stable. People were talking about it everywhere, even in the street and at the restaurant. Percy Vanstead! Percy Vanstead! It seemed impossible. It rang a knell to many hopes. For Vanstead was unique in having had no real Board of Directors to hamper him, no partner even in his financial schemes. His name upon a prospectus carried such weight that when the public knew he had taken up a majority of the shares they followed like a flock of sheep. Once a company was floated he had a genius for unloading himself of his own shares without raising suspicion. There are some men whose natural talents seem to be developed only by crime. It is probable that Vanstead could never have been a peaceable or virtuous citizen.

Crayshaw did not buy a paper to see if there were any more details. He was afraid of seeming too interested. He was growing afraid of everything. Though he did not know it his face had aged ten years since the morning, and his good looks were haggard. The waiter put down his appearance to the City smash in spite of his care, and said to himself, "That's one of Vanstead's goats or I'm d——d!" Some men at the next table were discussing it. "They'll never catch him. He's cleverer than Jabez Balfour or Whittaker Wright, or Hatry, or any of them!" Crayshaw's spirits rose with a bound, but then he remembered that even if Vanstead were safe it could not bring back his own lost capital. Such a few thousands! What were they to Vanstead? It seemed so hard. But Vanstead had been a hard man, and in that lay his quality of success. If he had faltered, for one kinder-hearted moment, over one of his victims, he might have lost his footing on the dangerous path he trod. His ruthlessness had never allowed a chance to slip for any consideration whatever.

Crayshaw went back to the hotel after lunch, and at last bought a paper. The headlines were of course the Great Shock to the City! Well-known Financier absconds with half a million! It was an exaggeration, and the details were likely to be as unauthenticated. Vanstead was reported to be on his way to South America, where he would be stopped and sent back on landing. (There was no warrant out against him as yet, and even his books were not in the hands of a Receiver.) All the staff of his office had already been arrested or detained! None of these things were really facts. The only reality was the collapse of the whole financial scheme of which Vanstead was the ingenious inventor. That had gone, and with it many of the bogus Companies in which he had gambled with the public's money.

There might be more in the stop press news. Crayshaw turned the page to look, and his eyes were caught by something else—a small paragraph about Monte Carlo. Had it not been for his association with the place he might have missed it. It was only a notice of the death of a well-known resident, the owner of one of the most beautiful villas on the Riviera—Madame Da Costa. She had died of pneumonia, following on an attack of influenza, in a few days. For some seasons she had been a well-known figure at the Sporting Club and the Casino, and was formerly known as the most beautiful woman in Santiago where her husband had been a merchant-millionaire. Her fortune was said to be fabulous, in spite of the inroads made on it by the tables. She had no family.

Crayshaw read the paragraph three times before he dropped the paper because his hand was too nerveless to hold it. A sudden sense of darkness and horror had descended on him that made him cringe. When he seemed on the crest of the wave, unassailable by reason of his good luck, it was as if an angry hand had struck him blow after blow out of vindictive revenge. He could not believe it. Cara's vitality, barely a week ago, seemed inexhaustible. She had looked less fleshy and material it is true, had complained of being ill in Paris and run down. He had not taken much notice of it. She had always represented herself as unable to face cold or bad weather, and he had ascribed her reluctance to come north as due to a darker motive—that shadow that lay over Da Costa's death. But she could not be dead, herself. Her beauty, her energy, her strong passions, made it impossible.

In three days—three or four—after he had left her—that

was why there was no letter. (His thoughts became dis-
jointed as his brain refused to take in more disaster.)
She had taken cold, or perhaps been sickening for the
epidemic even when he left. If he had only stayed, he
might have saved her—or (a baser thought) have persuaded her to make a will in his favor. . . .

He started up, crushing the paper in his hands like a
madman, and beginning to rave out loud. Fortunately,
he had the lounge to himself, for this season of the year
there was hardly any one staying in the hotel. What a
fool he had been to part from her, even for a short time.
What a fool to trust Vanstead, and prefer to depend on
his favor because it left him freer. Cara and her money.
Vanstead and his money. Both had failed him. It was
as if they grinned in his face and turned their backs on
him—leaving him penniless.

He would be penniless in a few weeks, when that balance
at the bank had gone. He could not face Noel and tell her.
He was oddly panic-stricken when he thought of her. He
could not think of a single friend who would lend him
money and go on lending it, for what he really wanted
was to be kept and not given a mere loan. Women had
helped to keep him before, but it meant a servitude that
was not well enough paid for. He wanted more now that
he had grown used to luxury. It was like offering pin-
money to a woman who has had a private income. . . .

He was down and out. Unless—unless Cara had had
time to do as she suggested and given him half her fortune.
She was generous and bold—she would fight even death
for him. He began to walk about the room distractedly.

"By God! she would do it. I believe she *did* do it!"
The reaction to optimism, more natural to him than
despair, made him laugh idiotically. "There will be a letter

for me to-morrow—if only in pencil—a few lines, telling me she has made arrangements."

He looked at the clock. It was no use going back to the post office to-day. To-morrow. If there were only not those interminable hours to get through—and the night. There was no refuge for him now in Monte Carlo—unless she had left him the Casa! He thought of it suddenly as a man dying of thirst does of drink. He fancied himself master of the Casa Caralyn with the money to keep it. A lazy, sensuous life, free from care and the beastly English climate—easily made friends—a life of summer and beauty and no worry. He almost licked his lips.

Then he remembered that all letters would be addressed to him in Curton's name, even by her executors, and by some remote chance might have been sent to Curton's office. It was unlikely, because he had never given Cara the address—but she knew the name of the firm. If Curton had heard he would be utterly mystified, and with the habit of duplicity Crayshaw began to concoct a story of their names getting mixed in the hotel in March, after Curton left, and of his having received a small account which had puzzled him at the time, but which, of course, he had paid before it dawned on him that it was his friend's. "That's it—because I took his letters to send on. There might be something intended for me at his office—manager of the hotel in fault—utter idiots. I can explain it—make him tell me if there's any further news, at any rate."

Yet he was reluctant to go to Curton, apart from the net that seemed to be entangling him on every side. Curton's liking for him had somehow waned since his return. They saw little of each other, and he sensed a hostility in Curton that had never been there before. Horace attributed it to Noel and to having made the initial slip of inviting Curton to Daisy Hill before he was there himself. Noel had no doubt represented things from her own point of view, and posed as a neglected wife. He did not think that she had actually confided in Curton, but she might have suggested that her husband kept her and the boy very short while he went abroad, or played golf in England. This was exactly what Crayshaw would have done himself in a like situation, and it is very difficult to believe in another course of action from a different nature. Anyhow, it made him more chary of approaching Curton, and he almost cursed his wife in his growing fury and desperation.

He paused with his hand actually on the telephone, saying to himself that Curton would be sure to be away at this time of year. Then he remembered that the senior partner was still abroad, and his own need was pressing. . . . The clerk answered him promptly—curtly, he thought, for his nerves were on edge for a rebuff. Name, please. He would ask if Mr. Curton were still there. Hold on a minute. . . . Then Curton's voice answering, pleasantly reserved as usual. "Is that you, Crayshaw? Yes, I can see you. Will you come round?" There was no avoiding it. He braced himself. Curton obviously suspected nothing. He must play his cards well, that was all. He had always been able to get round Curton. . . .

But his self-confidence faltered a little when he was shown into Curton's own room, by the clerk. It was just an ordinary solicitor's office, rather dark and not furnished nearly as well as Vanstead's had been. But then Vanstead had wished to create an impression, even by his surroundings. Crayshaw saw that now. There were rows of tin boxes with names on them, law books, a big desk with the tele-

phone standing at Curton's elbow, two office arm-chairs—
and Curton.

There was nothing to be read in the good-looking face
with its smooth hair and clean-shaven mouth. But Crayshaw had never noticed its hardness before. It might have
been cut out of granite. Not a man of whom to ask a
favor, or to confess a folly to. Crayshaw was conscious for
the first time of being at a physical disadvantage, and that
his face must be drawn and wild.

Curton shook hands with him and pointed to the chair
beside the writing-table.

"I say, Crayshaw, this is a big smash in the City!" he
said. "I hope it does not touch you at all?"

Crayshaw clutched at the opening at once. "That's just
what I came to you about," he exclaimed. "I'm in rather
a fix. You see I was a sort of confidential secretary to
Vanstead, and I want to know how I stand."

Curton had not expected this piece of information at
least, and for a moment his face showed his amazement.
Then it altered to the usual keen gravity with which he
listened to clients' muddled tales of their difficulties.

"Is there any warrant out against Vanstead?" he asked
sharply.

"No; not that I know of. I had no least idea—no suspicion—I thought he was a millionaire! I believe we were
all equally taken in, the whole staff. Morton, the head
clerk, was, I am sure."

"Were there other men implicated, outside the office?"

"I don't know. I should think not. He was very close
about the accounts. But I have heard nothing except from
Morton who was as knocked out as myself, and what I
saw in the papers. When I got to the office this morning
I found it closed and a crowd outside. I've been away for a

fortnight's leave and was to have joined Vanstead in Yorkshire for a shoot. God's truth! that's all I know!"

Curton settled himself a little more firmly in his chair, and began to ask questions. At the end of twenty minutes he had got the whole case from Crayshaw, including his own losses, and sat for a minute in silence, drawing figures on his blotting-paper with a pencil. His face had not softened, and he had not expressed any sympathy with Crayshaw; but then he had been merely the lawyer and business man throughout, getting all the details of the case.

"Unless Vanstead is caught and brought back I don't see that they are likely to come on you for any evidence," he said. "Even if they do you are not *particeps criminis*. Until the affair is gone into by the Receiver nobody knows how any one stands. I am afraid it is going to be a long business."

"My capital is gone at any rate. It was all in his hands."

"It looks rather black for investors. But with a man like Vanstead one can never tell. Extraordinary things may happen——" He paused a minute and added deliberately, "One happened to me to-day."

"Well, I hope it's of a different type to mine!" said Crayshaw with the ghost of his old laugh. He was wondering how to approach his real object and to speak of the possible interchange of letters.

"I had a fortune left me by a woman I hardly knew."

Crayshaw's face was out of control. It was so leaden in color that it looked like a man's with some fell disease. The faint laugh was still on his lips and twisted them as if with pain. A little drop of moisture ran down his forehead and lay like a bead on his temple.

"But *you* knew her, I think, at least by sight. I don't know if you ever spoke to her."

Curton's deliberate statements were absolutely unemotional. He went on as if Crayshaw had questioned him; but Crayshaw had not spoken because he could not.

"Madame Da Costa—that woman you noticed in the Casino at Monte Carlo. She is dead, and she has left a will in my favor."

Crayshaw spoke at last, slowly, like a man partly paralyzed. "You are sure there is no mistake?"

"None. The money is willed to me by name, and even this firm, Staine & Curton, is mentioned. I received a letter from the executors this morning. She has made it perfectly legal."

The two men looked at each other across the narrow space that lay between them, and each saw hate in his opponent's eyes. At that revealing moment they said all that was to be said between them, without words. A shudder seemed to convulse Crayshaw, that was all, and his body to crouch for a spring. He was the larger and heavier man. Curton did not move except to lay his hand on the bell at his elbow. The clerks were in the next room. Then Crayshaw gave a sudden ringing laugh—his own laugh this time and no shadow of itself.

"Well, old man, I congratulate you!" he said wildly. "What a thing it is to be a favorite with the ladies!" But it was as if he knew he was beaten.

Curton's self-possession had not left him, but he had never ceased to watch Crayshaw. "We only knew each other by sight," he said collectedly. "But I once did her a small service when her maid turned faint in the hall of the Casino. I did not think she knew my name, but I suppose she must have made inquiries. Women are romantic, even in this modern age." He spoke more lightly, but it sounded cynical.

"I did not know you had ever spoken to her!" said Crayshaw hoarsely. His muscles had relaxed. He fell back limply in his chair.

"Only on that occasion, and once afterwards when I stopped to ask her if the maid recovered. That was last year. This year she showed me no recognition, as you saw, and I did not try to renew the acquaintance."

"But you will, of course, have no hesitation in accepting her bequest!"

"I cannot help myself. It is willed to me by name, and the Firm is mentioned to prove my identity. She had no relations to dispute it—there is no one who can prove a better claim!"

Curton spoke now with the formality of the lawyer, informing a client of facts. For the minute he was simply Staine & Curton, Solicitors, presenting a steel wall of Law to Horace Crayshaw that could not be climbed over. He was not speaking to a friend. That pretense had fallen with his announcement of Madame Da Costa's will and his acceptance of her bequest, though no confession had been made by either man.

There was no formality about Crayshaw. He sat limply in his chair as if Curton had succeeded in pushing him there and crushing him down. His control over his face was gone again for the moment and it was dreadful. The flesh sagged and made new lines in place of the old ones that had meant laughter, his eyes were sunken since this morning, and his appearance was all at once unkempt in contrast to Curton's smooth hard surface. When he rose he rocked a little on his feet, and his gaze went round the office as if he wondered where he was.

"Thanks," he said with vague irony. "I'm afraid that's all that you can do for me——?"

"That is all that I can do for you," repeated Curton in his business voice. "If you wish to consult us later on as to being implicated in Vanstead's liquidation, I can advise you better when we have more information about him. At present——"

Crayshaw did not hear. He had walked blindly to the door and out of the office. He knew that he was ruined as far as Vanstead was concerned without Curton's telling him. What he had wanted was some ray of hope, some hint of help from the other man who had neatly stepped into his shoes and inherited the money that Cara had meant for him. He could not understand why Curton had suddenly turned vindictive, unless it was greed of money, but he knew that somehow the lawyer had ferreted out the whole of the snare he had unconsciously laid for himself, and was watching him struggle in it with cruel enjoyment. He, Horace Crayshaw, had stolen Curton's name for an intrigue, and it was through that fatal mistake that Cara Da Costa had willed her fortune to the wrong man. No getting out of it—no use standing up as he had felt he must do for one mad moment, and screaming that the money was his, that he had lied to Cara and called himself Curton but that it was Horace Crayshaw she had loved, and to Crayshaw that she had meant to leave those hundreds of thousands that she would not resign by marrying him!

The thing, put into words, sounded childish, sounded like a madman's invention to obtain the money. He could not dispute it, even if he could bring the evidence of the servants at the Casa and of Signora Gazzi and her husband to prove that he had stayed there as Curton, had been known to Cara as Curton, was the man to whom the money should be willed. It would mean nothing but fresh damning disclosures, and for the moment he could not face it or plan it. He was bewildered by one failure after another, and by Curton's cruel watching face. Curton had known it all, and had not even stretched out a helping hand to a man who was down and out.

"I'm not so mean as that," thought Horace with the habit of self-congratulation even in his misery. "If I had seen a man I knew and liked up against it, as I am, I'm too generous not to give him a leg up. It would be easy, too—just a few thousands out of this new fortune that's come to him—he could say it was a loan—to help me over —I'd have done it—Celtic blood——" He muttered to himself going out into the street so that people looked at his wild face suspiciously and drew away.

But he was right about Curton. When he had left the office the solicitor saw that he was as desperate as a man and as helpless as a child, and he was satisfied. Ever since Mrs. Staine had put the first clue into his hands from the two traveling Americans who had said they met him at Monte Carlo, he had been turning it over in his mind, following up the scent—sometimes a false one—like a sleuth, making inquiries until the whole folly of Crayshaw's intrigue in his identity was laid bare before him. He had not decided how to use the knowledge and whether it were a weapon to be of use to him against Crayshaw, when Fate suddenly took the matter out of his hands and diverted Madame Da Costa's fortune from Crayshaw to himself, for the use of his name! Her death was just in the nick of time, for had things gone on as they were much longer she would either have found out the deception for herself, or he would have unmasked Crayshaw in order to satisfy his own resentment. Cara would have forgiven Horace, in time, and have left him the fortune after all. But as things had turned out, it was a dramatic reprisal that nobody could foresee.

He sat at his table and thought, with that hard face, and he was not sorry for Crayshaw though it had come as an added surprise to hear that he was one of Vanstead's victims. Crayshaw's long years of subtle cruelty and neglect of his wife had wiped out everything else in Curton's mind. He thought that his triumph was for Noel, that his enjoyment of Crayshaw's retribution was on Noel's account, that his hardness to the man was merely justice to the woman. He did not realize that he was biased by his desire for her. He did not face himself as a would-be lover who is racked by the thought of the husband exercising his rights. But both these angles of his attitude were there if he had chosen to see his behavior as the result of them. There were others that were more justified, and it was those on which he took his stand. For he also, like Crayshaw, had fallen into the habit of self-approval and could find no fault in Hugh Curton.

## CHAPTER XVI

WHEN Crayshaw inquired at the bank, he found that he had a balance of fifty pounds. It would have been considerably more but for his visit to Monte Carlo, but he had spent money in those two weeks at the Casa, expecting to reimburse himself when he returned by a check for his salary, which was due to him. Cara had had baccarat parties, and they had proved more expensive than roulette at the Casino.

He drew the fifty pounds, and closed the account, without comment from the cashier. His bill at the hotel would be six or seven pounds for the two or three days he had spent there, and he did not dare to stay in London for fear of being detained in the Vanstead case. As yet the police had not called upon him, though they might know where he was. But he was known to have gone abroad before the smash came, and to have returned of his own free will, which was in his favor.

He packed one suit-case, and asked to have his heavier baggage kept at the hotel until he returned. His face and manner were more under control from the secret desperate fear in him, and the management agreed to keep his luggage and to reserve a room when he wired, thinking indeed that he looked a stricken man and vaguely attributing it to Vanstead's collapse because everything that looked ominous was attributed to Vanstead just then; but, on the whole, respecting Mr. Crayshaw for his restraint and reserve. He left the hotel the day after seeing Curton, and drove to Paddington where he took a third-class ticket to Newberry for no more definite reason than that he happened to see the name in large letters on a placard.

He had not the least idea where he was going or what he should do. All the money he had in the world was on him, and his brain refused to plan how he should make more. Several times in his life he had been reduced to a low limit of means (as Noel had cause to know, though she never knew when he had an access of good fortune) but he had always had a little capital behind him, something on which to fall back. His buoyancy had floated him up again, by the help of new friends. He was a man who was always making new friends, and who never kept old ones. Women more than men had helped to tide Crayshaw over bad places, but since his absorbing passion for Cara he had flicked away lesser loves, and had turned one or two into enemies in the carelessness of his success. They might have helped him now had he been more cautious.

Curiously enough it was his wife of whom he was most afraid, in his moment of difficulty. He could not bear the idea of facing Noel if she knew. Her face became a nightmare to him. All the grinding years through which he had drained her youth for the sake of the boy, came back on him like a flood and overwhelmed him. He had depended far more on the pity of a man like Curton than on Noel's, and when Curton had failed him it seemed to cut the ground from under his shiftless feet.

He left the train at a little station before Newberry, and carrying his suit-case walked into the country road that came and went nowhere to his frightened mind. All the money that he had in the world was with him, and he was nobody. The debauch of the last week's passion had no small share in having shaken his nerve, for he was like a demented person for the time being. He walked a mile along the sodden August road without meeting anything but a few cars and a cart. Across the fields he could see a group of cottages and a larger building that might be an inn. He was very thirsty, and the suit-case was heavy. He opened the gate to a field, and hid the suit-case under the hedge amongst some tall weeds and grasses. He could fetch it presently, but he should never reach the inn, and drink, with that weight to carry.

He reached it at last, and found that it was open for the licensing hours. He was dressed in golfing clothes to explain his departure for the country to the London hotel, and was dusty and tired. No one seemed to think him an unusual customer there, though the dark, strong-smelling bar was full of laborers and working men only. He said to some one—the barmaid, he thought—that he was on a walking tour and had missed his way. He ordered eggs and bacon and beer, and ate and drank mechanically to his own dull surprise. The woman who served him looked at him without curiosity or the least interest, and this was so unusual that it drove him to looking in the dim glass of the stuffy inn parlor. He saw then why she had not noticed him. His good looks were gone. In their place was a man with a haggard face and bloodshot eyes, roughened hair and dusty skin. He had tried to shave this morning, but his hand shook so that he had given it up, and being dark his chin showed a slight scrub. He had not slept last night. He should never forget last night—it must not happen again. He ought to have bought something at a chemist's to make him sleep.

He ordered more beer, but it had no effect upon him. He wished he had asked for whisky. Vile, no doubt, but it might bite. There was something in his pocket besides his money. His revolver. He did not know why it had been amongst his luggage, but he had found it when unpacking and put it in his jacket pocket.

But he knew, poor wretch, that it was only for the dramatic effect he had carried it about with him. He had not the will-power to take his own life. He remembered how he had once gone into the "Suicide's garden" at Monte Carlo and sat down on a particularly red seat, and thought—but only thought—of shooting himself. It was after one of his quarrels with Cara—he had laughed about it afterwards. . . .

"I believe they paint those seats bright red to avoid a stain if somebody cuts his throat!" he had said.

To his surprise Cara had suddenly blazed into anger.

"You don't know what you are talking about! Blood is not that post-box color, and it makes a darker stain," she said. And as if to illustrate her meaning she bit her underlip so fiercely that a bright drop fell and marked her gown. The wound took a day or so to heal. Was she thinking of Da Costa's death when she lacerated herself like that, and what ugly scene rose before her at the reference to shedding of blood? He had sometimes wondered if the power she had over her servants arose from their being her accomplices, for he knew that they had been with her in Santiago. . . .

He had always enjoyed his life, no matter who suffered for it. He remembered that old hag, his wife's aunt, calling him "The Miserable Sinner!" Dead in earnest she had been, too—though he had so often proved it false. She had told him once it would come home to him. She'd be glad, damn her, that it had! For what was he now but a miserable sinner? A sinner whose sins had played

him a trick, and paid him back! And most miserable—
most miserable——

For a few minutes he cried like a child in his self-pity.
"Lord, have mercy upon us Miserable Sinners!"

He did not believe in God, save for a superstitious fear
of finding Him somewhere in the dark when all the sunshine was gone, and the roses, and laughter and living. He
had been a pagan and a Celt. Curse that old woman,
Anstice York, and her croaking! "You—Miserable—Sinner!" He had believed in pleasure, and passion, and the
joys of the body, and beauty—he had loved his own—and
it was gone——

How beautiful Cara was! How perfect her smooth flesh
and the modeling of her limbs. It was impossible to think
of her as dead. What would she look like, dead? Beautiful
alabaster. Who was with her in those last feverish days?
He knew nothing. He should never know. He could not
ask Curton. Who would have the Casa? Curton? Probably. She had meant it for him, Horace, because it had
been their fairy palace beside her sea. They had been so
happy—amongst the carnations. He smelled carnations
now, even in this stuffy, horrible room, and looking round
him saw that somebody had put a vase of the same flowers
on the mantelpiece. Small, poor specimens compared to
those at Roquebrune, but—carnations! The scented thing
that had fallen between Cara's bare knees as he held her,
naked, in his arms before the mirror, to look at her own
beauty.

He wished he had not got up to look at the carnations
and smell them, for he caught sight of his face in the glass
again and it cowed him. Was that ugly fellow with the
sunken eyes Cara's handsome lover? He was forty—but
he had been accustomed to think of himself as ten years

younger. He looked fifty now, or more. That face in the glass!—Cara's triumphant lover.

Curton could not have the Casa—it was impossible. His set, self-sufficient figure against that background, in those haunting echoes of love and laughter—Curton going about appraising the value of things, thinking what it would cost to keep up—whether to sell it for a hotel or a club! For once, Crayshaw became imaginative in fitting Curton into such a picture, because he loathed it. The Casa that poor Cara had meant for him—for *him*——

How ugly and sordid this inn was! It smelt of beer and damp furniture. There was not even a sofa in the room where he could lie down, and he suddenly longed for sleep. The beer was taking effect after all. He pushed aside the common tray with his plate of cold egg and bacon-rind, and pulling the revolver out of his pocket laid it in the circle of his arm, and his head in his hands. Even then, he was careful not to run a risk—for it was loaded. His head began to droop lower. He pushed the revolver more on to one side, and strangely enough fell into the deep desired sleep that had eluded him last night.

No one came to disturb him. The inn was shut when the bar closed and they forgot the dusty tired man in the parlor, or perhaps thought he would wake and pay for his meal presently. He had looked like a gentlemen in spite of that wild, drawn face. He'd overdone it, walking in the heat.

Horace slept on, for some hours. No dreams came to trouble his peace, and his brain was refreshed when he woke, which he did suddenly, and for no particular cause. He felt perfectly happy, and he did not know where he was.

It was the revolver that brought it all back to him. The

happiness fled while he tried to hold on to it with all his will power. It faded, and the ghastly sequence of events of the past two days rolled back over his mind like a thick volume of smoke. It made him physically sick, so that he retched. It would not be dispelled again by blessed sleep. It was all true. . . .

He seized the revolver on impulse and thrust it into his mouth. He could never have done it if he had thought about it for a moment. But his actions all his life long had been impulses.

The solitary shot sounded through the empty inn like something that did not belong to it. The innkeeper was outside in the garden, hoeing his ground. His wife was picking the peas. They looked at each other, and said, "There's somebody's tire gone bust!"

.       .       .       .       .       .       .

When they found him at last he was unrecognizable. But no one would ever see the face that he had last seen in the glass, or know that he had lost his beauty before he took his life. Only the innkeeper's wife described him as a middle-aged man, dark, and ill-looking—nothing striking about him save his height. Yes, he had money on him—forty pounds odd. He owed them a trifle for his lunch.

## CHAPTER XVII

CURTON had been to Daisy Hill three times before
he found Noel.

She had of course left Sussex when It happened, for she
was mentioned as identifying her husband's body at the
inquest. Curton had seen It in the papers with a sense of
shock that affected even his iron purpose of bringing
Crayshaw to justice, and had known that she would be
summoned. But he could not offer himself to the police
as having information that bore on the case. The only
information he could have offered was that Crayshaw had
called upon him to ask advice as to his position as Vanstead's confidential secretary, though he had certainly not
been in Vanstead's confidence. The fact of his having been
in Vanstead's office, however, was considered as sufficient
to account for his taking his own life when he discovered that he was ruined. Possibly also the fear of having
been implicated in some of Vanstead's frauds and bogus
companies had driven him to panic. All this came out
at the inquest, but it was also stated that Mrs. Crayshaw
was actually ignorant of the fact that her husband was
associated with Vanstead at all, and knew nothing of his
losses.

Curton was less concerned with the ordeal that Noel
had to go through than with her position as Crayshaw's
widow. He had gathered that Crayshaw had left her
absolutely without means, and might have been in debt,
and he made it his business at once to find out how things

stood with her and to make provision for her. He did not add, even to himself "and the boy" because he did not mean Valentine to complicate the future, and he knew that for the present what was done for his mother was done for him.

On the second occasion when he went to Daisy Hill he encountered his old aversion, Captain Lewison, coming out of the bungalow which he locked behind him. Both men recognized each other with hostility, but Curton stopped Lewison as he was actually walking out of the garden gate.

"I came down to see Mrs. Crayshaw, if possible. I thought I might be of some use to her in this terrible business. I am a solicitor, and I knew her husband—we were abroad together this year."

"Mrs. Crayshaw is not here." Lewison's narrow face hardened to a look of asphalt or concrete, if such substance can be compared to human flesh, and he volunteered no further information.

"Do you know when she is coming back?"

"I do not."

"I have an address in Sussex—General Arthun's. Do you know if she is still there?"

"I can't say."

Curton would have liked to take the surly, limping man by his collar and throw him into the road. This being impossible, he turned on his heel without further speech, and got into his car again. But the rebuff had only made him more obstinate. He was determined to see Noel even if he had to go down to Sussex after her.

It was not necessary. The third time he went to the bungalow she opened the door herself, just as she had the first time he called. And it was again impossible to say that she was not at home, or refuse to see him, because they were face to face in the narrow space of the doorway.

"Pray let me come in, if only for a few minutes!" he said earnestly. "I hope it does not seem like forcing myself on you at such a time. There are things I must tell you——"

Her face was shockingly thin and her clear wholesome eyes had an unnatural look in them as though she still saw horror before her. He realized that they must have looked like that when she saw the battered head that had no likeness to Horace Crayshaw, the remains of what was once a handsome face, shot into fragments. . . . Crayshaw had not made a clean job of it. The papers said that he was unrecognizable save for his body and clothes.

"Come in," she said in a low voice. "I have only been home a few hours. My aunt is coming to stay with me to-night."

"Are you alone now?"

"Miss Lewison has been here—very kind. She has only gone home to attend to her brother——"

He came into the familiar little hall that somehow seemed different, as if it belonged to nobody and had never been a home. There were piles of books and personal belongings on the chairs and in the dining-room (all the doors stood open as if someone were in a hurry) and he realized before she told him that she was making a selection of such things as she wanted to keep, and that the little house would be sold as quickly as possible.

"Some men are coming to-morrow with cases to pack my books and our clothes, Val's and mine," she said in that low, flat voice. "And his couch is going down to Sussex."

"Where is the boy?"

"I left him with General Arthun."

"Quite the best place for him," said Curton cordially. It had occurred to him before that if the General could use his influence to get the boy to some suitable home or institution it would simplify the problem of his existence—and leave Noel free.

She looked at him for a moment but did not answer, and they went into the sitting room which was also littered with things that did not belong to it. Noel did not even offer her guest any hospitality on this occasion. She stood listlessly by the empty fireplace and looked down at it as if she were gazing into the fire as she did at Brighton, and Curton stood beside her, tall, too prosperous for the shabby room, and almost nervous in his earnestness.

"I have been down twice before," he said at last. "But you had not come back."

"Yes—it was very good of you. The neighbors told me a gentleman had been in a car. I knew it must be you. And you were busy too—your partner is still away." She spoke with an odd jerkiness as if her mind were almost unhinged.

"They are in South Africa. The climate is suiting Mr. Staine, or they would have come back before this." He moved restlessly. He did not want to think of John Staine, or of Sybil. He had pushed Sybil out of his life for the tremendous thing that had taken possession of him and altered even his sense of what was decent, what was due to his—partner's wife.

There was another silence that became so intolerable it made him desperate. He had a most unusual impulse to take this worn, tired woman in his arms and hold her strongly until she understood without further words. It was so unusual for Curton to have an impulse that he did not know what to do with it.

"I want you to let me help you," he said at last baldly.

She started a little and looked up at him with eyes which he now saw were quite sunk in her head. She might have been fifty, she was dusty and hot in her black gown, but it made no difference. He found that he wanted her just as she was.

"It is not necessary, thank you," she said, and a dull flush of color passed over her face. "I am selling this house—we shall go somewhere else."

"But I know that it *is* necessary. I know something of your husband's affairs. He came to see me—the very day he must have gone to that place—that inn."

"You saw him!—what did he say?—did he look——"

"He told me he was ruined through Vanstead. He asked me about his position."

"Did he—ask you to help him?"

"No. There was nothing certain. I could hardly advise him as to whether he were likely to be implicated."

"Did he say anything about——" She drew a deep breath and forced herself to speak—"about taking his own life?"

"Nothing. I never thought of his doing anything of the sort." He had an odd relief in telling the truth. "I think it must have been an impulse."

"But he must have looked unlike himself—very ill?"

"Yes, he looked ill. Like a man who has had a shock. I think he absolutely believed in Vanstead."

"Poor man!" She spoke under her breath, but as impersonally as if Horace Crayshaw had been nothing to her.

"But you must let me help you," he persisted, dragging her back to the issue at stake. "I cannot bear to think of you left like this—without any home, or any future. Call it a loan, or a gift, or anything you like—Noel, you know why I want to do this!"

It was out now, but he felt like a man who has just come through a bad accident, and his hands were trembling. He had never moved his eyes from her face, and she had never looked at him after that one startled minute when he admitted having seen Crayshaw.

"I love you—want to marry you—take you out of all this," he almost mumbled, and had to clear his throat before he could go on. "As soon as possible—as soon as I can get a license."

"Don't!" she said, flinching. She spoke as simply as a frightened child. "It is too soon—the other thing was too awful! I cant believe it, even now."

"Poor girl! My poor Noel!" He laid his hand on her shoulder and moved nearer to her. "Try to put it out of your mind and forget it. You could not help it. It was no fault of yours."

"I don't know. If we had been better friends he might have come and told me—I might have helped him through it."

He looked at her still, but with a harder face. "You are not going to put the ghost of Horace Crayshaw as a barrier between us, are you? Believe me you have no reason to do so! He was not faithful to you——"

"I know that. I have known it for years. This has nothing to do with it."

"It has something to do with it in one way," he said, angry that he could not move her and with a savage desire to make her understand Horace's treachery. "There was a woman in Monte Carlo—well, the less said about her the better. But she had money. Crayshaw stayed with her in her villa in April, and again this summer. I found this out because curious rumors began to reach me concerning myself, and I had to trace them. He had been using my name—he told this woman that he was Hugh Curton, and even gave the name of my firm as his own. She seems to have believed him. He was a clever liar!"

Again she shrank from him as if something in his hard face frightened her. "Did it—taking your name—do you any harm?"

"It might have done, if it had gone on," he said grimly. "As it happened it turned against Crayshaw with a kind of justice one hardly ever sees. The woman died—last week, of septic pneumonia—and had made a will in favor of Hugh Curton!"

"Meaning my husband—Horace Crayshaw?" She looked at him in a bewildered fashion as if she could not understand.

"What people mean does not always count in law. She left the money to me—Hugh Curton, of the firm of Staine & Curton. She was very particular to state the name of the firm that there might be no mistake. Her executors wrote to me. I had just had their letter when Crayshaw came to see me."

"Yes, but—I don't quite see—if the money were left to Horace——?"

"He could not touch it. He could not even dispute it. Don't you see? He had represented himself to be somebody else, which was actionable considering the use he made of it. When I told him what had happened it was a worse blow than Vanstead's decampment. I think he had counted on this woman either keeping him, or leaving him money. He would probably have gone to her, but that he saw her death in the papers."

The remembrance of that interview, of his satisfied

hatred, made his face momentarily triumphant. And Noel saw the situation between the two men in that look. She moved away out of his reach and her figure braced itself.

"You had him at your mercy, and you showed none," she said slowly. "You are a hard man. I don't know if you think that you were justified, but you sent him to his death."

"Noel!"

"Now you come to me, his widow, and you ask me to share the spoils with you. Is that it? This woman at Monte Carlo—however bad you may think her reputation—she must have loved Horace to wish to make him rich even if she could not live with him. She was more generous than you."

"I am not generous when I have been tricked and cheated. Would you be?"

"I was tricked and cheated for twelve years—but I would not have treated my worst enemy like that. And I loved him once. . . . Please go away, and do not try to help me again. I could not marry you—I should break my heart on your hardness some day if not now. And you would want to part me from Valentine. There is no room in your life for him, though you think there is for me."

He stood immovable, without taking the least notice of her request to him to go, but his face was broken out of its impassivity. "I did not think you would take it like this!" he said.

"No—or you would not have told me the bare truth. I respect you for that, anyway. But I feel as if I had had a great escape—for I nearly loved you."

"Then there is some hope for me," he said in a gentler voice. "If you nearly loved me—you are not a woman to change your mind for some fancied resentment against me.

You are not light or vacillating. You will get over this—
you have had a shock. I ought not to have tried to hurry
you. But I wanted to take care of you—to get you out of
it—so much!"

His voice was pleading, and those reserved eyes were
more expressive than she had ever seen them. He was
urging her with every atom of his will-power behind his
restraint. For he had not touched her, had not come any
nearer when she moved away.

"Yes, I shall get over it——" she said gravely. "In time
I hope I shall forget. If a woman remembered things like
that—like what I saw—she would go mad. But I shall
never get over you."

"How do you mean?"

"Your cruelty—your absolute hardness to a broken man.
Oh, I know he was weak and vile, and had fallen into
his own trap—but don't you see?—you drove him just
a little farther without any action on your part. You have
nothing to reproach yourself with—but you frighten me.
Some day I might come up against that side of you,
myself, and beat myself to death as if against an iron
door!"

"Noel darling, you are overwrought, unreasonable. Do
you think you could ever do such things as Crayshaw
did? Do you think I could be hard to *you*, even if you
did?"

"You are hard now in your thoughts, about Val."

"I will promise you never to try to part you from the
boy, if that will satisfy you." He meant what he said at
the moment. "I really thought it better for his own future,
for his character, that he should have a chance of some
specialized education."

"Yes, that is just the difficulty. You are quite wise; you

are no doubt justified—but you see I am his mother. More than that, I am his friend. I have had him to watch and train ever since he met with—an accident."

"Have you even forgiven Crayshaw that because he is dead?" he asked bitterly.

"No, I never forgave him. I don't think I do now. But I can see him from another point of view, like something which is clearer at a distance. When he was nearer to me he was blurred because I was always angry. I think in some ways he could not help himself. He had no moral sense. We needn't talk of that. It has not really anything to do with my feeling about you, except that it opened my eyes." She had been speaking quite patiently, but suddenly she raised her hands and pushed the limp hair from her forehead. "Oh, I am so tired! so tired!—I can't talk to you any more. Do please go away," she said, like a sick child.

"I'm a brute," he exclaimed remorsefully. "But I can't leave you alone like this. Mayn't I stay till Miss York comes? If I promise not to say a word you have forbidden, but just help you with those books?"

She looked at his tall figure, at his clothes, at the dusty books and small personal things lying about, and her wide mouth trembled to its old smile though her eyes filled with tears at the same moment.

"I can't," she gasped. "It's too impossible—you would make yourself in a mess. Oh, there *is* Aunt Anstice!"

"I can at least open the door to her," said Curton with relief in his voice. He was afraid that if he left Noel alone in the bungalow she might collapse, and yet he did not wish to stay and distress her. He had not the least intention of accepting her refusal and saying good-bye to her, except for the moment. He meant to return and talk and argue, and if necessary bully her into marrying him quickly; but for the minute he was glad to see Miss York.

Noel heard their voices in conversation at the door, and wondered how much or how little Curton was telling Anstice York. Then he came back into the sitting room for a moment to say good-bye, and held her hand in both his, and asked her to forgive him for worrying her at such a time. For one panic moment she thought he was going to kiss her, and that she was powerless to resist it, but she wanted to scream. He did not do anything of the kind however—just held her hands in his strong grasp and then left her to Miss York.

Anstice York closed the sitting room door and walked over to the window to watch Curton get into his car. When it had rolled away through the flat-roofed, odious bungalows and their exhausted gardens, she turned round and looked at her niece. Noel was sitting, almost crouching, by the fireplace, with her face buried in her hands. She was not crying, but she rocked her body to and fro as if to ease herself.

"What is it?" said Miss York gently. "What did he want?"

"He saw Horace—the same day It happened."

Miss York made an impatient sound in the roof of her mouth. "Did he come to tell you that, and rake it up again? I never thought Hugh Curton was a fool!" she said bitterly.

"No—not that. It came out, because he asked me to marry him, at once, quickly—and I refused. He wanted to explain to me that Horace did not stand in the way because he was not worth it."

"As if we did not know that!"

"And he told me of some woman in Monte Carlo who had kept Horace away so long in the spring and just lately." All this time Noel had never raised his face, but spoke from the hollow of her hands.

"That is nothing new," said Miss York.

"I know. But Horace had taken Mr. Curton's name, and had told her he was in the firm of solicitors—Staine & Curton—and a great deal more I expect. You know how he used to invent when he was once started on a lie. But Mr. Curton didn't know him, of course, as we did. Anyhow he was suspicious and he found out, and he was angry—very angry."

"He would be. That mouth of his is like hard steel. He could be far more angry than Horace."

"The woman died, just lately, thinking that Horace was Hugh Curton. She left all her money to him."

"Good God!—I see. And Horace could not claim it, he dared not state that he had used Curton's name to cover an intrigue—he was afraid of Curton; Curton knew the law and how far Horace was incriminated . . . the Miserable Sinner!"

"Oh Aunt Anstice, don't!—don't! He went to Hugh Curton when he knew that he was ruined through this man Vanstead, and he asked some questions about the Monte Carlo woman. I think he must have hoped that Hugh Curton would give him some loophole of escape and help him out——"

"You need not tell me that Curton did nothing of the sort. He hated Horace because of you, and he had him underfoot. Curton just sat still and did nothing—the money was his, legally—and Horace could do nothing either." Despite her control there was a faint sympathy with Curton in Anstice York's voice. She did not uphold his cruelty, but she knew that in his place she might have done the same.

"Yes, there was one thing that Horace could do—and he did it. He was on the edge of the precipice and there was no one to pull him back. Hugh did not push him over—he just sat still and did nothing, as you say."

"It was very difficult for anyone who loved you to see nothing in Horace but a fellow creature, Noel! You try Hugh Curton rather high."

"It is not that exactly—not his revenge—but his nature that frightens me. He is so hard, so deliberate. He would crush you in time. Val knows it by instinct. He told me Hugh did not like him, and wanted to get rid of him."

"I see." There was a pause. Miss York went into the kitchen and made the tea, and for once Noel made no effort to help her. She sat where she was, bowed forward, as if something had broken the springs of energy in her at last, and now and then she shivered in the flaccid heat of the room as if she were deadly sick.

When Miss York had made the tea she went deliberately into the dining room and opened the sideboard door. She knew that there was brandy there, kept for Horace, or in case Valentine were ill—but never for Noel. She measured a few teaspoonfuls into Noel's cup and then carried it to her and stood over her while she drank it.

"It tastes all wrong, Aunt Anstice," she gulped. "What did you put in it?"

"Brandy. Eat some biscuits. I had not time to make toast. I shall lace your next cup like the last. You need it. Your face is ghastly, Noel. You've had too much thrust on you."

"Leave me alone. I shall get through. If only Hugh had not come just now——"

"He will come again. He will never leave off coming. What are you going to do? You can't run away from him without money."

Noel's hand was steadier as she put down the cup, and her face was not quite so leaden. The brandy was helping her.

"I think there is one other thing I can do," she said. "I think there is a way out. Not Horace's way—and not Hugh's."

"You call him Hugh very naturally," said Miss York. "You think of him as Hugh."

Noel did not answer.

. . . . . .

Curton did not hurry himself, though for the first time in his life he would like to have done so beyond prudence. He wanted his marriage to be an accomplished fact before his partner came home, and he faced the future—and Sybil—with the same determined mouth that had told Noel he should not give her up. It galled him to be held back like this by her unexpected attitude about his meeting with Crayshaw, but he was a man who had learned to wait and to hold his purpose nevertheless.

He knew she could not get rid of the bungalow until the September quarter at least. He went to the agent about it himself, as a prospective buyer, and then learned for the first time that the little home was mortgaged. He might have expected it, for it was unlikely that Crayshaw would not raise money in any way he could during his shiftless career. He had bought the bungalow before his connection with Percy Vanstead, and he might have mortgaged it at any time—possibly when he went to Monte Carlo in February, to play golf with Curton. At any rate Curton was too late to shoulder that responsibility for Noel, and buy the place despite the mortgage. The agent had had an offer for it a week before, and had closed with it by Mrs. Crayshaw's instructions. It was not a good offer, as Curton suspected, and it would hardly clear such debts as Crayshaw had left, let alone leaving her with any capital to draw upon. He was not entirely sorry for this. It drew the net closer round her, and drove her into his arms eventually, whether she would or no.

Mrs. Crayshaw must come back to Daisy Hill for a few days at least before she left it. She had gone back to Sussex, but the agent assured him that she had arranged to return in September, before she finally vacated it. There were packing-cases there still belonging to her; probably she had nowhere to send them, and was settling as to whether she could afford to store them. Every small added expense meant another step towards the end he had in view. He did not want her to be harassed, but he accepted that also as inevitable before she gave way.

He had waited over a month before he saw her again, though he made periodical visits to the bungalow and had arranged with the agent to let him know of her return by telephone, on the understanding that he wished to buy certain tenant's fixtures not already disposed of. When he did not hear, he began to think that he should have to go down to Sussex, and force her to meet him again at General Arthun's house, though he saw the awkwardness of such an intrusion. He had written to her once or twice, and received very brief replies, one of them perhaps the briefest that he had ever received from a woman since it consisted of the word "No" and her signature. Then he had laughed, but it had not altered his determination. He would be a rich man now, when the necessary delay of probate in a foreign country was settled and Caralyn

Da Costa's fortune was handed over to him. There had been a good deal of litigation over it, but his own specialized knowledge helped him there, and Cara had no heirs or relations to turn up unexpectedly and dispute his inheritance. Da Costa had left the money and the Casa absolutely hers to bequeath; it was only during her lifetime that he had stretched out his dead hands to take it from her should she marry one of her inevitable lovers. Curton had no scruples in taking Crayshaw's legacy; but with a perverted sense of justice he wanted Noel to share in it. It would enable them to do nearly everything that seemed desirable to them—to travel, to live luxuriously, to have a house and land in England—and for the stress of domestic labor and poverty he meant to give her everything that wealth could afford in compensation. But there was no place for Valentine in the picture. They could not drag an invalid child round the world, and he ought not to be left at home, without supervision, just when he should be getting on with his education. For a time, perhaps, he must be with them, to satisfy the mother, but that would adjust itself in time. He was glad that Noel had not taken him at his word, a promise given in the heat of passion never to separate them. For the longer she kept him waiting the more greedy he grew of her—he wanted her all to himself and with no rival in the way, a shadowy likeness of Horace in his son.

It was the middle of September when one day the agent telephoned him that Mrs. Crayshaw was back, and he went to Daisy Hill to find the blinds drawn up in the bungalow and the place open. He had made a habit of leaving his car at a garage in the neighborhood of late, lest the neighbors should report on his persistent arrivals to her. He walked up to the door and found it was not closed—he had only to push it open—and he entered the house after a moment's hesitation and knocked on the sitting room door.

"Is there somebody there? Come in!" said Noel's voice, and he went in and found her busy setting things to rights in a final manner that made him realize that she was really going for good, more than when he found it all in disorder. The litter of books and clothes and pictures was gone. The poor basket-work furniture looked rather forlorn and almost too little for the room, small though it was. But the real change was in Noel herself. She looked so much better and more controlled that she seemed a different person to the poor woman he had left here four or five weeks since. She was grave still, and her face was too thin, but the bruises were gone from under her eyes, and the eyes themselves looked as clean and clear as they had done before they had looked on It. . . . Well, she had had a month of peace and security, he had forgotten that. If a short rest could make such a difference, what would not the years make with his love and care and no anxiety to wear her down? She was a young woman still.

"Noel!" he said. "I've come back—are you angry with me?"

He saw her large eyes dilate and one quick breath heave her bosom as if it tore its way from her heart. And he remembered how she had said, "I nearly loved you!"

"You had better not have come," she said in a low troubled voice. "Unless—you have only come to say—good-bye?"

"I have come to ask you what I did before—I want you to marry me. Nothing will ever make me accept that 'No' you wrote to me. It's no use, darling—I love you. I must have you. I've never wanted anything in my life like this. Noel—you must!"

"I can't, Hugh." She stood up stiffly and spoke with a jerk, as if she were suddenly changed to an automatic woman, with no life in her.

"You will come to it, in time." His confident face seemed to stagger her, and she looked at him as if frightened. "Don't be afraid of your happiness—our happiness. I will be so good to you! I will make you young again, and give you back the years that you have lost."

"You mustn't, Hugh—ah! don't touch me! I've put it out of your power—it's no use your asking me."

He began to feel a little chill of fear in his turn. She was so obviously afraid of him. "What do you mean?" he said on a laboring breath.

"I married General Arthun this morning."

**THE END.**